THE CHILDHOOD OF JESUS

SO BY J.M. COETZEE

J.M. COETZEE

The Childhood of Jesus

VINTAGE BOOKS
London

Published by Vintage 2014

2 4 6 8 10 9 7 5 3 1

First published in Great Britain in 2013 by
Harvill Secker

Vintage
Random House, 20 Vauxhall Bridge Road,
London SW1V 2SA

www.vintage-books.co.uk

Addresses for companies within The Random House Group Limited can be
found at: www.randomhouse.co.uk/offices.htm

The Random House Group Limited Reg. No. 954009

A CIP catalogue record for this book
is available from the British Library

ISBN 9780099581536

The Random House Group Limited supports the Forest Stewardship
Council® (FSC®), the leading international forest-certification
organisation. Our books carrying the FSC label are printed on FSC®-certified
paper. FSC is the only forest-certification scheme supported by the leading
environmental organisations, including Greenpeace. Our paper procurement
policy can be found at www.randomhouse.co.uk/environment

MIX
Paper from
responsible sources
FSC® C016897

Typeset by Palimpsest Book Production Limited,
Falkirk, Stirlingshire
Printed and bound by CPI Group (UK) Ltd, Croydon, CR0 4YY

For D.K.C.

Chapter 1

The man at the gate points them towards a low, sprawling building in the middle distance. 'If you hurry,' he says, 'you can check in before they close their doors for the day.'

They hurry. *Centro de Reubicación Novilla*, says the sign. *Reubicación*: what does that mean? Not a word he has learned.

The office is large and empty. Hot too – even hotter than outside. At the far end a wooden counter runs the width of the room, partitioned by panes of frosted glass. Against the wall is an array of filing drawers in varnished wood.

Suspended over one of the partitions is a sign: *Recién Llegados*, the words stencilled in black on a rectangle of cardboard. The clerk behind the counter, a young woman, greets him with a smile.

'Good day,' he says. 'We are new arrivals.' He articulates the words slowly, in the Spanish he has worked hard to master. 'I am looking for employment, also for a place to live.' He grips the boy under the armpits and lifts him so that she can see him properly. 'I have a child with me.'

The girl reaches out to take the boy's hand. 'Hello, young man!' she says. 'He is your grandson?'

'Not my grandson, not my son, but I am responsible for him.'

'A place to live.' She glances at her papers. 'We have a room free here at the Centre that you can use while you look for something better. It won't be luxurious, but perhaps you won't mind that. As for employment, let us explore that in the morning – you look tired, I am sure you want to rest. Have you travelled far?'

'We have been on the road all week. We have come from Belstar, from the camp. Are you familiar with Belstar?'

'Yes, I know Belstar well. I came through Belstar myself. Is that where you learned your Spanish?'

'We had lessons every day for six weeks.'

'Six weeks? You are lucky. I was in Belstar for three months. I almost perished of boredom. The only thing that kept me going was the Spanish lessons. Did you by any chance have señora Piñera as a teacher?'

'No, our teacher was a man.' He hesitates. 'May I raise a different matter? My boy' – he glances at the child – 'is not well. Partly it is because he is upset, confused and upset, and hasn't been eating properly. He found the food in the camp strange, didn't like it. Is there anywhere we can get a proper meal?'

'How old is he?'

'Five. That is the age he was given.'

'And you say he is not your grandson.'

'Not my grandson, not my son. We are not related. Here' – he takes the two passbooks from his pocket and proffers them.

She inspects the passbooks. 'These were issued in Belstar?'

'Yes. That is where they gave us our names, our Spanish names.'

She leans over the counter. 'David – that's a nice name,' she says. 'Do you like your name, young man?'

The boy regards her levelly but does not reply. What does she see? A slim, pale-faced child wearing a woollen coat buttoned to the throat, grey shorts covering his knees, black lace-up boots over woollen socks, and a cloth cap at a slant.

'Don't you find those clothes very hot? Would you like to take off your coat?'

The boy shakes his head.

He intervenes. 'The clothes are from Belstar. He chose them himself, from what they had to offer. He has become quite attached to them.'

'I understand. I asked because he seemed a bit warmly dressed for a day like today. Let me mention: we have a depository here at the Centre where people donate clothing that their children have outgrown. It is open every morning on weekdays. You are welcome to help yourself. You will find more variety than at Belstar.'

'Thank you.'

'Also, once you have filled in all the necessary forms you can draw money on your passbook. You have a settlement allowance of four hundred reals. The boy too. Four hundred each.'

'Thank you.'

'Now let me show you to your room.' She leans across and

whispers to the woman at the next counter, the counter labelled *Trabajos*. The woman pulls open a drawer, rummages in it, shakes her head.

'A slight hitch,' says the girl. 'We don't seem to have the key to your room. It must be with the building supervisor. The supervisor's name is señora Weiss. Go to Building C. I will draw you a map. When you find señora Weiss, ask her to give you the key to C-55. Tell her that Ana from the main office sent you.'

'Wouldn't it be easier to give us another room?'

'Unfortunately C-55 is the only room that is free.'

'And food?'

'Food?'

'Yes. Is there somewhere we can eat?'

'Again, speak to señora Weiss. She should be able to help you.'

'Thank you. One last question: Are there organizations here that specialize in bringing people together?'

'Bringing people together?'

'Yes. There must surely be many people searching for family members. Are there organizations that help to bring families together – families, friends, lovers?'

'No, I've never heard of such an organization.'

Partly because he is tired and disoriented, partly because the map the girl has sketched for him is not clear, partly because there are no signposts, it takes him a long time to find Building C and the office of señora Weiss. The door is closed. He knocks. There is no reply.

He stops a passer-by, a tiny woman with a pointy, mouse-like face wearing the chocolate-coloured uniform of the Centre. 'I am looking for señora Weiss,' he says.

'She's off,' says the young woman, and when he does not understand: 'Off for the day. Come back in the morning.'

'Then perhaps you can help us. We are looking for the key to room C-55.'

The young woman shakes her head. 'Sorry, I don't handle keys.'

They make their way back to the Centro de Reubicación. The door is locked. He raps on the glass. There is no sign of life inside. He raps again.

'I'm thirsty,' whines the boy.

'Hang on just a little longer,' he says. 'I will look for a tap.'

The girl, Ana, appears around the side of the building. 'Were you knocking?' she says. Again he is struck: by her youth, by the health and freshness that radiate from her.

'Señora Weiss seems to have gone home,' he says. 'Is there not something you can do? Do you not have a – what do you call it? – a *llave universal* to open our room?'

'*Llave maestra*. There is no such thing as a *llave universal*. If we had a *llave universal* all our troubles would be over. No, señora Weiss is the only one with a *llave maestra* for Building C. Do you perhaps have a friend who can put you up for the night? Then you can come back in the morning and speak to señora Weiss.'

'A friend who can put us up? We arrived on these shores six weeks ago, since when we have been living in a tent in a camp

5

out in the desert. How can you expect us to have friends here who will put us up?'

Ana frowns. 'Go to the main gate,' she orders. 'Wait for me outside the gate. I will see what I can do.'

They pass through the gate, cross the street, and sit down in the shade of a tree. The boy nestles his head on his shoulder. 'I'm thirsty,' he complains. 'When are you going to find a tap?'

'Hush,' he says. 'Listen to the birds.'

They listen to the strange birdsong, feel the strange wind on their skins.

Ana emerges. He stands up and waves. The boy gets to his feet too, arms stiffly by his sides, thumbs clenched in his fists.

'I've brought some water for your son,' she says. 'Here, David, drink.'

The child drinks, gives the cup back to her. She puts it in her bag. 'Was that good?' she asks.

'Yes.'

'Good. Now follow me. It's quite a walk, but you can look on it as exercise.'

Swiftly she strides along the track across the parkland. An attractive young woman, no denying that, though the clothes she wears hardly become her: a dark, shapeless skirt, a white blouse tight at the throat, flat shoes.

By himself he might be able to keep up with her, but with the child in his arms he cannot. He calls out: 'Please – not so fast!' She ignores him. At an ever-increasing distance he follows her across the park, across a street, across a second street.

Before a narrow, plain-looking house she pauses and waits.

'This is my place,' she says. She unlocks the front door. 'Follow me.'

She leads them down a dim corridor, through a back door, down rickety wooden stairs, into a small yard overgrown with grass and weeds, enclosed on two sides by a wooden fence and on the third by chain-link wire.

'Have a seat,' she says, indicating a rusty cast-iron chair half covered in grass. 'I'll get you something to eat.'

He has no wish to sit. He and the boy wait by the door.

The girl re-emerges bearing a plate and a pitcher. The pitcher holds water. The plate holds four slices of bread spread with margarine. It is exactly what they had for breakfast at the charity station.

'As a new arrival you are legally required to reside in approved lodgings, or else at the Centre,' she says. 'But it will be all right if you spend your first night here. Since I am employed at the Centre, we can argue that my home counts as approved lodging.'

'That's very kind of you, very generous,' he says.

'There are some leftover building materials in that corner.' She points. 'You can make yourself a shelter, if you like. Shall I leave you to it?'

He stares at her, nonplussed. 'I'm not sure I understand,' he says. 'Where exactly will we be spending the night?'

'Here.' She indicates the yard. 'I'll come back in a while and see how you are getting on.'

The building materials in question are half a dozen sheets of galvanized iron, rusted through in places – old roofing, no doubt – and some odds and ends of timber. Is this a test? Does she really mean that he and the child should sleep out in the open? He waits for her promised return, but she does not come. He tries the back door: it is locked. He knocks; there is no response.

What is going on? Is she behind the curtains, watching to see how he will react?

They are not prisoners. It would be an easy matter to scale the wire fence and make off. Is that what they should do; or should he wait and see what will happen next?

He waits. By the time she reappears the sun is setting.

'You haven't done much,' she remarks, frowning. 'Here.' She hands him a bottle of water, a hand towel, a roll of toilet paper; and, when he looks at her questioningly: 'No one will see you.'

'I have changed my mind,' he says. 'We will go back to the Centre. There must be a public room where we can spend the night.'

'You can't do that. The gates at the Centre are closed. They close at six.'

Exasperated, he strides over to the stack of roofing, drags out two sheets, and leans them at an angle against the wooden fence. He does the same with third and fourth sheets, making a rude lean-to. 'Is that what you have in mind for us?' he says, turning to her. But she is gone.

'This is where we are going to sleep tonight,' he tells the boy. 'It will be an adventure.'

'I'm hungry,' says the boy.

'You haven't eaten your bread.'

'I don't like bread.'

'Well, you will have to get used to it, because that is all there is. Tomorrow we will find something better.'

Mistrustfully the boy picks up a slice of bread and nibbles at it. His fingernails, he notices, are black with dirt.

As the last daylight wanes, they settle down in their shelter, he on a bed of weeds, the boy in the crook of his arm. Soon the boy is asleep, his thumb in his mouth. In his own case sleep is slow in coming. He has no coat; in a while the cold begins to seep up into his body; he begins to shiver.

It is not serious, it is only cold, it will not kill you, he says to himself. *The night will pass, the sun will rise, the day will come. Only let there not be crawling insects. Crawling insects will be too much.*

He is asleep.

In the early hours he wakes up, stiff, aching with cold. Anger wells up in him. Why this pointless misery? He crawls out of the shelter, gropes his way to the back door, and knocks, first discreetly, then more and more loudly.

A window opens above; by moonlight he can faintly make out the girl's face. 'Yes?' she says. 'Is something wrong?'

'Everything is wrong,' he says. 'It is cold out here. Will you please let us into the house.'

There is a long pause. Then: 'Wait,' she says.

He waits. Then: 'Here,' says her voice.

An object falls at his feet: a blanket, none too large, folded in four, made of some rough material, smelling of camphor.

'Why do you treat us like this?' he calls out. 'Like dirt?'

9

The window thuds to.

He crawls back into the shelter, wraps the blanket around himself and the sleeping child.

He is woken by a clamour of birdsong. The boy, still sound asleep, lies turned away from him, his cap under his cheek. His own clothes are damp with dew. He dozes away again. When next he opens his eyes the girl is gazing down on him. 'Good morning,' she says. 'I have brought you some breakfast. I have to leave soon. When you are ready I will let you out.'

'Let us out?'

'Let you out through the house. Please be quick. Don't forget to bring the blanket and the towel.'

He wakes the child. 'Come,' he says, 'time to get up. Time for breakfast.'

They pee side by side in a corner of the yard.

Breakfast turns out to be more bread and water. The child disdains it; he himself is not hungry. He leaves the tray untouched on the step. 'We are ready to go,' he calls out.

The girl leads them through the house into the empty street. 'Goodbye,' she says. 'You can come back tonight if you need to.'

'What about the room you promised at the Centre?'

'If the key can't be found, or the room has been taken in the meantime, you can sleep here again. Goodbye.'

'Just a minute. Can you help us with some money?' Thus far he has not had to beg, but he does not know where else to turn.

'I said I would help you, I didn't say I would provide you with money. For that you will have to go to the offices of the

Asistencia Social. You can catch a bus in to the city. Be sure to take your passbook along, and your proof of residence. Then you can draw your relocation allowance. Alternatively you can find a job and ask for an advance. I won't be at the Centre this morning, I have meetings, but if you go there and tell them you are looking for a job and want *un vale*, they will know what you mean. *Un vale.* Now I really must run.'

The track he and the boy follow across the empty parklands turns out to be the wrong one; by the time they reach the Centre the sun is already high in the sky. Behind the *Trabajos* counter is a woman of middle age, stern-faced, her hair drawn back over her ears and tied tightly behind.

'Good morning,' he says. 'We checked in yesterday. We are new arrivals, and I am looking for work. I understand you can give me *un vale.*'

'*Vale de trabajo,*' says the woman. 'Show me your passbook.'

He gives her his passbook. She inspects it, returns it. 'I will write you a *vale*, but as for the line of work you do, that is up to you to decide on.'

'Have you any suggestions for where I should begin? This is foreign territory to me.'

'Try the docks,' says the woman. 'They are usually on the lookout for workers. Catch the Number 29 bus. It leaves from outside the main gate every half-hour.'

'I don't have money for buses. I don't have money at all.'

'The bus is free. All buses are free.'

'And a place to stay? May I raise the question of a place to stay? The young lady who was on duty yesterday, Ana she is called, reserved a room for us, but we haven't been able to gain access.'

'There are no rooms free.'

'There was a room free yesterday, room C-55, but the key was mislaid. The key was in the care of señora Weiss.'

'I know nothing about that. Come back this afternoon.'

'Can't I speak to señora Weiss?'

'There is a meeting of senior staff this morning. Señora Weiss is at the meeting. She will be back in the afternoon.'

Chapter 2

On the 29 bus he examines the *vale de trabajo* he has been given. It is nothing but a leaf torn from a notepad, on which is scribbled: 'Bearer is a new arrival. Please consider him for employment.' No official stamp, no signature, simply the initials P.X. It all seems very informal. Will it be enough to get him a job?

They are the last passengers to dismount. Considering how extensive the docks are – wharves stretch upriver as far as the eye can see – they are strangely desolate. On only one quay does there seem to be activity: a freighter is being loaded or unloaded, men are ascending and descending a gangplank.

He approaches a tall man in overalls who seems to be supervising operations. 'Good day,' he says. 'I am looking for work. The people at the Relocation Centre said I should come here. Are you the right person to speak to? I have a *vale*.'

'You can speak to me,' says the man. 'But are you not a little old for an *estibador*?'

Estibador? He must look baffled, for the man (the foreman?)

mimes swinging a load onto his back and staggering under the weight.

'Ah, *estibador*!' he exclaims. 'I am sorry, my Spanish is not good. No, not too old at all.'

Is it true, what he has just heard himself say? Is he really not too old for heavy work? He does not feel old, just as he does not feel young. He does not feel of any particular age. He feels ageless, if that is possible.

'Try me out,' he proposes. 'If you decide I am not up to it, I will quit at once, with no hard feelings.'

'Good,' says the foreman. He screws the *vale* into a ball and lobs it into the water. 'You can start at once. The youngster is with you? He can wait here with me, if you like. I'll keep an eye on him. As for your Spanish, don't worry, persist. One day it will cease to feel like a language, it will become the way things are.'

He turns to the boy. 'Will you stay with this gentleman while I help carry the bags?'

The boy nods. He has his thumb in his mouth again.

The gangplank is wide enough for only one man. He waits while a stevedore, bearing a bulging sack on his back, descends. Then he climbs up to the deck and down a stout wooden ladder into the hold. It takes a while for his eyes to adjust to the half-light. The hold is heaped with identical bulging sacks, hundreds of them, maybe thousands.

'What is in the sacks?' he asks the man beside him.

The man regards him oddly. '*Granos*,' he says.

He wants to ask what the sacks weigh, but there is no time. It is his turn.

Perched on top of the heap is a big fellow with brawny fore-arms and a wide grin whose job it evidently is to drop a sack onto the shoulders of the stevedore waiting in line. He turns his back, the sack descends; he staggers, then grips the corners as he sees the other men do, takes a first step, a second. Is he really going to be able to climb the ladder bearing this heavy weight, as the other men are doing? Does he have it in him?

'Steady, *viejo*,' says a voice behind him. 'Take your time.'

He places his left foot on the lowest rung of the ladder. It is a matter of balance, he tells himself, of keeping steady, of not letting the sack slide or the contents shift. Once things begin to shift or slide, you are lost. You go from being a stevedore to being a beggar shivering in a tin shelter in a stranger's backyard.

He brings up his right foot. He is beginning to learn some-thing about the ladder: that if you rest your chest against it then the weight of the sack, instead of threatening to topple you off balance, will stabilize you. His left foot finds the second rung. There is a light ripple of applause from below. He grits his teeth. Eighteen rungs to go (he has counted them). He will not fail.

Slowly, a step at a time, resting at each step, listening to his racing heart (What if he has a heart attack? What an embarrass-ment that will be!), he ascends. At the very top he teeters, then slumps forward so that the sack sags onto the deck.

He gets to his feet again, indicates the sack. 'Can someone give me a hand?' he says, trying to control his panting, trying to sound casual. Willing hands heave the sack onto his back.

The gangplank presents its own difficulties: it rocks gently from side to side as the ship moves, offering none of the support that the ladder did. He tries his best to hold himself erect as he descends, even though this means he cannot see where he is placing his feet. He fixes his eyes on the boy, who stands stock-still beside the foreman, observing. *Let me not shame him!* he says to himself.

Without a stumble he reaches the quayside. 'Turn left!' calls out the foreman. Laboriously he turns. A cart is in the process of drawing up, a low flat-bottomed cart hauled by two huge horses with shaggy fetlocks. Percherons? He has never seen a Percheron in the flesh. Their rank, urinous smell envelops him.

He turns and lets the sack of grain fall into the bed of the cart. A young man wearing a battered hat leaps lightly aboard and drags the sack forward. One of the horses drops a load of steaming dung. 'Out of the way!' calls out a voice behind him. It is the next of the stevedores, the next of his workmates, with the next sack.

He retraces his steps into the hold, returns with a second load, then a third. He is slower than his mates (they have sometimes to wait for him), but not much slower; he will improve as he gets used to the work and his body toughens. Not too old, after all.

Though he is holding them up, he senses no animus from the other men. On the contrary, they give him a cheery word or two, and a friendly slap on the back. If this is stevedoring, it is not such a bad job. At least one is accomplishing something. At least one is helping to move grain, grain that will be turned into bread, the staff of life.

A whistle blows. 'Break-time,' explains the man beside him. 'If you want to – you know.'

The two of them urinate behind a shed, wash their hands at a tap. 'Is there someplace one can get a cup of tea?' he asks. 'And perhaps something to eat?'

'Tea?' says the man. He seems amused. 'Not that I know of. If you are thirsty you can use my mug; but bring your own tomorrow.' He fills his mug at the tap, proffers it. 'Bring a loaf too, or half a loaf. It's a long day on an empty stomach.'

The break lasts only ten minutes, then the work of unloading resumes. By the time the foreman blows his whistle for the end of the day, he has carried thirty-one sacks out of the hold onto the wharf. In a full day he could carry perhaps fifty. Fifty sacks a day: two tons, more or less. Not a great deal. A crane could move two tons in one go. Why do they not use a crane?

'A good young man, this son of yours,' says the foreman. 'No trouble at all.' No doubt he calls him a young man, *un jovencito*, to make him feel good. A good young man who will grow up to be a stevedore too.

'If you were to bring in a crane,' he observes, 'you could get the unloading done in a tenth of the time. Even a small crane.'

'You could,' agrees the foreman. 'But what would be the point? What would be the point of getting things done in a tenth of the time? It is not as if there is an emergency, a food shortage for example.'

What would be the point? It sounds like a genuine question, not a slap in the face. 'So that we could devote our energies to some better task,' he suggests.

'Better than what? Better than supplying our fellow man with bread?'

He shrugs. He should have kept his mouth shut. He is certainly not going to say: *Better than lugging heavy loads like beasts of burden*.

'The boy and I need to hurry,' he says. 'We must be back at the Centre by six, otherwise we will have to sleep in the open. Shall I come back tomorrow morning?'

'Of course, of course. You have done well.'

'And can I get an advance on my pay?'

'Not possible, I'm afraid. The paymaster doesn't do his round until Friday. But if you are short of money' – he burrows into his pocket and comes out with a handful of coins – 'here, take what you need.'

'I am not sure what I need. I am new here, I have no idea of prices.'

'Take it all. You can pay me back on Friday.'

'Thank you. It is very kind of you.'

It is true. To keep an eye on your *jovencito* while you work and then to cap it all by lending you money: not what you would expect of a foreman.

'It's nothing. You would do the same. Goodbye, young man,' he says, turning to the boy. 'See you bright and early in the morning.'

They reach the office just as the woman with the dour face is closing up. Of Ana there is no sign.

'Any news of our room?' he asks. 'Have you found the key?'

The woman frowns. 'Follow the road, take the first turn

right, look for a long, flat building, it is called C Building. Ask for señora Weiss. She will show you your room. And ask señora Weiss whether you can use the laundry room to wash your clothes.'

He picks up the hint and flushes. After a week without a bath the child has begun to smell; no doubt he smells even worse.

He shows her his money. 'Can you tell me how much is this?'

'Can't you count?'

'I mean, what can I buy with it? Can I buy a meal?'

'The Centre does not provide meals, only breakfast. But speak to señora Weiss. Explain your situation. She may be able to help you.'

C-41, señora Weiss's office, is closed and locked as before. But in the basement, in a nook under the stairs lit by a single bare bulb, he comes upon a young man sprawled in a chair reading a magazine. As an addition to the chocolate-coloured Centre uniform the fellow wears a tiny round hat with a strap under the chin, like a performing monkey's.

'Good evening,' he says. 'I am looking for the elusive señora Weiss. Have you any idea where she is? We have been allocated a room in this building, and she has the key, or at least the master key.'

The young man gets to his feet, clears his throat, and responds. His response is polite but in the end not helpful. If señora Weiss's office is locked then the señora has probably gone home. As for any master key, if one exists then it is likely to be in the same locked office. Similarly for the key to the laundry room.

'Can you at least direct us to room C-55?' he asks. 'C-55 is the room allocated to us.'

Without a word the young man leads them down a long corridor, past C-49, C-50 . . . C-54. They reach C-55. He tries the door. It is not locked. 'Your troubles are over,' he remarks with a smile, and withdraws.

C-55 is small, windowless, and exceedingly simply furnished: a single bed, a chest of drawers, a washbasin. On the chest of drawers is a tray holding a saucer with two and a half cubes of sugar in it. He gives the sugar to the boy.

'Do we have to stay here?' asks the boy.

'Yes, we have to stay here. It will only be for a short time, while we look for something better.'

At the far end of the corridor he locates a shower cubicle. There is no soap. He undresses the child, undresses himself. Together they stand under a thin stream of tepid water while he does his best to wash them. Then, while the child waits, he holds their underwear under the same stream (which soon turns cool and then cold) and wrings it out. Defiantly naked, with the child beside him, he pads down the bare corridor back to their room and bolts the door. With their one and only towel he dries the boy. 'Now get into bed,' he says.

'I'm hungry,' complains the boy.

'Be patient. We will have a big breakfast in the morning, I promise. Think about that.' He tucks him into bed, gives him a goodnight kiss.

But the boy is not sleepy. 'What are we here for, Simón?' he asks quietly.

'I told you: we are here just for a night or two, till we find a better place to stay.'

'No, I mean, why are we *here*?' His gesture takes in the room, the Centre, the city of Novilla, everything.

'You are here to find your mother. I am here to help you.'

'But after we find her, what are we here for?'

'I don't know what to say. We are here for the same reason everyone else is. We have been given a chance to live and we have accepted that chance. It is a great thing, to live. It is the greatest thing of all.'

'But do we have to live here?'

'Here as opposed to where? There is nowhere else to be but here. Now close your eyes. It is time to sleep.'

Chapter 3

He wakes up in a good mood, full of energy. They have a place to stay, he has a job. It is time to set about the chief task: finding the boy's mother.

Leaving the boy asleep, he steals out of the room. The main office has just opened. Ana, behind the counter, greets him with a smile. 'Did you have a good night?' she asks. 'Have you settled in?'

'Thank you, we have settled in. But now I have another favour to ask. You may remember, I asked you about tracking down family members. I need to find David's mother. The trouble is, I don't know where to start. Do you keep records of arrivals in Novilla? If not, is there some central registry I can consult?'

'We keep a record of everyone who passes through the Centre. But records won't help if you don't know what you are looking for. David's mother will have a new name. A new life, a new name. Is she expecting you?'

'She has never heard of me so she has no reason to expect

me. But as soon as the child sees her he will recognize her, I am sure of that.'

'How long have they been separated?'

'It is a complicated story, I won't burden you with it. Let me simply say I promised David I would find his mother. I gave him my word. So may I have a look at your records?'

'But without a name, how will that help you?'

'You keep copies of passbooks. The boy will recognize her from a photograph. Or I will. I will know her when I see her.'

'You have never met her but you will recognize her?'

'Yes. Separately or together, he and I will recognize her. I am confident of that.'

'What about this anonymous mother herself? Are you sure she wants to be reunited with her son? It may seem heartless to say, but most people, by the time they get here, have lost interest in old attachments.'

'This case is different, truly. I can't explain why. Now: may I look at your records?'

She shakes her head. 'No, that I can't permit. If you had the mother's name it would be a different matter. But I can't let you hunt through our files at will. It is not just against regulations, it is absurd. We have thousands of entries, hundreds of thousands, more than you can count. Besides, how do you know she passed through the Novilla centre? There is a reception centre in every city.'

'I concede, it makes no sense. Nevertheless, I plead with you. The child is motherless. He is lost. You must have seen how lost he is. He is in limbo.'

'In limbo. I don't know what that means. The answer is no. I am not going to give in, so don't press me. I am sorry for the boy, but this is not the correct way to proceed.'

There is a long silence between them.

'I can do it late at night,' he says. 'No one will know. I will be quiet, I will be discreet.'

But she is not attending to him. 'Hello!' she says, looking over his shoulder. 'Have you just got up?'

He turns. In the doorway, tousle-haired, barefoot, in his underwear, his thumb in his mouth, still half asleep, stands the boy.

'Come!' he says. 'Say hello to Ana. Ana is going to help us in our quest.'

The boy ambles across to them.

'I will help you,' says Ana, 'but not in the way you ask. People here have washed themselves clean of old ties. You should be doing the same: letting go of old attachments, not pursuing them.' She reaches down, ruffles the boy's hair. 'Hello, sleepy head!' she says. 'Aren't you washed clean yet? Tell your dad you are washed clean.'

The boy looks from her to him and back again. 'I'm washed clean,' he mumbles.

'There!' says Ana. 'Didn't I tell you?'

They are in the bus, on their way to the docks. After a substantial breakfast the boy is decidedly more cheerful than yesterday.

'Are we going to see Álvaro again?' he says. 'Álvaro likes me. He lets me blow his whistle.'

'That's nice. Did he say you could call him Álvaro?'

'Yes, that's his name. Álvaro Avocado.'

'Álvaro Avocado? Well, remember, Álvaro is a busy man. He has lots of things to do besides child-minding. You must take care not to get in his way.'

'He's not busy,' says the boy. 'He just stands and looks.'

'It may seem to you like standing and looking, but in fact he is supervising us, seeing to it that ships get unloaded in time, seeing to it that everyone does what he is supposed to do. It is an important job.'

'He says he is going to teach me chess.'

'That's good. You will like chess.'

'Will I always be with Álvaro?'

'No, soon you will find other boys to play with.'

'I don't want to play with other boys. I want to be with you and Álvaro.'

'But not all the time. It's not good for you to be with grown-ups all the time.'

'I don't want you to fall into the sea. I don't want you to drown.'

'Don't worry, I'll take great care not to drown, I promise you. You can shoo away dark thoughts like that. You can let them fly away like birds. Will you do that?'

The boy does not respond. 'When are we going to go back?' he says.

'Back across the sea? We are not going back. We are here now. This is where we live.'

'For ever?'

'For good. Soon we will begin our search for your mother. Ana will help us. Once we have found your mother, you won't have any more thoughts about going back.'

'Is my mother here?'

'She is somewhere nearby, waiting for you. She has been waiting a long time. All will become clear as soon as you lay eyes on her. You will remember her and she will remember you. You may think you are washed clean, but you aren't. You still have your memories, they are just buried, temporarily. Now we must get off. This is our stop.'

The boy has befriended one of the carthorses, to whom he has given the name El Rey. Though he is tiny compared with El Rey, he is quite unafraid. Standing on tiptoe, he proffers handfuls of hay, which the huge beast bends down lazily to accept.

Álvaro cuts a hole in one of the bags they have unloaded, allowing grain to trickle out. 'Here, feed this to El Rey and his friend,' he tells the boy. 'But be careful not to feed them too much, otherwise their tummies will blow up like balloons and we will have to prick them with a pin.'

El Rey and his friend are in fact mares, but Álvaro, he notes, does not correct the boy.

His fellow stevedores are friendly enough but strangely incurious. No one asks where they come from or where they are staying. He guesses that they take him to be the boy's father – or perhaps, like Ana at the Centre, his grandfather. *El viejo*.

No one asks where the boy's mother is or why he has to spend all day hanging around the docks.

There is a small wooden shed at the quayside which the men use as a dressing room. Though the door has no lock, they seem happy to store their overalls and boots there. He asks one of the men where he can buy overalls and boots of his own. The man writes an address on a scrap of paper.

What can one expect to pay for a pair of boots? he asks.

'Two, maybe three reals,' says the man.

'That seems very little,' he says. 'By the way, my name is Simón.'

'Eugenio,' says the man.

'May I ask, Eugenio, are you married? Do you have children?'

Eugenio shakes his head.

'Well, you are still young,' he says.

'Yes,' says Eugenio non-committally.

He waits to be asked about the boy – the boy who may seem to be his son or grandson but in fact is not. He waits to be asked the boy's name, his age, why he is not at school. He waits in vain.

'David, the child I am looking after, is still too young to go to school,' he says. 'Do you know anything about schools around here? Is there' – he hunts for the term – 'un jardin para los niños?'

'Do you mean a playground?'

'No, a school for the younger children. A school before proper school.'

'Sorry, I can't help you.' Eugenio rises. 'Time to get back to work.'

The next day, just as the whistle blows for the lunch break, a stranger comes riding up on a bicycle. With his hat, black suit and tie he looks out of place on the quayside. He dismounts, greets Álvaro familiarly. His trouser-cuffs are pinned back with bicycle clips, which he neglects to remove.

'That's the paymaster,' says a voice beside him. It is Eugenio.

The paymaster slackens the straps on his bicycle rack and removes an oilcloth, revealing a green-painted metal cashbox, which he sets down on an upended drum. Álvaro beckons the men over. One by one they step forward, speak their names, and are given their wages. He joins the end of the line, waits his turn. 'Simón is the name,' he says to the paymaster. 'I am new, I may not be on your list yet.'

'Yes, here you are,' says the paymaster, and ticks off his name. He counts out the money in coins, so many that they weigh down his pockets.

'Thank you,' he says.

'You're welcome. It's your due.'

Álvaro rolls the drum away. The paymaster straps the cashbox back on his bicycle, shakes hands with Álvaro, dons his hat, and pedals off down the quay.

'What are your plans for the afternoon?' asks Álvaro.

'I have no plans. I might take the boy for a walk; or if there is a zoo, I might take him there, to see the animals.'

It is Saturday, noon, the end of the working week.

'Would you like to come along to the football?' asks Álvaro. 'Does your young man like football?'

'He is still a bit young for football.'

'He has to start sometime. The game starts at three. Meet me at the gate at, say, two forty-five.'

'All right, but which gate, and where?'

'The gate to the football ground. There is only one gate.'

'And where is the football ground?'

'Follow the footpath along the riverfront and you can't miss it. About twenty minutes from here, I would guess. Or if you don't feel like walking you can catch the Number 7 bus.'

The football ground is further away than Álvaro said; the boy gets tired and dawdles; they arrive late. Álvaro is at the gate, waiting for them. 'Hurry,' he says, 'they will be kicking off at any moment.'

They pass through the gate into the ground.

'Don't we need to buy tickets?' he asks.

Álvaro regards him oddly. 'It's football,' he says. 'It's a game. You don't need to pay to watch a game.'

The ground is more modest than he had expected. The playing field is marked off with rope; the covered stand holds at most a thousand spectators. They find seats without difficulty. The players are already on the pitch, kicking the ball around, warming up.

'Who is playing?' he asks.

'That's Docklands in blue, and in red are North Hills. It is a league game. Championship games are played on Sunday mornings. If you hear the hooters sounding on a Sunday morning, that means there is a championship game being played.'

'Which team do you support?'

'Docklands, of course. Who else?'

Álvaro seems in a good mood, excited, even ebullient. He is glad of that, grateful too for being singled out to accompany him. Álvaro strikes him as a good man. In fact, all of his fellow stevedores strike him as good men: hard-working, friendly, helpful.

In the very first minute of the game the team in red makes a simple defensive error and Docklands scores. Álvaro throws up his arms and lets out a cry of triumph, then turns to the boy. 'Did you see that, young fellow? Did you see?'

The young fellow has not seen. Ignorant of football, the young fellow does not grasp that he should be attending to the men running back and forth on the pitch rather than to the sea of strangers around them.

He lifts the boy onto his lap. 'See,' he says, pointing, 'what they are trying to do is to kick the ball into the net. And the man over there, wearing the gloves, is the goalkeeper. He has to stop the ball. There is a goalkeeper at each end. When they kick the ball into the net, it is called a goal. The team in blue has just scored a goal.'

The boy nods, but his mind seems to be elsewhere.

He lowers his voice. 'Do you need to go to the toilet?'

'I'm hungry,' the boy whispers back.

'I know. I'm hungry too. We must just get used to it. I'll see if I can get us some potato crisps at half-time, or some peanuts. Would you like peanuts?'

The boy nods. 'When is half-time?' he asks.

'Soon. First the footballers must play some more, and try to score more goals. Watch.'

Chapter 4

Returning to their room that evening, he finds a note pushed under the door. It is from Ana: *Would you and David like to come to a picnic for new arrivals? Meet at noon tomorrow, in the park, by the fountain. A.*

They are at the fountain at noon. It is already hot – even the birds seem lethargic. Away from the noise of traffic they settle beneath a spreading tree. After a while Ana arrives, bearing a basket. 'Sorry,' she says, 'something came up.'

'How many of us are you expecting?' he asks.

'I don't know. Perhaps half a dozen. Let us wait and see.'

They wait. No one comes. 'Looks like it is just us,' says Ana at last. 'Shall we start?'

The basket turns out to contain no more than a packet of crackers, a pot of saltless bean paste, and a bottle of water. But the child wolfs down his share without complaint.

Ana yawns, stretches out on the grass, closes her eyes.

'What did you mean, the other day, when you used the

words *washed clean*?' he asks her. 'You said David and I should wash ourselves clean of old attachments.'

Lazily Ana shakes her head. 'Another time,' she says. 'Not now.'

In her tone, in the hooded glance she casts him, he senses an invitation. The half-dozen guests who have failed to turn up – were they just a fiction? If the child were not here he would lie down on the grass beside her and then perhaps let his hand rest ever so lightly on hers.

'No,' she murmurs, as if reading his mind. The ghost of a frown crosses her brow. 'Not that.'

Not that. What is he to make of this young woman, now warm, now cool? Is there something in the etiquette of the sexes or the generations in this new land that he is failing to understand?

The boy nudges him and points to the nearly empty packet of crackers. He spreads paste on a cracker and passes it across.

'He has a healthy appetite,' says the girl without opening her eyes.

'He is hungry all the time.'

'Don't worry, he will adapt. Children adapt quickly.'

'Adapt to being hungry? Why should he adapt to being hungry when there is no shortage of food?'

'Adapt to a moderate diet, I mean. Hunger is like a dog in your belly: the more you feed it, the more it demands.' She sits up abruptly, addresses the child. 'I hear you are looking for your mama,' she says. 'Do you miss your mama?'

The boy nods.

'And what is your mama's name?'

The boy casts him an interrogative glance.

'He doesn't know her by name,' he says. 'He had a letter with him when he boarded the boat, but it was lost.'

'The string broke,' says the boy.

'The letter was in a pouch,' he explains, 'which was hanging around his neck on a string. The string broke and the letter was lost. There was a hunt for it all over the ship. That was how David and I met. But the letter was never found.'

'It fell in the sea,' says the boy. 'The fishes ate it.'

Ana frowns. 'If you don't remember your mama's name, can you tell us what she looks like? Can you draw a picture of her?'

The boy shakes his head.

'So your mama is lost and you don't know where to look for her.' Ana pauses to reflect. 'Then how would you feel if your *padrino* began looking for another mama for you, to love and take care of you?'

'What is a *padrino*?' asks the boy.

'You keep slotting me into roles,' he interrupts. 'I am not David's father, nor am I his *padrino*. I am simply helping him to be reunited with his mother.'

She ignores the rebuke. 'If you found yourself a wife,' she says, 'she could be a mother to him.'

He bursts out laughing. 'What woman would want to marry a man like me, a stranger without even a change of clothing to his name?' He waits for the girl to disagree, but she does not. 'Besides, even if I did find myself a wife, who is to say she would want – you know – a foster child? Or that our young friend here would accept her?'

'You never know. Children adapt.'

'As you keep saying.' Anger flares up in him. What does this cocksure young woman know about children? And what entitles her to preach to him? Then suddenly the elements of the picture come together. The unbecoming clothes, the baffling severity, the talk of godfathers – 'Are you a nun, Ana, by any chance?' he asks.

She smiles. 'What makes you say that?'

'Are you one of those nuns who have left the convent behind to live in the world? To take on jobs that no one else wants to do – in jails and orphanages and asylums? In refugee reception centres?'

'That is ridiculous. Of course not. The Centre isn't a jail. It isn't a charity. It is part of Social Welfare.'

'Even so, how could anyone put up with a never-ending stream of people like us, helpless and ignorant and needy, without faith of some kind to give her strength?'

'Faith? Faith has nothing to do with it. Faith means believing in what you do even when it does not bear visible fruit. The Centre is not like that. People arrive needing help, and we help them. We help them and their lives improve. None of that is invisible. None of it requires blind faith. We do our job, and everything turns out well. It is as simple as that.'

'Nothing is invisible?'

'Nothing is invisible. Two weeks ago you were in Belstar. Last week we found you a job at the docks. Today you are having a picnic in the park. What is invisible about that? It is progress, visible progress. Anyway, to come back to your question, no, I am not a nun.'

'Then why the asceticism that you preach? You tell us to subdue our hunger, to starve the dog inside us. Why? What is wrong with hunger? What are our appetites for if not to tell us what we need? If we had no appetites, no desires, how would we live?'

It seems to him a good question, a serious question, one that might trouble the best-schooled young nun.

Her answer comes easily, so easily and in so low a voice, as if the child were not meant to hear, that for a moment he misunderstands her: 'And where, in your case, do your desires lead you?'

'My own desires? May I be frank?'

'You may.'

'With no disrespect to you or to your hospitality, they lead me to more than crackers and bean paste. They lead, for instance, to beefsteak with mashed potatoes and gravy. And I am sure this young man' — he reaches out and grips the boy's arm — 'feels the same way. Don't you?'

The boy nods vigorously.

'Beefsteak dripping with meat juices,' he goes on. 'Do you know what surprises me most about this country?' A reckless tone is creeping into his voice; it would be wiser to stop, but he does not. 'That it is so bloodless. Everyone I meet is so decent, so kindly, so well-intentioned. No one swears or gets angry. No one gets drunk. No one even raises his voice. You live on a diet of bread and water and bean paste and you claim to be filled. How can that be, humanly speaking? Are you lying, even to yourselves?'

Hugging her knees, the girl stares at him wordlessly, waiting for the tirade to end.

'We are hungry, this child and I.' Forcefully he draws the boy to him. 'We are hungry all the time. You tell me our hunger is something outlandish that we have brought with us, that it doesn't belong here, that we must starve it into submission. When we have annihilated our hunger, you say, we will have proved we can adapt, and we can then be happy for ever after. But I don't want to starve the dog of hunger! I want to feed it! Don't you agree?' He shakes the boy. The boy burrows in under his armpit, smiling, nodding. 'Don't you agree, my boy?'

A silence falls.

'You really are angry,' says Ana.

'I am not angry, I am hungry! Tell me: What is wrong with satisfying an ordinary appetite? Why must our ordinary impulses and hungers and desires be beaten down?'

'Are you sure you want to carry on like this in front of the child?'

'I am not ashamed of what I am saying. There is nothing in it that a child needs to be protected from. If a child can sleep outdoors on the bare earth, then surely he can hear a robust exchange between adults.'

'Very well, I will give you robust exchange back. What you want from me is something I don't do.'

He stares in puzzlement. 'What I want from you?'

'Yes. You want me to let you embrace me. We both know what that means: *embrace*. And I don't permit it.'

'I said nothing about embracing you. And what is wrong with embraces anyway, if you are not a nun?'

'Refusing desires has nothing to do with being or not being a nun. I just don't do that. I don't permit it. I don't like it. I don't have an appetite for it. I don't have an appetite for it in itself and I don't wish to see what it does to human beings. What it does to a man.'

'What do you mean, *what it does to a man*?'

She glances pointedly at the child. 'You are sure you want me to go on?'

'Go on. It is never too early to learn about life.'

'Very well. You find me attractive, I can see that. Perhaps you even find me beautiful. And because you find me beautiful, your appetite, your impulse, is to embrace me. Do I read the signs correctly, the signs you give me? Whereas if you did not find me beautiful you would feel no such impulse.'

He is silent.

'The more beautiful you find me, the more urgent becomes your appetite. That is how these appetites work which you take as your lodestar and blindly follow. Now reflect. What – pray tell me – has beauty to do with the embrace you want me to submit to? What is the connection between the one and the other? Explain.'

He is silent, more than silent. He is dumbfounded.

'Go on. You said you would not mind if your godson heard. You said you wanted him to learn about life.'

'Between a man and a woman,' he says at last, 'there sometimes springs up a natural attraction, unforeseen, unpremeditated. The two find each other attractive or even, to use the other word, beautiful. The woman more beautiful than the man, usually. Why the one should follow from the other, the attraction and the desire to embrace from the beauty, is a mystery which I cannot explain except to say that being drawn to a woman is the only tribute that I, my physical self, know how to pay to the woman's beauty. I call it a tribute because I feel it to be an offering, not an insult.'

He pauses. 'Go on,' she says.

'That is all I want to say.'

'That is all. And as a tribute to me – an offering, not an insult – you want to grip me tight and push part of your body into me. As a tribute, you claim. I am baffled. To me the whole business seems absurd – absurd for you to want to perform, and absurd for me to permit.'

'It is only when you put it that way that it seems absurd. In itself it is not absurd. It cannot be absurd, since it is a natural desire of the natural body. It is nature speaking in us. It is the way things are. The way things are cannot be absurd.'

'Really? What if I were to say that to me it seems not just absurd but ugly too?'

He shakes his head in disbelief. 'You cannot mean that. I myself may seem old and unattractive – I and my desires. But surely you cannot believe that nature itself is ugly.'

'Yes, I can. Nature can partake of the beautiful but nature can partake of the ugly too. Those parts of our bodies that you modestly do not name, not in your godson's hearing: do you find them beautiful?'

'In themselves? No, in themselves they are not beautiful. It is the whole that is beautiful, not the parts.'

'And these parts that are not beautiful – you want to push them inside me! What should I think of that?'

'I don't know. Tell me what you think.'

'That all your fine talk of paying tribute to beauty is *una tontería*. If you found me to be an incarnation of the good, you would not want to perform such an act upon me. So why wish to do so if I am an incarnation of the beautiful? Is the beautiful inferior to the good? Explain.'

'*Una tontería*: what's that?'

'Nonsense. Rubbish.'

He gets to his feet. 'I am not going to excuse myself further, Ana. I don't find this to be a profitable discussion. I don't believe you know what you are talking about.'

'Really? You think I am some ignorant child?'

'You may not be a child but, yes, I do think you are ignorant of life. Come,' he says to the boy, taking his hand. 'We have had our picnic, now it is time to thank the lady and go off and find ourselves something to eat.'

Ana reclines, stretches out her legs, folds her hands in her lap, smiles up at him mockingly. 'Too close to the bone, was it?' she says.

Under a blazing sun he strides across the empty parklands, the boy trotting to keep up with him.

'What is a *padrino*?' asks the boy.

'A *padrino* is someone who acts as your father when for some reason your father cannot be there.'

'Are you my *padrino*?'

'No, I am not. No one invited me to be your *padrino*. I am just your friend.'

'I can invite you to be my *padrino*.'

'That is not up to you, my boy. You can't choose a *padrino* for yourself, as you can't choose your father. There isn't a proper word for what I am to you, just as there isn't a proper word for what you are to me. However, if you like, you can call me Uncle. When people say, *Who is he to you?* you can say, *He is my uncle. He is my uncle and he loves me.* And I will say, *He is my boy.*'

'But is that lady going to be my mother?'

'Ana? No. Being a mother would not interest her.'

'Are you going to marry her?'

'Of course not. I am not here to find a wife, I am here to help you find your mother, your real mother.'

He is trying to keep his voice even, his tone light; but the truth is, the attack by the girl has shaken him.

'You were cross with her,' says the boy. 'Why were you cross?'

He halts in his tracks, lifts the boy up, gives him a kiss on the brow. 'I'm sorry I was cross. I wasn't cross with you.'

'But you were cross with the lady and she was cross with you.'

'I was cross with her because she treats us badly and I don't understand why. We had an argument, she and I, a heated argument. But it's all over now. It was not important.'

'She said you wanted to push something inside her.'

He is silent.

'What did she mean? Do you really want to push something inside her?'

'It was only a manner of speaking. She meant that I was trying to force my ideas on her. And she was right. One should not try to force ideas upon people.'

'Do I force ideas on you?'

'No, of course not. Now let us find something to eat.'

They scour the streets east of the parkland, hunting for an eating place of some kind. It is a neighbourhood of modest villas, with now and again a low apartment building. They happen on only a single shop. *NARANJAS* says the sign, in large letters. The steel shutters are closed, so he cannot see whether it indeed sells oranges or whether Naranjas is just a name.

He stops a passer-by, an elderly man walking a dog on a lead. 'Excuse me,' he says, 'my boy and I are looking for a café or restaurant where we can get a meal, or failing that a provisions shop.'

'On a Sunday afternoon?' says the man. His dog sniffs the boy's shoes, then his crotch. 'I don't know what to suggest, unless you are prepared to go in to the city.'

'Is there a bus?'

'Number 42, but it doesn't run on Sundays.'

'So we cannot in fact go in to the city. And there is nowhere nearby where we can eat. And all the shops are closed. What then do you suggest we do?'

The man's features harden. He tugs at the dog's lead. 'Come, Bruno,' he says.

In a sour mood he heads back to the Centre. Their progress is slow, since the boy keeps hesitating and hopping to avoid cracks in the paving.

'Come on, hurry up,' he says irritably. 'Keep your game for another day.'

'No. I don't want to fall into a crack.'

'That's nonsense. How can a big boy like you fall down a little crack like that?'

'Not that crack. Another crack.'

'Which crack? Point to the crack.'

'I don't know! I don't know which crack. Nobody knows.'

'Nobody knows because nobody can fall through a crack in the paving. Now hurry up.'

'I can! You can! Anyone can! You don't know!'

Chapter 5

During the midday break at work the next day he takes Álvaro aside. 'Forgive me if I raise a private matter,' he says, 'but I am becoming more and more concerned about the youngster's health, and specifically about his diet, which – as you can see – consists of bread and bread and yet more bread.'

And indeed they can see the boy, sitting among the stevedores in the lee of the shed, munching dolefully on his half-loaf moistened with water.

'It seems to me,' he continues, 'that a growing child needs more variety, more nourishment. One cannot live on bread alone. It is not a universal food. You don't know where I can buy meat, do you, without making a trip to the city centre?'

Álvaro scratches his head. 'Not around here, not around the docklands. There are people who catch rats, I have heard tell. There is no shortage of rats. But for that you will need a trap, and I don't know offhand where you would lay your hands on a good rat trap. You would probably have to make it yourself. You could use wire, with some kind of trip mechanism.'

'Rats?'

'Yes. Haven't you seen them? Wherever there are ships there are rats.'

'But who eats rats? Do you eat rats?'

'No, I wouldn't dream of it. But you asked where you could get meat, and that is all I can suggest.'

He stares long into Álvaro's eyes. He can see no sign that he is joking. Or if it is a joke, it is a very deep joke.

After work he and the boy make their way straight back to the enigmatic Naranjas. They arrive as the proprietor is about to let down the shutters. Naranjas is indeed a shop, as it turns out, and does indeed sell oranges, as well as other fruits and vegetables. While the proprietor waits impatiently, he selects as much as the two of them can carry: a small pocket of oranges, half a dozen apples, some carrots and cucumbers.

Back in their room at the Centre he slices an apple for the boy and peels an orange. While the boy is eating these he cuts a carrot and a cucumber into slim cartwheels and lays them out on a plate. 'There!' he says.

Suspiciously the boy prods the cucumber, sniffs it. 'I don't like it,' he says. 'It smells.'

'Nonsense. Cucumber has no smell at all. The green part is just the rind. Taste it. It's good for you. It will make you grow.' He eats half the cucumber himself, and a whole carrot, and an orange.

The next morning he revisits Naranjas and buys more fruit – bananas, pears, apricots – which he brings back to the room. Now they have quite a stock.

He is late for work, but Álvaro does not remark on it.

Despite the welcome additions to their diet, the feeling of bodily exhaustion does not leave him. Rather than building up his strength, the daily labour of lifting and carrying seems to be draining him. He is beginning to feel quite wraithlike; he fears he is going to faint in front of his comrades and shame himself.

He seeks out Álvaro again. 'I'm not feeling well,' he says. 'I haven't been feeling well for a while. Is there a doctor you can recommend?'

'There is a clinic on Wharf Seven that is open in the afternoons. Go there at once. Tell them you work here; then you won't have to pay.'

He follows the signs to Wharf Seven, where there is indeed a little clinic, called simply *Clínica*. The door is open, the counter unmanned. He presses the buzzer, but it does not work.

'Hello!' he calls out. 'Is anyone here?'

Silence.

He crosses behind the counter and raps on the closed door marked *Cirugía*. 'Hello!' he calls.

The door opens and he is confronted by a large, florid-faced man in a white laboratory coat on whose collar there is a lush smear of what looks like chocolate. The man is sweating heavily.

'Good afternoon,' he says. 'Are you the doctor?'

'Come in,' says the man. 'Sit down.' He indicates a chair, removes his glasses, wipes the lenses carefully with a tissue. 'Do you work here at the docks?'

'On Wharf Two.'

'Ah, Wharf Two. And what can I do for you?'

'For the past week or two I have not been feeling well. There are no specific symptoms except that I get tired easily and now and again have dizzy spells. I think it is probably because of my diet, the lack of nourishment in my diet.'

'When do you have these dizzy spells? At any particular time of day?'

'No particular time. They come when I am tired. I work as a stevedore, loading and unloading, as I told you. It is not work I am accustomed to. In the course of a day I have to cross a gangplank many times. Sometimes as I look down into the space between the quay and the ship's side, at the waves slapping against the quay, I feel dizzy. I feel I am going to slip and fall and perhaps hit my head and drown.'

'That doesn't sound to me like undernourishment.'

'Maybe not. But if I were better nourished I would be better able to resist the dizziness.'

'Have you ever had such fears before, fears of falling and drowning?'

'This is not a psychological matter, Doctor. I am a labourer. I do hard work. I carry heavy loads hour after hour. My heart hammers. I am continually at the limit of my powers. It is only natural, surely, that my body should sometimes get to the point of failing, of letting me down.'

'Of course it is natural. But if it is natural why have you come to the clinic? What do you expect from me?'

'Don't you think you should listen to my heart? Don't you

47

think you should test me for anaemia? Don't you think we should discuss possible deficiencies in my diet?'

'I will check your heart as you suggest but I cannot test you for anaemia. This is not a medical laboratory, it is just a clinic, a first-aid clinic for dock workers. Take off your shirt.'

He removes his shirt. The doctor presses a stethoscope to his chest, directs his gaze to the ceiling, listens. His breath smells of garlic. 'There is nothing wrong with your heart,' he says at last. 'It is a good heart. It will last you many years. You can go back to work.'

He rises. 'How can you say that? I am exhausted. I am not myself. My general health deteriorates with every passing day. This was not what I expected when I arrived. Illness, exhaustion, unhappiness – I expected none of these. I have presentiments – not mere intellectual presentiments but actual bodily presentiments – that I am about to collapse. My body is signalling to me, in every way it can, that it is failing. How can you say there is nothing wrong with me?'

There is silence. Carefully the doctor folds his stethoscope into its black bag and puts it away in a drawer. He sets his elbows on his desk, clasps his hands, rests his chin on his hands, speaks. 'Good sir,' he says, 'I am sure you did not come to this little clinic expecting a miracle. If you were hoping for a miracle, you would have gone to a proper hospital with a proper laboratory. All I can offer you is advice. My advice is simple: don't look down. You have these attacks of vertigo because you look down. Vertigo is a psychological matter, not a medical matter. Looking down is what sets off the attack.'

'Is that all you can suggest: don't look down?'

'That is all, unless you have symptoms of an objective nature that you can share with me.'

'No, no such symptoms. No such symptoms at all.'

'How did it go?' asks Álvaro when he returns. 'Did you find the clinic?'

'I found the clinic and I spoke to the doctor. He says that I should look up. As long as I keep looking up, all will be well with me. Whereas if I look down, I may fall.'

'That sounds like good, common-sense advice,' says Álvaro. 'Nothing fancy. Now why not take the day off and have a bit of a rest?'

Despite the fresh fruit from Naranjas, despite the assurance of the doctor that his heart is sound and that there is no reason why he should not live for many years, he continues to feel exhausted. Nor does the dizziness go away. Though he heeds the doctor's advice not to look down as he crosses the gangplank, he cannot block out the menacing sound that the waves make as they slap against the oily quayside.

'It is just vertigo,' Álvaro reassures him, giving him a pat on the back. 'Lots of people suffer from it. Fortunately it is only in the mind. It is not real. Ignore it and soon enough it will go away.'

He is not convinced. He does not believe that what oppresses him will go away.

'Anyway,' says Álvaro, 'if by some chance you do slip and fall, you won't drown. Someone will save you. I will save you. What else are comrades for?'

'You would jump in and save me?'

'If necessary. Or throw you a rope.'

'Yes, throwing a rope would be more efficient.'

Álvaro ignores the edge to the remark, or perhaps does not pick it up. 'More practical,' he says.

'Is this all we ever unload — wheat?' he asks Álvaro on another occasion.

'Wheat and rye,' replies Álvaro.

'But is this all we import through the docks: grain?'

'It depends on what you mean by *we*. Wharf Two is for grain cargoes. If you worked on Wharf Seven you would be unloading mixed cargoes. If you worked on Wharf Nine you would be unloading steel and cement. Haven't you been around the docks? Haven't you explored?'

'I have. But the other wharves have always been empty. As they are now.'

'Well, that makes sense, doesn't it? You don't need a new bicycle every day. You don't need new shoes every day, or new clothes. But you do have to eat every day. So we need lots of grain.'

'Therefore if I were to transfer to Wharf Seven or Wharf Nine I would have an easier time. I could take whole weeks off work.'

'Correct. If you worked on Seven or Nine you would have an easier time. But you would also not have a full-time job. So, on the whole, you are better off on Two.'

'I see. So it is for the best, after all, that I am here, on this wharf, in this port, in this city, in this land. All is for the best in this best of all possible worlds.'

Álvaro frowns. 'This isn't a possible world,' he says. 'It is the only world. Whether that makes it the best is not for you or for me to decide.'

He can think of several replies, but refrains from airing them. Perhaps, in this world that is the only world, it would be prudent to put irony behind him.

Chapter 6

As he promised, Álvaro has been teaching the boy chess. When
work is slack, they can be seen hunched over a pocket set in
some patch of shade, absorbed in a game.

'He has just beaten me,' reports Álvaro. 'Only two weeks
and already he is better than me.'

Eugenio, the most bookish of the stevedores, issues the boy
with a challenge. 'A lightning game,' he says. 'We each have
five seconds to make our move. One-two-three-four-five.'

Ringed by spectators, they play their lightning game. In a
matter of minutes the boy has Eugenio backed into a corner.
Eugenio gives his king a tap and it falls on its side. 'I'll think
twice before taking you on again,' he says. 'You've got a real
devil in you.'

In the bus that evening he tries to discuss the game, and
Eugenio's strange remark; but the boy is reticent.

'Would you like me to buy you a chess set of your own?' he
offers. 'Then you can practise at home.'

The boy shakes his head. 'I don't want to practise. I don't like chess.'

'But you are so good at it.'

The boy shrugs.

'If one is blessed with a talent, one has a duty not to hide it,' he presses on doggedly.

'Why?'

'Why? Because the world is a better place, I suppose, if each of us can excel at something.'

The boy stares moodily out of the window.

'Are you upset about what Eugenio said? You shouldn't be. He didn't mean it.'

'I'm not upset. I just don't like chess.'

'Well, Álvaro will be disappointed.'

The next day a stranger makes his appearance at the docks. He is small and wiry; his skin is burned a deep walnut shade; his eyes are deep set, his nose hooked like a hawk's beak. He wears faded jeans streaked with machine oil, and scarred leather boots.

From his breast pocket he takes a scrap of paper, hands it to Álvaro, and without a word stands staring into the distance.

'Right,' says Álvaro. 'We will be unloading for the rest of the day and most of tomorrow. When you are ready, join the line.'

From the same breast pocket the stranger produces a pack of cigarettes. Without offering it around, he lights himself one and takes a deep puff.

'Remember,' says Álvaro, 'no smoking in the hold.'

The man gives no sign that he has heard. Tranquilly he gazes around. The smoke from his cigarette rises into the still air.

His name, Álvaro lets it be known, is Daga. No one calls him anything else, not 'the new man', not 'the new guy'.

Despite his small stature, Daga is strong. He staggers not a millimetre when the first sack is dropped onto his shoulders; he ascends the ladder swiftly and steadily; he lopes down the gangplank and heaves the sack into the waiting cart with no sign of effort. But then he retreats into the shadow of the shed, squats on his heels, and lights another cigarette.

Álvaro marches up to him. 'No breaks, Daga,' he says. 'Get on with it.'

'What's the quota?' says Daga.

'There is no quota. We are paid by the day.'

'Fifty sacks a day,' says Daga.

'We move more than that.'

'How many?'

'More than fifty. No quota. Each man carries what he can.'

'Fifty. No more.'

'Get up. If you have to smoke, wait for the break.'

Things come to a head at noon that Friday, when they are being paid. As Daga approaches the wooden board that serves as a table, Álvaro leans down and whispers in the paymaster's ear. The paymaster nods. He sets Daga's money on the board before him.

'What's this?' says Daga.

'Your pay for the days you have worked,' says Álvaro.

Daga picks up the coins and with a quick, contemptuous movement flings them back in the paymaster's face.

'What's that for?' says Álvaro.

'Rat's wage.'

'That's the rate. That's what you earned. That's what we all earn. Do you want to say we are all rats?'

The men crowd around. Discreetly the paymaster shuffles his papers together and closes the lid of his cashbox.

He, Simón, feels the boy gripping his leg. 'What are they doing?' he whines. His face is pale and anxious. 'Are they going to fight?'

'No, of course not.'

'Tell Álvaro not to fight. Tell him!' The boy tugs at his fingers, tugs and tugs.

'Come, let's move away,' he says. He draws the boy towards the breakwater. 'Look! Do you see the seals? The big one with his nose in the air is the male, the bull seal. And the others, the smaller ones, are his wives.'

From the crowd comes a sharp cry. There is a flurry of motion.

'They are fighting!' whines the boy. 'I don't want them to fight!'

A half-circle of men has formed around Daga, who crouches down, a faint smile on his lips, one arm stretched forward. In his hand glints the blade of a knife. 'Come!' he says, and makes a beckoning motion with the knife. 'Who is next?'

Álvaro sits on the ground, hunched over. He seems to be clutching his chest. There is a streak of blood on his shirt.

'Who is next?' repeats Daga. No one stirs. He comes erect, folds the knife, slips it into his hip pocket, lifts the cashbox, upends it on the board. Coins shower everywhere. 'Pussies!' he says. He counts out what he wants, gives the drum a derisory kick. 'Help yourselves,' he says, and turns his back on the men. Leisurely he mounts the paymaster's bicycle and pedals away.

Álvaro gets to his feet. The blood on his shirt comes from his hand, oozing from a slash across the palm.

He, Simón, is the senior man or at least the eldest: he should take the lead. 'You need a doctor,' he tells Álvaro. 'Let's go.' He gestures to the boy. 'Come – we are going to take Álvaro to the doctor.'

The boy does not stir.

'What's wrong?'

The boy's lips move but he can hear no word. He bends closer. 'What's wrong?' he asks.

'Is Álvaro going to die?' whispers the boy. His whole body is rigid. He is shivering.

'Of course not. He has a cut on his hand, that's all. He needs a plaster to stop the bleeding. Come. We will take him to the doctor and the doctor will fix him up.'

In fact Álvaro is already on his way, accompanied by another of the men.

'He was fighting,' says the boy. 'He was fighting and now the doctor is going to cut off his hand.'

'Nonsense. Doctors don't cut off hands. The doctor is going to wash the cut and put a plaster on it, or maybe sew it shut with needle and thread. Tomorrow Álvaro will be back at work and we will have forgotten all about it.'

The boy stares at him piercingly.

'I am not fibbing,' he says. 'I would not fib to you. Álvaro's wound is not serious. That man, señor Daga or whatever his name is, didn't mean to hurt him. It was an accident. The knife slipped. Sharp knives are dangerous. That is the lesson to remember: not to play with knives. If you play with knives you can get hurt. Álvaro got hurt, fortunately not seriously. And señor Daga has left us, taken his money and gone. He won't be back. He didn't belong here, and he knows it.'

'*You* mustn't fight,' says the boy.

'I won't, I promise you.'

'You must never fight.'

'I am not in the habit of fighting. And Álvaro wasn't fighting. He was just trying to protect himself. He tried to protect himself and he got cut.' He stretches out his hand, to show how Álvaro tried to protect himself, how Álvaro suffered the cut.

'Álvaro was fighting,' says the boy, pronouncing the words with solemn finality.

'Protecting yourself isn't fighting. Protecting yourself is a natural instinct. If someone tried to hit you, you would protect yourself. You wouldn't think twice. Look.'

In all their time together he has never laid a finger on the boy. Now, suddenly, he raises a threatening hand. The boy does not bat an eyelid. He feints a slap to his cheek. He does not flinch.

'All right,' he says. 'I believe you.' He lets his hand drop. 'You are right, I was wrong. Álvaro should not have tried to protect himself. He should have been like you. He should have been brave. Now shall we stroll over to the clinic and see how he is getting on?'

Álvaro comes to work the next day with the injured hand in a sling. He refuses to discuss the incident. Taking their lead from him, the men too do not talk about it. But the boy keeps nagging. 'Is señor Daga going to bring the bicycle back?' he asks. 'Why is he called señor Daga?'

'No, he won't be coming back,' he replies. 'He doesn't like us, he doesn't enjoy the kind of work we do, he has no reason to come back. I don't know if Daga is his real name. It doesn't matter. Names don't matter. If he wants to call himself Daga, then let him.'

'But why did he steal the money?'

'He didn't *steal* the money. He didn't *steal* the bicycle. Stealing means taking what doesn't belong to you while no one is looking. We were all looking while he took the money. We could have stopped him, but we didn't. We chose not to fight with him. We chose to let him go. Surely you approve. You are the one who says we shouldn't fight.'

'The man should have given him more money.'

'The paymaster? The paymaster should have given him whatever he wanted?'

The boy nods.

'He couldn't do that. If the paymaster paid each of us whatever we wanted, he would run out of money.'

'Why?'

'Why? Because we all want more than is due to us. That's

human nature. Because we all want more than we are worth.'

'What is human nature?'

'It means the way human beings are built, you and I and Álvaro and señor Daga and everyone else. It means the way we are when we come into the world. It means what we all have in common. We like to believe we are special, my boy, each of us. But, strictly speaking, that cannot be so. If we were all special, there would be no specialness left. Yet we continue to believe in ourselves. We go down into the ship's hold, into the heat and dust, we heave sacks onto our backs and lug them up into the light, we see our friends toiling just like us, doing exactly the same work, nothing special about it, and we feel proud of them and of ourselves, all comrades labouring together with a common goal; yet in a little corner of our hearts, which we keep hidden, we whisper to ourselves, *Nevertheless, nevertheless, you are special, you will see! One day, when we are least expecting it, there will be a blast on Álvaro's whistle and we will all be summoned to assemble on the quayside, where a great crowd will be waiting, and a man in a black suit with a tall hat; and the man in the black suit will call on you to step forward, saying,* Behold this singular worker, in whom we are well pleased! *and he will shake your hand and pin a medal on your chest* – For Service Beyond the Call of Duty, *the medal will say* – *and everyone will cheer and clap.*

'It is human nature to have dreams like that, even if it would be wise to keep them to ourselves. Like all of us, señor Daga thought he was special; but he didn't keep the thought to himself. He wanted to be singled out. He wanted to be recognized.'

He halts. There is no sign on the boy's face that he has understood a word. Is today one of his stupid days or is he just being stubborn?

'Señor Daga wanted to be praised and given a medal,' he says. 'When we didn't give him the medal he dreamed of, he took money instead. He took what he thought he was worth. That's all.'

'Why didn't he get a medal?' says the boy.

'Because if we all got medals then medals would be worth nothing. Because medals have to be earned. Like money. You don't get a medal just because you want one.'

'I would give señor Daga a medal.'

'Well, maybe we should ask you to be our paymaster. Then we will all get medals and as much money as we want and next week there will be nothing left in the moneybox.'

'There's always money in the moneybox,' says the boy. 'That's why it is called the moneybox.'

He throws up his hands. 'I won't argue with you if you are going to be silly.'

Chapter 7

Some weeks after they first presented themselves at the Centre, a letter arrives from the office of the Ministerio de Reubicación in Novilla informing him that he and his family have been allocated an apartment in the East Village, occupation to be effected no later than noon on the coming Monday.

East Village, familiarly known as the East Blocks, is an estate to the east of the parklands, a cluster of apartment blocks separated by expanses of lawn. He and the boy have already explored there, as they have explored its twin estate, West Village. The blocks making up the village are of identical pattern, four floors high. On each floor six apartments face upon a square that holds such communal amenities as a children's playground, a paddle pool, a bicycle rack, and washing lines. East Village is generally held to be more desirable than West Village; they can count themselves lucky to be sent there.

The move from the Centre is easily effected, for they own few possessions and have made no friends. Their neighbours have been, on one side, an old man who dodders around in his dressing gown talking to himself, and on the other a stand-offish couple who pretend not to understand the Spanish he speaks.

The new apartment, on the second floor, is modest in scale and sparsely furnished: two beds, a table and chairs, a chest of drawers, steel shelving. A tiny annexe contains an electric cooker on a stand and a basin with running water. A sliding screen hides a shower and toilet.

For their first supper in the Blocks he makes the boy's favourite food, pancakes with butter and jam. 'We are going to like it here, aren't we?' he says. 'It will be a new chapter in our life.'

Having advised Álvaro that he is not well, he has no qualms about taking days off from work. He is earning more than enough for their needs, there is little to spend his money on, he does not see why he should exhaust himself to no purpose. Besides, there are always new arrivals looking for casual work who can fill in for him at the docks. So some mornings he spends simply lazing abed, dozing and waking, enjoying the sunny warmth that pours in through the windows of their new home.

I am girding my loins, he tells himself. *I am girding my loins for the next chapter in this enterprise.* By the next chapter he means the quest for the boy's mother, the quest that he does not yet know where to commence. *I am concentrating my energies; I am making plans.*

While he relaxes, the boy plays outdoors in the sandpit or on the swings, or else roams among the washing lines, humming to himself, winding himself like a cocoon in drying bedsheets, then gyrating and unwinding himself. It is a game he never seems to tire of.

'I don't think our neighbours will be pleased to see you handling their freshly laundered washing,' he says. 'What do you find so attractive about it?'

'I like the way it smells.'

The next time he crosses the courtyard, he discreetly presses his face into a sheet and draws a deep breath. The smell is clean and warm and comforting.

Later that day, glancing out of the window, he sees the boy sprawled on the lawn head to head with another, bigger boy. They seem to be conversing intimately.

'I see you have a new friend,' he remarks over lunch. 'Who is he?'

'Fidel. He can play the violin. He showed me his violin. Can I get a violin too?'

'Does he live in the Blocks?'

'Yes. Can I have a violin too?'

'We will see. Violins cost a lot of money, and you will need a teacher, you can't just pick up a violin and play.'

'Fidel's mother teaches him. She says she can teach me too.'

'It's good that you have made a new friend, I am glad for you. As for violin lessons, perhaps I should first have a chat with Fidel's mother.'

'Can we go now?'

'We can go later, after your nap.'

Fidel's apartment is on the far side of the courtyard. Even before he can knock, the door is thrown open and Fidel stands before them, sturdy, curly-headed, smiling.

Though no larger than theirs and not as sunny, the apartment has a more welcoming air, perhaps because of its bright curtains with their cherry-blossom motif repeated across the bedspreads.

Fidel's mother comes forward to greet him: an angular, even gaunt young woman with prominent teeth and hair drawn tight behind her ears. In an obscure way he is disappointed by this first sight of her, though he has no reason to be.

'Yes,' she confirms, 'I have told your son he can join Fidelito in his music lessons. Later we can reassess and see if he has the aptitude and the will to progress.'

'That is very kind of you. Actually, David is not my son. I don't have a son.'

'Where are his parents?'

'His parents . . . That is a difficult question. I will explain when we have more time. About the lessons: will he need a violin of his own?'

'With beginners I usually start on the recorder. Fidel' – she draws her son closer, he hugs her affectionately – 'Fidel learned the recorder for a year before he began the violin.'

He turns to David. 'Do you hear that, my boy? First you learn to play the recorder, then after that the violin. Agreed?'

The boy pulls a face, shoots a glance at his new friend, is silent.

'It is a big undertaking, to become a violinist. You won't succeed if your heart isn't in it.' He turns to Fidel's mother. 'May I ask, how much do you charge?'

She gives him a surprised look. 'I don't charge,' she says. 'I do it for the music.'

Her name is Elena. It is not the name he would have guessed. He would have guessed Manuela, or even Lourdes.

He invites Fidel and his mother on a bus ride out to the New Forest, a ride that Álvaro has recommended ('It was once a plantation, but it has been allowed to go wild – you will like it'). From the bus terminus the two boys race ahead up the path, while he and Elena stroll behind.

'Do you have many students?' he asks her.

'Oh, I'm not a proper music teacher. I have just a few children whom I help with the basics.'

'How do you make a living if you don't charge?'

'I take in sewing. I do this and that. I get a small grant from the Asistencia. I have enough. There are more important things than money.'

'Do you mean music?'

'Music, yes, but also how one lives. How one is to live.'

A good answer, a serious answer, a philosophic answer. He is, for a moment, silenced.

'Do you see lots of people?' he asks. 'I mean' – he grasps the nettle – 'is there a man in your life?'

She frowns. 'I have friends. Some are women, some are men. I don't distinguish between them.'

The path narrows. She goes ahead; he falls behind, eyeing the sway of her hips. He prefers a woman with more flesh on her bones. Nevertheless, he likes Elena.

'As for me, it is not a distinction I can give up,' he says. 'Or would wish to give up.'

She slows to let him catch up, gives him a straight look. 'No one should have to give up what is important to him,' she says.

The two boys return, panting after their run, glowing with health. 'Have we got anything to drink?' demands Fidel.

It is not until they are in the bus, going home, that he has another chance to speak to Elena.

'I don't know about you,' he says, 'but the past is not dead in me. Details may have grown fuzzy, but the feel of how life used to be is still quite vivid. Men and women, for instance: you say you have got beyond that way of thinking; but I haven't. I still feel myself to be a man, and you to be a woman.'

'I agree. Men and women are different. They have different roles to play.'

The two boys, in the seat in front of them, are whispering together, giggling. He takes Elena's hand in his. She does not pull free. Nevertheless, by the inscrutable means by which the body speaks, her hand gives answer. It dies in his grasp like a fish out of water.

'May I ask,' he says: 'Are you beyond feeling anything for a man?'

'I don't feel nothing,' she replies slowly and carefully. 'On the contrary, I feel goodwill, much goodwill. Towards both you and your son. Warmth and goodwill.'

'By goodwill do you mean you wish us well? I am struggling to grasp the concept. You feel benevolent towards us?'

'Yes, exactly.'

'Benevolence, I must tell you, is what we keep encountering here. Everyone wishes us well, everyone is ready to be kind to us. We are positively borne along on a cloud of goodwill. But it all remains a bit abstract. Can goodwill by itself satisfy our needs? Is it not in our nature to crave something more tangible?'

Deliberately Elena extracts her hand from his. 'You may want more than goodwill; but is what you want better than goodwill? That is what you should be asking yourself.' She pauses. 'You keep referring to David as "the boy". Why don't you use his name?'

'David is a name they gave him at the camp. He doesn't like it, he says it is not his true name. I try not to use it unless I have to.'

'It is quite easy to change a name, you know. You go to the registry office and fill out a name-change form. That's all. No questions.' She leans forward. 'And what are you two whispering about?' she demands of the boys.

Her son smiles back at her, raises his fingers to his lips, pretending that what occupies the two of them is secret business.

The bus deposits them outside the Blocks. 'I would have liked to invite you in for a cup of tea,' says Elena, 'but unfortunately it is time for Fidelito's bath and supper.'

'I understand,' he says. 'Goodbye, Fidel. Thank you for the walk. We had a good time.'

'You and Fidel seem to get on well together,' he remarks to the boy once they are alone.

'He is my best friend.'

'So Fidel feels goodwill towards you, does he?'

'Lots of goodwill.'

'How about you? Do you feel goodwill too?'

67

The boy nods vigorously.

'Anything else besides?'

The boy gives him a puzzled look. 'No.'

So there he has it, out of the mouths of babes and sucklings. From goodwill come friendship and happiness, come companionable picnics in the parklands or companionable afternoons strolling in the forest. Whereas from love, or at least from longing in its more urgent manifestations, come frustration and doubt and heartsore. It is as simple as that.

And what is he up to, anyway, with Elena, a woman he barely knows, the mother of the child's new friend? Is he hoping to seduce her, because in memories that are not entirely lost to him seducing one another is something that men and women do? Is he insisting on the primacy of the personal (desire, love) over the universal (goodwill, benevolence)? And why is he continually asking himself questions instead of just living, like everyone else? Is it all part of a far too tardy transition from the old and comfortable (the personal) to the new and unsettling (the universal)? Is the round of self-interrogation nothing but a phase in the growth of each new arrival, a phase that people like Álvaro and Ana and Elena have by now successfully passed through? If so, how much longer before he will emerge as a new, perfected man?

Chapter 8

'You were telling me about goodwill the other day, goodwill as a universal balm for our ills,' he says to Elena. 'But don't you sometimes find yourself missing plain old physical contact?'

They are in the parklands, beside a field on which half a dozen disorderly football games are being played. Fidel and David have been allowed to join in one of the games, though they are really too young. Dutifully they surge back and forth with the other players, but the ball is never passed to them.

'Anyone who brings up a child does not lack for physical contact,' replies Elena.

'By physical contact I mean something different. I mean loving and being loved. I mean sleeping with someone every night. Don't you miss that?'

'Do I miss it? I am not the kind of person who suffers from memories, Simón. What you speak of seems very far away. And – if by sleeping with someone you mean sex – quite strange too. A strange thing to be preoccupied with.'

'But surely there is nothing like sex for bringing people closer. Sex would bring the two of us closer. For example.'

Elena turns away. 'Fidelito!' she calls, and waves. 'Come! We have to leave now!'

Is he mistaken, or is there a flush on her cheek?

The truth is, he finds Elena only mildly attractive. He does not like her boniness, her strong jaw and prominent front teeth. But he is a man, she is a woman; and the children's friendship keeps drawing them together. So, despite one polite brush-off after another, he continues to permit himself mild freedoms, freedoms that seem to amuse more than anger her. Willy-nilly he finds himself slipping into daydreams in which some or other stroke of fortune impels Elena into his arms.

That stroke of fortune, when it comes, takes the guise of a power cut. Power cuts are not infrequent across the city. Usually they are announced a day in advance, and apply either to even-numbered or to odd-numbered dwellings. In the case of the Blocks, they are applied to whole buildings according to a rota.

On the evening in question, however, there is no announcement, just Fidel knocking at the door, asking whether he can come in and do his homework, since there is no electric light in their apartment.

'Have you eaten yet?' he asks the boy.

Fidel shakes his head.

'Run back at once,' he says. 'Tell your mother that you and she are invited to supper.'

The supper he provides for them is no more than bread and soup (barley and squash boiled up with a can of beans; he has yet to find a shop that sells spices), but it is adequate. Fidel's homework is soon done. The boys settle down with picture books; then suddenly, as if poleaxed, Fidel falls asleep.

'He has been like that since he was a baby,' says Elena. 'Nothing will wake him. I'll carry him back and put him to bed. Thank you for the meal.'

'You can't go back to that dark apartment. Stay the night. Fidel can share David's bed. I'll sleep in a chair. I am used to it.'

It is a lie, he is not used to sleeping in chairs, and on the little straight-backed kitchen chair he doubts that sleep is humanly possible. But he gives Elena no chance to refuse. 'You know where the bathroom is. Here is a towel.'

By the time he himself returns from the bathroom she is in his bed and the two boys are asleep side by side. He wraps himself in the spare blanket and switches off the light.

For a while there is silence. Then, out of the dark, she speaks: 'If you are uncomfortable, as I am sure you are, I can make space.'

He slips into bed with her. Quietly, discreetly, they do the business of sex, mindful of the children asleep an arm's length away.

It is not what he had hoped it would be. Her heart is not in it, he feels that at once; as for himself, the reserve of pent-up desire that he had counted on proves to be an illusion.

'You see what I mean?' she whispers when it is over. With

a finger she brushes his lips. 'It doesn't advance us, does it?'

Is she right? Should he take this experience to heart and bid farewell to sex, as Elena appears to have done? Perhaps. Yet merely to hold a woman in his arms, even if she is no ship-stirring beauty, buoys him.

'I don't agree,' he murmurs back. 'In fact, I think you are quite wrong.' He pauses. 'Have you ever asked yourself whether the price we pay for this new life, the price of forgetting, may not be too high?'

She does not reply, but rearranges her underwear and turns away from him.

Though they do not live together, he likes to think of himself and Elena, after that first shared night, as a couple, or a couple in the making, and therefore of the two boys as brothers or stepbrothers. It becomes more and more of a habit for the four of them to have their evening meal together; at weekends they go shopping or go on picnics or excursions into the countryside; and though he and Elena do not spend another whole night together, she now and again, when the boys are out of the way, allows him to make love to her. He begins to grow used to her body, with its jutting hipbones and tiny breasts. She has little sexual feeling for him, that is clear; but he likes to think of his lovemaking as a patient and prolonged act of resuscitation, of bringing back to life a female body that for all practical purposes has died.

When she invites him to make love to her, it is without the slightest coquetry. 'If you like, we can do it now,' she will say, and close the door and take off her clothes.

Such matter-of-factness might once have put him off, just as her unresponsiveness might once have humiliated him. But he decides he will neither be put off nor humiliated. What she offers he will accept, as readily and as gratefully as he can.

Usually she refers to the act simply as *doing it*, but sometimes, when she wants to tease him, she uses the word *descongelar*, thaw: 'If you like, you can have another go at thawing me.' It was a word he once let slip in a heedless moment: 'Let me thaw you!' The notion of being thawed back into life struck her then and strikes her now as limitlessly funny.

Between the two of them there is growing up, if not intimacy, then a friendship that he feels to be quite solid, quite reliable. Whether friendship would have grown up between them anyway, on the ground of the children's friendship and of the many hours they spend together, whether *doing it* has contributed anything at all, he cannot say.

Is this, he asks himself, how families come into being, here in this new world: founded on friendship rather than on love? It is not a condition he is familiar with, being mere friends with a woman. But he can see its benefits. He can even, cautiously, enjoy it.

'Tell me about Fidel's father,' he asks Elena.

'I don't remember much about him.'

'But he must have had a father.'

'Of course.'

'Was the father at all like me?'

'I don't know. I can't say.'

'Would you, just hypothetically, consider someone like me as a husband?'

'Someone like you? Like you in what respects?'

'Would you marry someone like me?'

'If that is your way of asking whether I would marry you, then the answer is yes, I would. It would be good for Fidel and David, both of them. When would you want to do it? Because the registry office is open only on weekdays. Can you get time off?'

'I am sure I can. Our foreman is very understanding.'

After this strange offer, and this strange acceptance (about which he does nothing), he begins to feel a certain wariness on Elena's part, and a new tension in their relations. Yet he does not regret asking. He is finding his way. He is making a new life.

'How would you feel,' he asks on another day, 'if I were to see another woman?'

'By *see* do you mean have sex with?'

'Perhaps.'

'And whom do you have in mind?'

'No one in particular. I am simply exploring possibilities.'

'Exploring? Hasn't the time come for you to settle down? You are no longer a young man.'

He is silent.

'You ask how I would feel. Do you want a short answer or a full answer?'

'A full answer. The fullest.'

'Very well. Our friendship has been good for the boys, we

can agree on that. They have grown close. They see us as guardian presences, or even as a single guardian presence. So it would not be good for them if our friendship were to come to an end. And I see no reason why it should, just because you are seeing some hypothetical other woman.

'However, I suspect that with this woman you will want to conduct the same kind of experiment you have been conducting with me, and that in the course of the experiment you will lose touch with Fidel and with me.

'Therefore I am going to put in words something I was hoping you would come to understand by yourself. You want to see this other woman because I do not provide what you feel you need, namely storms of passion. Friendship by itself is not good enough for you. Without the accompaniment of storms of passion it is somehow deficient.

'To my ear that is an old way of thinking. In the old way of thinking, no matter how much you may have, there is always something missing. The name you choose to give this *something-more* that is missing is passion. Yet I am willing to bet that if tomorrow you were offered all the passion you wanted – passion by the bucketful – you would promptly find something new to miss, to lack. This endless dissatisfaction, this yearning for the something-more that is missing, is a way of thinking we are well rid of, in my opinion. *Nothing is missing*. The nothing that you think is missing is an illusion. You are living by an illusion.

'There. You asked for a full answer and I have given you one. Is it enough, or is there yet more that you long for?'

It is a warm day, this day of the full answer. The radio is playing softly; they are lying on the bed in her apartment, fully clothed.

'For my part –' he commences; but Elena interrupts him. 'Hush,' she says. 'No more talk, at least not today.'

'Why not?'

'Because next thing we will be bickering, and I don't want that.'

So they hush, and lie in silence side by side, listening now to the gulls cawing as they circle the courtyard, now to the boys laughing together in their play, now to the music from the radio, whose unremitting, even-tempered melodiousness used once to soothe him but today simply irritates him.

What he wants to say, *for his part*, is that life here is too placid for his taste, too lacking in ups and downs, in drama and tension – is too much, in fact, like the music on the radio. *Anodina*: is that a Spanish word?

He remembers asking Álvaro once why there was never any news on the radio. 'News of what?' inquired Álvaro. 'News of what is going on in the world,' he replied. 'Oh,' said Álvaro, 'is something going on?' As before, he was ready to suspect irony. But no, there was none.

Álvaro does not trade in irony. Nor does Elena. Elena is an intelligent woman but she does not see any doubleness in the world, any difference between the way things seem and the way things are. An intelligent woman and an admirable woman too, who out of the most exiguous of materials – seamstressing, music lessons, household chores – has put together a new life, a life from which she claims – with justice? – that nothing is missing. It is the same with Álvaro and the stevedores: they have no secret yearnings he can detect, no hankerings after another kind of life. Only he is the exception, the dissatisfied one, the misfit. What is wrong with him? Is it, as Elena says, just the old way of thinking and feeling that has not yet died in him, but kicks and shudders in its last throes?

Things do not have their due weight here: that is what he would like, in the end, to say to Elena. The music we hear lacks weight. Our lovemaking lacks weight. The food we eat, our dreary diet of bread, lacks substance – lacks the substantiality of animal flesh, with all the gravity of bloodletting and sacrifice behind it. Our very words lack weight, these Spanish words that do not come from our heart.

The music reaches its graceful end. He gets up. 'I must be going,' he says. 'Do you remember how the other day you told me you didn't suffer from memories?'

'Did I?'

'Yes, you did. While we were watching football in the park. Well, I am not like you. I suffer from memories, or the shadows of memories. I know we are all supposed to be washed clean by the passage here, and it is true, I don't have a great repertoire to call on. But the shadows linger nevertheless. That is what I suffer from. Except that I don't use the word *suffer*. I hold onto them, those shadows.'

'That's good,' says Elena. 'It takes all kinds to make a world.'

Fidel and David rush into the room, flushed, sweaty, bursting with life. 'Are there any biscuits?' demands Fidel.

'In the jar in the cupboard,' says Elena.

The two boys disappear into the kitchen. 'Are you having a good time?' Elena calls out.

'Mm,' says Fidel.

'That's good,' says Elena.

Chapter 9

'How are the music lessons going?' he asks the boy. 'Are you enjoying them?'

'Mm. Do you know what? When Fidel grows up he is going to buy himself a tiny, tiny violin' – he shows how tiny the violin will be: a mere two handbreadths – 'and he is going to wear a clown suit and play the violin in the circus. Can we go to the circus?'

'When the circus next comes to town we can go, all of us. We can invite Álvaro along, and maybe Eugenio too.'

The boy pouts. 'I don't want Eugenio to come. He says things about me.'

'He said only one thing, that you had a devil in you, and that was just a manner of speaking. He meant you have a spark inside you that makes you good at chess. An imp.'

'I don't like him.'

'All right, we won't invite Eugenio. What are you learning in your music lessons besides scales?'

'Singing. Do you want to hear me sing?'

'I would love to. I didn't know Elena taught singing. She is full of surprises.'

They are on the bus, heading out of the city into the countryside. Though there are several other passengers, the boy is not shy to sing. In his clear young voice he chants:

Wer reitet so spät durch Dampf und Wind?
Er ist der Vater mit seinem Kind;
Er halt den Knaben in dem Arm,
Er füttert ihn Zucker, er küsst ihm warm.

'That's all. It's English. Can I learn English? I don't want to speak Spanish any more. I hate Spanish.'

'You speak very good Spanish. You sing beautifully too. Maybe you will be a singer when you grow up.'

'No. I'm going to be a magician in a circus. What does it mean, *Wer reitet so*?'

'I don't know. I don't speak English.'

'Can I go to school?'

'You will have to wait a while for that, until your next birthday. Then you can go to school along with Fidel.'

They get off at the stop marked *Terminal*, where the bus turns back. The map he has picked up at the bus station shows tracks and footpaths up into the hills; his plan is to follow a winding path that leads to a lake, which on the map has a starburst next to it, signifying that it is a beauty spot.

They are the last passengers to get off, and the sole walkers on the footpath. The countryside through which they pass is empty. Though the land seems lush and fertile, there is no sign of human habitation.

'Isn't it peaceful here in the country!' he remarks to the boy, though in truth the emptiness strikes him as desolate rather than peaceful. It would be better if there were animals he could point out, cattle or sheep or pigs, going about their animal business. Even rabbits would do.

Now and again they see birds in flight, but too far away and too high in the sky for him to be sure what kind they are.

'I'm tired,' announces the boy.

He inspects the map. They are halfway to the lake, he guesses. 'I will carry you for a while,' he says, 'until your strength comes back.' He swings the boy onto his shoulders. 'Sing out as soon as you see a lake. That will be where the water comes from that we drink. Sing out if you see it. In fact, sing out if you see any water. Or if you see any country folk.'

They press on. But either he has misread the map or the map itself is at fault, for after rising sharply and then plunging as steeply, the track terminates without warning at a brick wall and a rusty gate overgrown with ivy. Beside the gate is a weather-beaten painted sign. He pushes aside the ivy. '*La Residencia*,' he reads.

'What is a *residencia*?' asks the boy.

'A *residencia* is a house, a grand one. But this particular *residencia* may be nothing but a ruin.'

'Can we look?'

They try the gate, but it will not budge. Just as they are about to turn back, there comes, carried on the breeze, the faint sound of laughter. Following the sound, beating their way through heavy undergrowth, they come to a point where the brick wall gives way to a high wire-netting fence. On the other side of the fence is a tennis court, and on the court are three players, two men and a woman, dressed in white, the men in shirts and long trousers, the woman in a full skirt and a blouse with the collar turned up, and a cap with a green visor.

The men are tall, broad-shouldered, slim-hipped; they look like brothers, perhaps even twin brothers. The woman has teamed up with one of them to play against the other. They are all practised players, he sees that at once, dextrous and swift of foot. The sole man is particularly good, holding his own with ease.

'What are they doing?' whispers the boy.

'It's a game,' he replies in a low voice. 'It is called tennis. You try to hit the ball past your opponent. Like scoring a goal in football.'

The ball thuds into the fence. Turning to retrieve it, the woman sees them. 'Hello,' she says, and gives the boy a smile.

Something stirs inside him. Who is this woman? Her smile, her voice, her bearing – there is something obscurely familiar about her.

'Good morning,' he says, his throat dry.

'Come, hurry up!' her partner calls. 'Game point!'

No further words pass. In fact, when her partner comes a minute later to fetch a ball, he gives the pair of them a glowering look, as if to make it clear they are not welcome, not even to watch.

'I'm thirsty,' whispers the boy.

He offers the flask of water he has brought.

'Haven't we got anything else?'

'What do you want – nectar?' he hisses back, then at once regrets his irritation. From his pack he takes an orange and tears a hole in the peel. The boy sucks greedily.

'Is that better?' he asks.

The boy nods. 'Are we going to the Residencia?'

'This must be the Residencia. The tennis court must be part of it.'

'Can we go in?'

'We can try.'

Leaving the tennis players behind, they plunge on through the undergrowth, following the wall, until they emerge onto a dirt road leading to a pair of high iron gates. Behind the bars, through trees, they can glimpse an imposing building in dark stone.

Though closed, the gates are not locked. They slip through and walk up a driveway ankle-deep in fallen leaves. A sign with an arrow points to an arched entranceway that opens into a courtyard at whose centre stands a marble statue, a larger-than-life figure of a woman or perhaps an angel in flowing robes gazing at the horizon, holding up a flaming torch.

'Good afternoon, sir,' says a voice. 'Can I help you?'

The speaker is an elderly man, his face lined, his back bent. He wears a faded black uniform; he has emerged from a little office or lodge in the entranceway.

'Yes. We have just come from the city. I wonder if we may

have a word with one of the residents, a lady who is playing tennis on the court at the back.'

'And would the lady in question wish to speak to you, sir?'

'I believe so. There is a matter of importance that I need to discuss with her. A family matter. But we can wait until their game is over.'

'And the lady's name?'

'That I can't tell you, because I don't know it. But I can describe her. I would say she is about thirty years old, of medium height, with dark hair which she wears swept away from her face. She is in the company of two young men. And she is dressed all in white.'

'There are a number of ladies of that general appearance in La Residencia, sir, several of whom play tennis. Tennis is quite a popular recreation.'

The boy tugs at his sleeve. 'Tell him about the dog,' he whispers.

'The dog?'

The boy nods. 'The dog they had with them.'

'My young friend says they have a dog,' he repeats. He himself cannot recollect any dog.

'Aha!' says the porter. He retreats into his lair, pulling the glass door to behind him. In the dim light they can make him out shuffling through papers. Then he picks up a telephone, dials a number, listens, lays down the receiver, and returns. 'I'm sorry, sir, there is no reply.'

'That is because she is out on the tennis court. Can't we just go to the courts?'

'I'm sorry, but that is not allowed. Our facilities are off limits to visitors.'

'Then may we wait here until she has finished playing?'

'You may.'

'May we walk in the garden while we wait?'

'You may.'

They wander off into the overgrown garden.

'Who is the lady?' asks the boy.

'Didn't you recognize her?'

The boy shakes his head.

'Didn't you feel a strange movement in your breast when she spoke to us, when she said hello – a kind of tug at the heart-strings, as if you might have seen her before, in some other place?'

Doubtfully the boy shakes his head.

'I ask because the lady may be the very person we are looking for. That, at least, is the feeling I have.'

'Is she going to be my mother?'

'I don't know for sure. We will have to ask her.'

They complete a circuit of the garden. Back at the porter's lodge, he taps at the glass. 'Would you mind ringing the lady again?' he asks.

The porter dials a number. This time there is a reply. 'A gentleman at the gate to see you,' he hears him say. 'Yes . . . yes . . .' He turns to them. 'You did say it was a family matter, did you not, sir?'

'Yes, a family matter.'

'And the name?'

'The name is of no concern.'

The porter closes the door and resumes his conversation. At last he emerges. 'The lady will see you, sir,' he says. 'However, there is a slight difficulty. Children are not allowed into the Residencia. I am afraid your little boy will have to wait here.'

'That's strange. Why are children not allowed?'

'No children in the Residencia, sir. That's the rule. I don't make the rules, I just apply them. He will have to stay behind while you pay your family visit.'

'Will you stay with this gentleman?' he asks the boy. 'I'll be back as soon as I can.'

'I don't want to,' says the boy. 'I want to come with you.'

'I understand that. But I am sure, as soon as the lady hears you are waiting out here, she will want to come out and meet you. So will you make a big sacrifice and stay behind with this gentleman, just for a short while?'

'Will you come back? Do you promise?'

'Of course.'

The boy is silent, will not meet his eye.

'Can't you make an exception in this case?' he asks the porter. 'He will be very quiet, he won't disturb anyone.'

'Sorry, sir, no exceptions. Where would we be if we began making exceptions? Soon everyone would want to be an exception, and then there would be no rules left, would there?'

'You can play in the garden,' he tells the boy. To the porter: 'He can play in the garden, can't he?'

'Of course.'

'Go and climb a tree,' he tells the boy. 'There are lots of trees good for climbing. I'll be back in no time.'

Following the porter's instructions, he crosses the quadrangle, passes through a second entranceway, and knocks at a door with the word *Una* on it. There is no reply. He enters.

He is in a waiting room. The walls are papered in white, with a motif of a lyre and lily in pale green. From hidden lamps white light is cast discreetly upward. There is a sofa in white imitation leather, and two easy chairs. On a small table by the door are half a dozen bottles, and glasses of all shapes.

He sits down, waits. The minutes pass. He rises and peers down the corridor. No sign of life. Idly he examines the bottles. Cream sherry, dry sherry. Vermouth. Alcohol content by volume 4%. Oblivedo. Where is Oblivedo?

Then suddenly she is there, still in her tennis clothes, solider than she had seemed on the court, almost heavy-set. She bears a plate, which she places on the table. Without greeting him she seats herself on the sofa, crosses her legs under her long skirt. 'You wanted to see me?' she says.

'Yes.' His heart is beating fast. 'Thank you for coming. My name is Simón. You don't know me, I am of no importance. I come on behalf of someone else, bearing a proposal.'

'Won't you sit?' she says. 'Something to eat? A glass of sherry?'

With an unsteady hand he pours a glass of sherry and takes one of the flimsy little triangular sandwiches. Cucumber. He sits opposite her, downs the sweet liquor. It goes straight to his head. The tension lifts, and words come in a rush.

'I have brought someone here. In fact the child you saw at the tennis court. He is outside, waiting. The porter would not allow him in. Because he is a child. Will you come and meet him?'

'You have brought a child to meet me?'

'Yes.' He rises and pours himself another glass of the liberating sherry. 'I am sorry – this must be confusing, strangers arriving without announcement. But I can't tell you how important it is. We have been –'

Without warning the door swings open and the boy himself is before them, out of breath, panting.

'Come here,' he beckons to the boy. 'Do you recognize the lady now?' He turns to her. Her face is frozen in alarm. 'May he take your hand?' And to the boy: 'Come, take the lady's hand.'

The boy stands stock-still.

Now the porter himself arrives on the scene, clearly upset. 'I'm sorry, sir,' he says, 'but this is against the rules, as I warned you. I must ask you to leave.'

He turns to the woman in appeal. Surely she does not have to submit to this porter and his rules. But she utters no word of protest.

'Have a heart,' he says to the porter. 'We have travelled a long way. What if we all retired to the garden? Would that still be against the rules?'

'No, sir. But note, the gates close at five o'clock sharp.'

He addresses the woman. 'Can we go out into the garden? Please! Give me a chance to explain.'

In silence, the boy holding his hand, the three of them cross the quadrangle into the tangled garden.

'This must once have been a magnificent establishment,' he remarks, trying to clear the air, trying to sound like a sensible adult. 'A pity the garden is so neglected.'

'We have only one full-time gardener. It is too much for him.'

'And you yourself? Have you been resident here long?'

'For a while. If we follow that path there, we come out at a pond with goldfish. Your son may like that.'

'In fact I am not his father. I look after him. I am a guardian of sorts. Temporarily.'

'Where are his parents?'

'His parents . . . That is the reason why we are here today. The boy does not have parents, not in the usual way. There was a mishap on board the boat during the voyage here. A letter went missing that might have explained everything. As a result, his parents are lost, or, more accurately, he is lost. He and his mother have been separated, and we are trying to find her. His father is a different matter.'

They have reached the promised pond, in which there are indeed goldfish, both small and large. The boy kneels down at the edge, using a frond of sedge in an attempt to lure them.

'Let me be more precise,' he says, speaking softly and rapidly. 'The boy has no mother. Ever since we got off the boat we have been searching for her. Will you consider taking him?'

'Taking him?'

'Yes, being a mother to him. Being his mother. Will you take him as your son?'

'I don't understand. In fact I understand nothing at all. Are you suggesting that I adopt your boy?'

'Not adopt. Be his mother, his full mother. We have only one mother, each of us. Will you be that one and only mother to him?'

Up to this point she has been listening attentively. But now she begins to glance around a little wildly, as if hoping that someone – the porter, one of her tennis companions, anyone – will come to her rescue.

'What of his real mother?' she says. 'Where is she? Is she still alive?'

He had thought the child was too absorbed in the goldfish to be listening. But now he suddenly pipes up: 'She's not dead!'

'Then where is she?'

The child is silent. For a while he too is silent. Then he speaks. 'Please believe me – please take it on faith – this is not a simple matter. The boy is without mother. What that means I cannot explain to you because I cannot explain it to myself. Yet I promise you, if you will simply say Yes, without forethought, without afterthought, all will become clear to you, as clear as day, or so I believe. Therefore: will you accept this child as yours?'

She glances at her wrist, on which there is no wristwatch. 'It's getting late,' she says. 'My brothers will be expecting me.' She turns and strides swiftly back towards the residence, her skirt swishing through the grass.

He runs after her. 'Please!' he says. 'One moment more. Here. Let me write down his name. His name is David. That is the name he goes by, the name he was given in the camp. And this is where we live, just outside the city, in the East Village. Please think about it.' He presses the scrap of paper into her hand. Then she is gone.

'Doesn't she want me?' asks the child.

'Of course she wants you. You are such a handsome, clever boy, who would not want you? But first she must get used to the idea. We have planted the seed in her mind; now we must be patient and allow it to grow. As long as you and she like each other, it is certain to grow and flower. You do like the lady, don't you? You can see how kind she is, kind and gentle.'

The boy is silent.

By the time they have found their way back to the terminus it is nearly dark. In the bus the boy falls asleep in his arms; he has to carry him, asleep, from the bus stop to the apartment.

In the middle of the night he is roused from a deep sleep. It is the boy, standing by his bedside, tears streaming down his face. 'I'm hungry!' he whines.

He gets up, warms some milk, butters a slice of bread.

'Are we going to live there?' asks the boy, his mouth full.

'At La Residencia? I don't think so. There would be nothing for me to do. I would become like one of those bees that just hangs around the hive waiting for mealtimes. But we can discuss it in the morning. There is lots of time.'

'I don't want to live there. I want to live here, with you.'

'No one is going to force you to live where you don't want to. Now let us go back to bed.'

He sits with the child, stroking him softly until he is asleep.

I want to live with you. What if that wish comes bitterly true? Does he have it in him to be both father and mother to the child, to bring him up in the ways of goodness while all the time holding down a job at the docks?

He curses himself inwardly. If only he had presented their case more calmly, more rationally! But no, he must behave like a madman, bursting in upon the poor woman with his pleas and his demands. *Take this child! Be his one and only mother!* Better if he had found a way of giving the boy into her arms, body to body, flesh to flesh. Then memories lying deeper than all thought might have been reawoken, and all would have been well. But alas, it came too suddenly for her, this great moment, as it had come too suddenly for him. It had burst on him like a star, and he had failed it.

Chapter 10

As it turns out, however, all is not lost. Just as noon is striking, the boy comes rushing upstairs in a state of great excitement. 'They are here, they are here!' he shouts.

'Who is here?'

'The lady from the Residencia! The lady who is going to be my mother! She came in a car.'

The lady, who arrives at the door wearing a rather formal dark blue dress, a curious little hat with a gaudy gold hatpin, and – he cannot believe his eyes – white gloves, as if she were visiting a lawyer, does not come alone. She is accompanied by the tall, rangy young man who had so capably taken on two adversaries on the tennis court. 'My brother Diego,' she explains.

Diego nods to him but says no word.

'Please sit down,' he says to his guests. 'If you don't mind using the bed . . . We haven't bought furniture yet. Can I offer you a glass of water? No?'

The lady from La Residencia perches side by side with her brother on the bed; she plucks nervously at her gloves, clears her throat. 'Will you repeat for us what you said yesterday?' she says. 'Start at the beginning, the very beginning.'

'If I started at the very beginning we would be here all day,' he replies, trying to sound deliberate, trying above all to sound sane. 'Let me rather say the following. We, David and I, came here, as everyone does, for the sake of a new life, a new beginning. What I want for David, what David wants too, is a normal life like any other youngster's. But – it stands to reason – to lead a normal life he needs a mother, needs to be born to a mother, so to speak. I am right, am I not?' he says, turning to the boy. 'That is what you want. You want your very own mother.'

The boy nods vigorously.

'I have always been sure – don't ask me why – that I would know David's mother when I saw her; and now that I have met you I know I was right. It could not have been chance that led us to La Residencia. Some hand must have been guiding us.'

It is Diego, he can see, who is going to be the hard nut to crack: Diego, not the woman, whose name he does not know and does not want to ask. The woman would not be here if she were not ready to be swayed.

'Some unseen hand,' he repeats. 'Truly.'

Diego's gaze bores into him. *Liar!* it says.

He takes a deep breath. 'You have doubts, I can see. *How can this child whom I have never laid eyes on be my child?* you ask yourself. I plead with you: put doubt aside, listen instead to what your heart says. Look at him. Look at the boy. What does your heart say?'

The young woman gives no answer, does not look at the boy at all, but turns to her brother, as if to say, *Do you see? It is as I told you. Listen to this unbelievable, this mad proposal of his! What shall I do?*

In a low voice the brother speaks. 'Is there somewhere private we can go, you and I?'

'Of course. We can go outdoors.'

He leads Diego downstairs, across the courtyard, across the lawn, to a bench in the shade of a tree. 'Sit down,' he says. Diego ignores the invitation. He himself sits down. 'How can I help you?' he says.

Diego props a leg on the bench and leans down over him. 'First, who are you, and why are you after my sister?'

'Who I am doesn't matter. I am not important. I am a kind of manservant. I look after the child. And I am not after your sister. I am after the child's mother. There is a difference.'

'Who is this child? Where did you pick him up? Is he your grandson? Where are his parents?'

'He is neither my grandson nor my son. He and I are not kin. We were brought together by accident on the boat when he lost some documents he was carrying. But why should any of that matter? We arrive here, all of us, you, me, your sister, the boy, washed clean of the past. The boy happens to be in my care. That may not be a destiny I chose for myself, but I accept it. Over time he has come to depend on me. We have grown close. But I cannot be everything to him. I cannot be his mother.

'Your sister – I am sorry, I don't know her name – is his

mother, his natural mother. I cannot explain how that happens, but it is so, it is as simple as that. And in her heart she knows it. Why else do you think she is here today? On the surface she may seem calm, but beneath the surface I can see it thrills her, this great gift, the gift of a child.'

'Children are not allowed in La Residencia.'

'No one would dare separate a mother from her child, no matter what the rule book says. Nor does your sister have to go on living at La Residencia. She could take over the apartment here. It is hers. I give it over to her. I will find somewhere else to live.'

Leaning forward as if to speak confidentially, Diego gives him a sudden slap across the head. Shocked, trying to shield himself, he is struck a second blow. They are not heavy blows, but they jolt him.

'Why do you do that!' he exclaims, rising.

'I am not a fool!' hisses Diego. 'Do you think I am a fool?' Again he raises a threatening hand.

'Not for a moment do I take you for a fool.' He needs to placate this young man, who must be upset – as who would not be? – by this queer intervention in his life. 'It is an unusual story, I admit. But spare a thought for the child. He is the one whose needs are paramount.'

His plea has no effect: Diego glares as belligerently as before. He plays his last card. 'Come on, Diego,' he says, 'look into your heart! If there is goodwill in your heart, surely you will not keep a child from his mother!'

'It's not for you to doubt my goodwill,' says Diego.

'Then prove it! Come back with me and prove to the child how much goodwill you are capable of. Come!' And he rises and takes Diego's arm.

A strange spectacle greets them. Diego's sister is kneeling on the bed with her back to them, straddling the boy – who lies flat on his back beneath her – her dress hoisted up to allow a glimpse of solid, rather heavy thighs. 'Where is the spider, where is the spider . . . ?' she croons in a high, thin voice. Her fingers drift down his chest to his belt buckle; she tickles him, convulsing him in helpless laughter.

'We are back,' he announces in a loud voice. She scrambles off the bed, her face flushed.

'Inés and I are playing a game,' says the boy.

Inés! So that is the name! And in the name the essence!

'Inés!' says the brother, and beckons to her curtly. Smoothing her dress down, she hurries after him. From the corridor come furious whisperings.

Inés comes marching back, her brother trailing behind. 'We want you to go through all of it again,' she says.

'You want me to repeat my proposal?'

'Yes.'

'Very well. I propose that you become David's mother. I give up all claim to him (he has a claim on me, but that is a different matter). I will sign any paper you put before me to confirm it. You and he can live together as mother and child. It can happen as soon as you like.'

Diego gives an exasperated snort. 'This is all nonsense!' he exclaims. 'You can't be this child's mother, he already has a mother, the mother he was born to! Without his mother's permission you can't adopt him. Listen to me!'

He exchanges a silent glance with Inés. 'I want him,' she says, addressing not him but her brother. 'I want him,' she repeats. 'But we can't stay at La Residencia.'

'As I told your brother, you are welcome to move in here. It can happen today. I will move out at once. This will be your new home.'

'I don't want you to go,' says the boy.

'I won't go far, my boy. I will go and stay with Elena and Fidel. You and your mother can come visiting whenever you like.'

'I want you to stay here,' says the boy.

'That is sweet of you, but I can't come between you and your mother. From now on, you and she are going to be together. You will be a family. I can't be part of that family. But I will be a helper, a servant and a helper. I promise.' He turns to Inés. 'Are we agreed?'

'Yes.' Now that she has made up her mind, Inés has become quite imperious. 'We will come back tomorrow. We will bring our dog. Will your neighbours object to a dog?'

'They would not dare.'

By the time Inés and her brother return the next morning, he has swept the floors, scrubbed the tiles, changed the sheets; his own belongings are bundled up and ready to go.

Diego heads the incoming procession, bearing a large suitcase on his shoulder. He drops it on the bed. 'There's more to come,' he announces ominously. And indeed there is: a trunk, even larger, and a stack of bedclothes that include a vast eiderdown bedcover.

He, Simón, does not linger over his leavetaking. 'Be good,' he tells the boy. 'He doesn't eat cucumber,' he tells Inés. 'And leave a light on when he goes to bed, he doesn't like to sleep in the dark.'

She gives no sign of having heard him. 'It's cold in here,' she says, rubbing her hands together. 'Is it always so cold?'

'I'll buy an electric fire. I'll bring it in the next day or two.' To Diego he offers his hand, which Diego reluctantly takes. Then he picks up his bundle and without a backward glance strides off.

He had announced he would be staying with Elena, but in fact he has no such plan. He makes his way to the docks, deserted over the weekend, and stows his belongings in the little hut off Wharf Two where the men keep their gear. Then he walks back to the Blocks and knocks at Elena's door. 'Hello,' he calls, 'can you and I have a chat?'

Over tea he outlines to her the new dispensation. 'I am sure David will flourish now that he has a mother to look after him. It wasn't good for him to be brought up just by me. He was under too much pressure to become a little man himself. A child needs his childhood, don't you think?'

'I can't believe my ears,' replies Elena. 'A child is not like a chick that you can stuff under the wing of some strange hen to raise. How could you hand David over to someone you have never laid eyes on before, some woman who is probably acting on a whim and will lose interest before the week is over and want to give him back?'

'Please, Elena, don't pass judgment on this Inés before you have met her. She is not acting on a whim; on the contrary, I believe she is acting under a force stronger than herself. I am counting on you to help us, to help her. She is in unknown territory; she has no experience of motherhood.'

'I am not passing judgment on this Inés of yours. If she asks for help, I will give it. But she is not your boy's mother and you should stop calling her that.'

'Elena, she *is* his mother. I arrived in this land bare of everything save one rock-solid conviction: that I would know the boy's mother when I saw her. And the moment I beheld Inés I knew it was she.'

'You followed an intuition?'

'More than that. A conviction.'

'A conviction, an intuition, a delusion – what is the difference when it cannot be questioned? Has it occurred to you that if we all lived by our intuitions the world would fall into chaos?'

'I don't see why that follows. And what is wrong with a little chaos now and again if good follows from it?'

Elena shrugs. 'I don't want to get into an argument. Your son missed his lesson today. It is not the first lesson he has missed. If he is going to give up his music, please let me know.'

'That is no longer for me to decide. And once again, he is not my son, I am not his father.'

'Really? You keep denying it, but sometimes I wonder. I say

no more. Where are you going to spend tonight? In the bosom of your new-found family?'

'No.'

'Do you want to sleep here?'

He rises from the table. 'Thank you, but I have made other arrangements.'

Considering that the doves nesting in the gutter scratch and rustle and coo without cease, he sleeps quite well that night, on his bed of sacks in his little hideout. He goes without breakfast, yet is able to work a full day and feel fine at the end of it, if a little ethereal, a little ghostly.

Álvaro asks after the boy, and so touched is he by Álvaro's concern that for a moment he considers telling him the good news, the news that the boy's mother has been found. But then, mindful of Elena's reaction to the very same news, he checks himself and tells a lie: David has been taken by his teacher to a big music concourse.

A music concourse, says Álvaro, looking dubious: what is that, and where is it being held?

No idea, he replies, and changes the subject.

It would be a pity, it seems to him, if the boy were to lose touch with Álvaro and never again see his friend El Rey the draft horse. He hopes that, once she has strengthened her bond with him, Inés will allow the boy to visit the docks. The past is so shrouded in clouds of forgetting that he cannot be sure his memories are true memories rather than mere stories he makes up; but he does know that he would have loved it if, as a child, he had been allowed to set off of a morning in the company of grown men and spend the day helping them load and unload great ships. A dose of the real cannot but be good for the child, it seems to him, so long as the dose is not too sudden or too large.

He had intended to call at Naranjas for supplies, but he has left it too late: by the time he gets there the shop is closed. Hungry, and lonely too, he knocks once again at Elena's door. The door is opened by Fidel, in his pyjamas. 'Hello, young Fidel,' he says, 'may I come in?'

Elena is sitting at the table, sewing. She does not greet him, does not raise her eyes from her work.

'Hello,' he says. 'Is something wrong? Has something happened?'

She shakes her head.

'David can't come here any more,' says Fidel. 'The new lady says he can't come.'

'The new lady,' says Elena, 'has announced that your son is not allowed to play with Fidel.'

'But why?'

She shrugs.

'Give her time to settle down,' he says. 'Being a mother is new to her. She is bound to be a little erratic at first.'

'Erratic?'

'Erratic in her judgments. Over-cautious.'

'Like forbidding David to play with his friends?'

'She does not know you or Fidel. Once she gets to know you, she will see what a good influence you are.'

'And how do you propose that she get to know us?'

'You and she are bound to bump into each other. You are neighbours, after all.'

'We'll see. Have you eaten?'

'No. The shops were closed by the time I got there.'

'You mean Naranjas. Naranjas is closed on Mondays, I could have told you that. I can offer you a bowl of soup, if you don't mind a repeat of last night. Where are you living now?'

'I have a room near the docks. It's a bit primitive, but it will do for the time being.'

Elena warms up the pot of soup and cuts bread for him. He tries to eat slowly, though in fact his appetite is wolfish.

'You can't stay the night, I'm afraid,' she says. 'You know why.'

'Of course. I'm not asking to stay. My new quarters are perfectly comfortable.'

'You have been expelled, haven't you? From your home. That's the truth, I can see it. You poor thing. Cut off from your boy, whom you love so much.'

He gets up from the table. 'It has to be,' he says. 'It's the nature of things. Thank you for the meal.'

'Come again tomorrow. I'll feed you. It's the least I can do. Feed you and console you. Though I think you have made a mistake.'

He takes his leave. He ought to go straight to his new home at the docks. But he hesitates, then crosses the court-yard, climbs the stairs, and taps softly at the door of his old apartment. There is a crack of light under the door: Inés must still be up. After a long wait he taps again. 'Inés?' he whispers.

A handsbreadth away on the other side he hears her: 'Who is there?'

'It's Simón. Can I come in?'

'What do you want?'

'Can I see him? Just for a minute.'

'He's asleep.'

'I won't wake him. I just want to see him.'

Silence. He tries the door. It is locked. A moment later the light clicks off.

Chapter 11

By taking up residence at the docks he is probably infringing some regulation or other. That does not concern him. However, he does not want Álvaro to find out, for out of the goodness of his heart Álvaro is then bound to feel he has to offer him a home. So before leaving the toolshed each morning he takes care to tuck his few possessions away in the rafters where they will not be seen.

Keeping neat and clean is a problem. He visits the gymnasium at the East Blocks to shower; he washes his clothes by hand and hangs them on the East Blocks lines. He has no qualms about this – he is, after all, still on the list of residents – but out of prudence, not wishing to run into Inés, he pays his visits only after dark.

A week passes during which he gives all his energies to his work. Then on the Friday, with his pockets full of money, he knocks at the door of his old apartment.

The door is thrown open by a smiling Inés. Her face falls

when she sees him. 'Oh, it's you,' she says. 'We are just on our way out.'

From behind her the boy emerges. There is something odd about his appearance. It is not just that he wears a new white shirt (in fact more blouse than shirt – it has a frilly front and hangs over his pants): he stands clutching Inés's skirt, not responding to his greeting, staring at him with great eyes.

Has something happened? Has it been a calamitous mistake to hand him over to this woman? And why does he tolerate this eccentric, girlish blouse – he who has been so attached to his little-man outfit, his coat and cap and lace-up boots? For the boots are gone too, replaced by shoes: blue shoes with straps instead of laces, and brass buttons on the side.

'Lucky I caught you, in that case,' he says, trying to keep his tone light. 'I have brought the electric heater I promised.'

Inés casts a dubious eye on the little one-bar heater he holds out. 'At La Residencia there is an open fire in each apartment,' she says. 'A man brings logs every evening and makes the fire.' She pauses abstractedly. 'It is lovely.'

'I am sorry. It must be a comedown, having to live in the Blocks.' He turns to the boy. 'So you are going out for the evening. And where is it you are going?'

The boy does not answer directly, but casts a look up to his new mother as if to say, *You tell him*.

'We're going to La Residencia for the weekend,' says Inés. And as though to confirm her, Diego, dressed in tennis whites, comes striding up the corridor.

'That's nice,' he says. 'I thought they didn't allow children at La Residencia. I thought that was the rule.'

'That is the rule,' says Diego. 'But it's a free weekend for the staff. There is no one to check.'

'No one checks,' Inés echoes.

'Well, I just dropped by to see if everything is all right, and perhaps to help with the shopping. Here: I brought a small contribution.'

Without a word of thanks Inés accepts the money. 'Yes, all is well with us,' she says. She presses the child tight against her side. 'We had a big lunch and then we had a nap, and now we are going off in the car to meet Bolívar, and in the morning we are going to play tennis and have a swim.'

'That sounds exciting,' he says. 'And we have a nice new shirt too, I see.'

The boy does not reply. His thumb is in his mouth, he has not stopped staring at him with those great eyes. More and more he is convinced there is something wrong.

'Who is Bolívar?' he asks.

For the first time the boy speaks. 'Bolívar is an Assación.'

'An Alsatian,' says Inés. 'Bolívar is our dog.'

'Ah yes, Bolívar,' he says. 'He was with you at the tennis court, wasn't he? I don't want to be an alarmist, Inés, but Alsatians don't have a good reputation around children. I hope you will take care.'

'Bolívar is the gentlest dog in the world.'

He knows she does not like him. Up to this moment he has assumed it is because she is in debt to him. But no, the dislike is more personal and more immediate than that, and therefore more intractable. What a pity! The child will learn to look on him as an enemy, the enemy of their mother–child bliss.

'Have a wonderful time,' he says. 'Perhaps I will drop by again on Monday. Then you can tell me the whole story. Agreed?'

The boy nods.

'Goodbye,' he says.

'Goodbye,' says Inés. From Diego not a word.

He trudges back to the docks feeling that something has expired in him, feeling like an old man. He had one great task, and that task is discharged. The boy has been delivered to his mother. Like one of those drab male insects whose sole function is to pass on his seed to the female, he may as well wither away now and die. There is nothing left to build his life around.

He misses the boy. Waking up the next morning with the empty weekend before him is like waking after surgery to find a limb has been cut off – a limb or perhaps even his heart. He spends the day drifting about, killing time. He wanders around the empty docks; he roams back and forth across the parklands, where hosts of children are throwing balls or flying kites.

The feel of the boy's sweaty little hand in his is still vividly alive to him. Whether the boy loved him he does not know, but certainly he needed and trusted him. A child belongs with his mother: he would not for a moment deny that. But what if the mother is not a good mother? What if Elena is right? Out of what complex of private needs did this Inés, of whose history he knows not a jot, grasp a chance to have a child of her own? Perhaps there is wisdom in the law of nature which says that, before it can emerge into the world as a living soul, the embryonic being, the being-to-be, must for a term be borne in its mother's womb. Perhaps, like the weeks of inwardness that the mother bird spends sitting on her eggs, a period of seclusion and self-absorption is necessary not only for an animalcule to turn into a human being but also for a woman to turn from virgin into mother.

Somehow the day passes. He thinks of calling in at Elena's, then at the last minute changes his mind, unable to face the nagging interrogation that awaits him there. He has not eaten, has no appetite. He settles down on his bed of sacks, restless, fretting.

The next morning, at the crack of dawn, he is at the bus station. An hour passes before the first bus arrives. From the terminus he follows the uphill track to La Residencia, to the tennis court. The court is deserted. He settles down to wait.

At ten o'clock the second brother, the one he has not yet had the pleasure of being introduced to, arrives in his whites and begins to set up the net. He pays no attention to the stranger in plain sight not thirty paces away. After a while the rest of the party makes its appearance.

The boy sees him at once. In his knock-kneed way (he is an awkward runner) he dashes across the court. 'Simón! We are going to play tennis!' he calls out. 'Do you want to play too?'

He grips the boy's fingers through the mesh. 'I'm not much of a tennis player,' he says, 'I'd rather watch. Are you enjoying yourself? Are you getting enough to eat?'

The boy nods vigorously. 'I had tea for breakfast. Inés says I am big enough to drink tea.' He turns and calls out, 'I can drink tea, can't I, Inés?' then without a pause plunges on: 'And I gave Bolívar his food and Inés says we can take Bolívar for a walk after tennis.'

'Bolívar the Alsatian? Please be careful around Bolívar. Don't provoke him.'

'Alsatians are the best dogs. When they catch a thief they never let go. Would you like to watch me play tennis? I'm not very good yet, I have to practise first.' With that he whirls around and dashes back to where Inés and her brothers stand conferring. 'Can we practise now?'

They have outfitted him in brief white shorts. So, with the white blouse, he is all in white, save for the blue shoes with the straps. But the tennis racquet they have given him is far too large: even with two hands he can barely swing it.

Bolívar the Alsatian slinks across the court and settles down in the shade. Bolívar is a male, with huge shoulders and a black ruff. In looks he is not far removed from a wolf.

'Come here, big man!' calls Diego. He stands over the boy, his hands enclosing the boy's hands as they hold the racquet. The other brother lobs a ball. Together they swing; they hit the ball cleanly. The brother lobs another ball. Again they hit it. Diego backs away. 'There's nothing I can teach him,' he calls to his sister. 'He is a natural.' The brother lobs a third ball. The boy swings the heavy racquet and misses, almost falling over in the effort.

'You two play,' calls Inés to her brothers. 'David and I will go and throw balls.'

With easy competence the two brothers knock a ball back and forth over the net, while Inés and the boy disappear behind the little wooden pavilion. He, *el viejo*, the silent watcher, is simply ignored. It could not be made more clear that he is unwanted.

Chapter 12

He has vowed to keep his woes to himself, but when Álvaro asks a second time what has become of the boy ('I miss him — we all miss him'), the whole story comes pouring out.

'We went searching for his mother and — behold! — we found her,' he says. 'Now the two of them are reunited, and they are very happy together. Unfortunately the kind of life Inés has in mind for him doesn't include hanging around the docks with the menfolk. It includes nice clothes and good manners and regular meals. Which is fair enough, I suppose.'

Of course it is fair enough. What right has he to complain?

'It must come as a blow to you,' says Álvaro. 'The youngster is special. Anyone can see that. And you and he were close.'

'Yes, we were close. But it's not as if I won't see him again. It's just that his mother feels that he and she will restore their bond more easily if I stay out of the picture for a while. Which, again, is fair enough.'

'Indeed,' says Álvaro. 'But it does ignore the urgings of the heart, doesn't it?'

The urgings of the heart: who would have thought Álvaro had it in him to talk like that? A man strong and true. A comrade. Why can he not bare his heart frankly to Álvaro? But no: 'I have no right to make demands,' he hears himself say. *Hypocrite!* 'Besides, the rights of the child always trump the rights of grown-ups. Isn't that a principle in law? The rights of the child as bearer of the future.'

Álvaro gives him a sceptical look. 'I've never heard of such a principle.'

'A law of nature then. Blood is thicker than water. A child belongs with his mother. Particularly a young child. By comparison, my claims are very abstract, very artificial.'

'You love him. He loves you. That isn't artificial. It's the law that is artificial. He should be with you. He needs you.'

'It's good of you to say so, Álvaro, but does he truly need me? Perhaps the truth is, I am the one who needs him. Perhaps I lean on him more than he leans on me. Who knows how we elect those we love anyway? It is all a great mystery.'

That afternoon he has a surprise visitor: young Fidel, who arrives at the docks on his bicycle, bearing a scrawled note: *We have been expecting you. I hope there is nothing wrong. Would you like to come to dinner this evening? Elena.*

'Say to your mother, *Thank you, I'll be there*,' he tells Fidel.

'Is this your work?' asks Fidel.

'Yes, this is what I do. I help to load and unload ships like this one. I'm sorry I can't take you on board, but it is a bit dangerous. One day when you are older, perhaps.'

'Is it a galleon?'

'No, it doesn't have sails so it can't qualify as a galleon. It is what we call a coal-fired ship. That means it burns coal to work the engines that make it go. Tomorrow they will be loading coal for the return voyage. That will be done at Wharf Ten, not here. I won't be involved. I'm glad of it. It's a nasty job.'

'Why?'

'Because coal leaves black dust all over you, including in your hair. Also because coal is very heavy to carry.'

'Why can't David play with me?'

'It's not that he can't play with you, Fidel. It's just that his mother wants him to herself for a while. She hasn't seen him in a long time.'

'I thought you said she had never seen him.'

'In a manner of speaking. She saw him in her dreams. She knew he was coming. She was waiting for him. Now he has come, and she is overjoyed. Her heart is full.'

The boy is silent.

'Fidel, I have to get back to work now. I'll see you and your mother this evening.'

'Is her name Inés?'

'David's mother? Yes, her name is Inés.'

'I don't like her. She's got a dog.'

'You don't know her. Once you get to know her you will like her.'

'I won't. It's a fierce dog. I'm scared of it.'

'I have seen the dog. Its name is Bolívar, and I agree, you should steer clear of it. It is an Alsatian. Alsatians tend to be unpredictable. I'm surprised she has brought it to the Blocks.'

'Does it bite?'

'It can.'

'And where exactly are you living,' asks Elena, 'now that you have given up your nice apartment?'

'I told you: I have taken a room near the docks.'

'Yes, but where exactly? In a boarding house?'

'No. It doesn't matter where it is or what kind of room. It is good enough for my purposes.'

'Does it have cooking facilities?'

'I don't need cooking facilities. I wouldn't use them if I had them.'

'So you are living on bread and water. I thought you were sick of bread and water.'

'Bread is the staff of life. He who has bread shall not want. Elena, please stop this interrogation. I am perfectly capable of caring for myself.'

'I doubt that. I doubt it very much. Can the people at the arrivals centre not find you a new apartment?'

'As far as the Centre is aware, I am still happily situated in my old apartment. They are not about to award me a secondary residence.'

'And Inés — did you not say that Inés has rooms at La Residencia? Why can't she and the child stay there?'

'Because children aren't allowed at La Residencia. La Residencia is a kind of resort, as far as I can work out.'

'I know La Residencia. I have visited there. Do you know she has brought a dog with her? It's one thing keeping a small dog in an apartment, but this is a great big wolfhound. It's not hygienic.'

'It's not a wolfhound, it's an Alsatian. I admit, it makes me nervous. I've warned David to be careful. I've warned Fidel too.'

'I will certainly not allow Fidel anywhere near it. Are you sure you have done the right thing, giving your child away to a woman like that?'

'To a woman with a dog?'

'To a childless woman in her thirties. A woman who spends her time playing sports with men. A woman who keeps dogs.'

'Inés plays tennis. Lots of women play tennis. It's enjoyable. It keeps you fit. And she has only one dog.'

'Has she told you anything about her background, her past?'

'No. I didn't ask her.'

'Well, in my opinion you are out of your mind, handing over your child to a stranger who for all you know has a dubious past.'

'That's nonsense, Elena. Inés has no past, none that counts. None of us has a past. We start anew here. We start with a blank slate, a virgin slate. And Inés is not a stranger. I recognized her as soon as I set eyes on her, which means I must have some kind of prior knowledge.'

'You arrive here with no memories, with a blank slate, yet you claim to recognize faces from the past. It makes no sense.'

'It is true: I have no memories. But images still persist, shades of images. How that is I can't explain. Something deeper persists too, which I call the memory of having a memory. It is not from the past that I recognize Inés but from elsewhere. It is as if the image of her were embedded in me. I have no doubts about her, no second thoughts. At least, I have no doubt that she is the boy's true mother.'

'Then what doubts do you have?'

'I only hope she will be good for him.'

Chapter 13

In retrospect that day, the day when Elena sent her son to the docks to call him, marks the moment when he and she, whom he had thought of as two ships on a near-windless ocean, adrift perhaps, but drifting on the whole towards each other, began to drift apart. There is much that he still likes about Elena, not least her readiness to give ear to his complaints. But the feeling hardens that something that ought to be between them is missing; and if Elena does not share that feeling, if she believes that nothing is missing, then she cannot be what is missing from his life.

Sitting on a bench outside the East Blocks, he writes a note to Inés.

I have grown friendly with a woman who lives across the courtyard, in Block C. Her name is Elena. She has a son named Fidel who has become David's closest friend and a steadying influence on him. For a youngster Fidel has a good heart, you will find.

David has been taking music lessons with Elena. See if

you can persuade him to sing for you. He sings beautifully. My feeling is that he should go on with his lessons, but of course the decision is yours.

David also gets on well with my foreman at work, Álvaro, another good friend. Having good friends encourages one to be good too, or so I find. To follow in the ways of goodness – isn't that what we both desire for David?

If there is any way in which I can help [he concludes] you have only to raise a finger. I am at the docks most days, on Wharf Two. Fidel will take messages; David knows the way too.

He drops the note in Inés's letter box. He expects no reply and indeed receives none. He has no clear sense of what kind of woman Inés is. Is she the kind of woman prepared to accept well-meant advice, for instance, or is she the kind that gets irritated when strangers tell her how to run her life, and tosses their communications in the trash? Does she even check her letter box?

Located in the basement of Block F of East Village, the same block that houses the communal gymnasium, is a bakery outlet for which his private name is the Commissariat. Its doors are open on weekday mornings from nine until noon. Besides bread and other baked goods, it sells at laughably low prices such basic foodstuffs as sugar, salt, flour, and cooking oil.

From the Commissariat he buys a stock of canned soup, which he carries back to his hideout at the docks. His evening meal, when he is by himself, is bread and bean soup, cold. He grows used to its unvaryingness.

Since most tenants of the Blocks use the Commissariat, he guesses that Inés will use it too. He toys with the idea of hanging around there of a morning in the hope of seeing her and the boy, but then thinks better of it. It would be too humiliating if she stumbled on him lurking among the shelves, spying on her.

He does not want to turn into a ghost unable to quit its old haunts. He is ready to accept that the best way for Inés to build up trust with the child is to have him for a while all to herself. But there is a nagging fear he cannot dismiss: that the child may be lonely and unhappy, pining for him. He cannot forget the look in the child's eyes when he visited, full of mute doubt. He longs to see him again as he used to be, wearing his little peaked cap and black boots.

Now and again he gives in to temptation and dawdles around the outskirts of the Blocks. On one such visitation he glimpses Inés gathering up the washing from the line. Though he cannot be sure, she seems tired, tired and perhaps sad. Can it be that things are going badly with her?

He recognizes the boy's clothing on the line, including the blouse with the frilly front.

On another – and, as it turns out, the last – of these surreptitious visits he observes the family trio – Inés, the child, the dog – emerge from the Blocks and set off across the lawns in the direction of the parklands. What surprises him is that the boy, clad in his grey coat, is not walking but being pushed in a stroller. Why does a five-year-old need to be wheeled? Why indeed does he permit it?

He catches up with them in the wildest part of the park-lands, where a wooden footbridge crosses a stream choked with rushes. 'Inés!' he calls out.

Inés stops and turns. The dog turns too, cocking its ears, tugging at its leash.

He puts on a smile as he approaches. 'What a coincidence! I was on my way to the shops when I saw you. How are you getting on?' And then, without waiting for her reply, 'Hello,' he says to the child, 'I see you are going for a ride. Like a young prince.'

The child's eyes fix on his and lock. A sense of peace invades him. All is well. The link between them is not broken. But the thumb is in the mouth again. Not a promising sign. The thumb in the mouth means insecurity, means a troubled heart.

'We're taking a walk,' says Inés. 'We need some air. It is so stuffy in that apartment.'

'I know,' he says. 'It is badly designed. I keep the window open day and night to air it. I mean, I used to keep the window open.'

'I can't do that. I don't want David catching cold.'

'Oh, he doesn't catch cold easily. He's a tough fellow – aren't you?'

The boy nods. The coat is buttoned all the way up to his chin, no doubt so that wind-borne germs won't get in.

A long silence. He would like to come closer, but the dog has not relaxed its vigilant glare.

'Where did you get that' – he gestures – 'that vehicle?'

'At the family depot.'

'The family depot?'

'There is a depot in the city where you can get things for children. We got him a cot too.'

'A cot?'

'A cot with sides. So that he doesn't fall out.'

'That's strange. He has been sleeping in a bed ever since I can remember, and he has never fallen out.'

Even before he has finished, he knows it was the wrong thing to say. Inés's lips clamp tight, she swings the vehicle around, she would march off but for the fact that the dog's leash has become tangled in the wheels and has to be unwound.

'I'm sorry,' he says, 'I don't mean to interfere.'

She does not deign to reply.

Going back over the episode afterwards, he wonders why it is that he has no feeling for Inés as a woman, not the slightest flicker, even though there is nothing wrong with her looks. Is it because she is so hostile to him and has been from the start; or is she unattractive simply because she refuses to be attractive, refuses to open herself up? May she indeed be, as Elena asserts, a virgin, or at least the virginal type? What he knew of virgins is lost in clouds of forgetting. Does the aura of the virginal stifle a man's desire or on the contrary sharpen it? He thinks of Ana, from the Relocation Centre, who strikes him as a virgin of a rather fierce kind. Ana he certainly found attractive. What does Ana have that Inés does not? Or should the question be phrased contrariwise: What does Inés have that Ana does not?

★ ★ ★

'I bumped into Inés and young David yesterday,' he tells Elena. 'Do you see much of them?'

'I see her around the Blocks. We haven't spoken. I don't think she wants much to do with the residents.'

'I suppose, if one is used to life in La Residencia, it must be hard to find oneself living in the Blocks.'

'Living in La Residencia doesn't make her better than us. We all started from nowhere, from nothing. It's just a matter of luck that she landed up there.'

'How do you think she is coping with motherhood?'

'She's very protective of the child. Over-protective, in my opinion. She watches him like a hawk, won't let him play with other children. You know that. Fidel can't understand. He feels hurt.'

'I'm sorry. What else have you seen?'

'Her brothers spend a lot of time visiting. They have a car – one of those little four-seaters with a roof that you can roll back, a cabriolet I think it is called. They all go off in the car and come back after dark.'

'The dog too?'

'The dog too. Everywhere Inés goes, the dog goes. It gives me the shivers. It is like a coiled spring. One of these days it is going to attack someone. I just pray it isn't a child. Can't she be persuaded to muzzle it?'

'No chance of that.'

'Well, I think it is madness to keep a vicious dog when you have a young child.'

'It's not a vicious dog, Elena, just a bit unpredictable.

Unpredictable but faithful. That is what seems to matter most to Inés. Fidelity, queen of the virtues.'

'Really? I wouldn't call it that. I would call it a middle-ranking virtue, like temperance. The sort of virtue you look for in a soldier. Inés strikes me as a bit of a watchdog herself, hovering around David, warding off harm. Why on earth did you choose a woman like that? You were a better father to him than she is a mother.'

'That's not true. A child can't grow up without a mother. Didn't you say so yourself: to the mother the child owes his substance, whereas the father merely provides the idea? Once the idea has been transmitted, the father is dispensable. And in this case I am not even the father.'

'A child needs a mother's womb to come into the world. After he has left the womb the mother as life-giver is as much a spent force as the father. What the child needs from then on is love and care, which a man can provide as well as a woman. Your Inés knows nothing about love and care. She is like a little girl with a doll – an unusually jealous and selfish little girl who won't let anyone else touch her toy.'

'Nonsense. You are ready to condemn Inés, yet you barely know her.'

'And you? How well did you know her before you handed over your precious charge? Investigating her qualifications as a mother was not necessary, you said: you could rely on intuition. You would know the true mother in a flash, the moment you laid eyes on her. Intuition: what sort of basis is that for deciding a child's future?'

'We have been through this before, Elena. What is wrong with native intuition? What else is there we can trust, finally?'

'Common sense. Reason. Any reasonable person would have warned you that a thirty-year-old virgin used to a life of idleness, insulated from the real world, guarded by two thuggish brothers, would not make a reliable mother. Also, any reasonable person would have made inquiries about this Inés, explored her past, assessed her character. Any reasonable person would have imposed a trial period, to make sure they got on together, the child and his nurse.'

He shakes his head. 'You still misunderstand. My task was to bring the boy to his mother. It was not to bring him to *a* mother, to a woman who passed some or other motherhood test. It does not matter if by your standards or mine Inés is not a particularly good mother. The fact is, she is *his* mother. He is with *his* mother.'

'But Inés is not *his* mother! She did not conceive him! She did not carry him in her womb! She did not bring him into the world in blood and pain! She is just someone you picked out on a whim, for all I know because she reminded you of your own mother.'

He shakes his head again. 'The moment I saw Inés, I knew. If we don't trust the voice that speaks inside us, saying, *This is the one!* then there is nothing left to trust.'

'Don't make me laugh! Inner voices! People lose their savings at the horse races obeying inner voices. People plunge into calamitous love affairs obeying inner voices. It –'

'I am not in love with Inés, if that is what you imply. Far from it.'

'You may not be in love with her but you are unreasonably fixated on her, which is worse. You are convinced she is your child's destiny. Whereas the truth is Inés has no relation, mystical or otherwise, to you or your boy. She is just a random woman on whom you have projected some private obsession of yours. If the child was predestined, as you say, to be united with his mother, why could you not leave it to destiny to bring them together? Why did you have to inject yourself into the act?'

'Because it is not enough to sit around waiting for destiny to act, Elena, just as it is not enough to have an idea and then sit back waiting for it to materialize. Someone has to bring the idea into the world. Someone has to act on behalf of destiny.'

'That is just what I said. You arrive with some private idea of what a mother is, which you then project onto this woman.'

'This is no longer a reasonable discussion, Elena. It is just animosity I hear, animosity and prejudice and jealousy.'

'It is neither animosity nor prejudice, and to call it jealousy is even more absurd. I am trying to help you understand where this sacred intuition of yours comes from, which you trust above the evidence of your senses. It comes from inside you. It has its origin in a past that you have forgotten. It has nothing to do with the boy or his welfare. If you had any interest in the boy's welfare you would reclaim him right away. This woman is bad for him. He is going backwards under her care. She is turning him into a baby.

'You could get him back today if you wanted to. You could simply walk in and take him away. She has no legal right over him. She is a complete stranger. You could reclaim your child, you could reclaim your apartment, and the woman could go back to La Residencia, where she belongs – to her brothers and her tennis games. Why don't you do it? Or are you too frightened – frightened of her brothers, frightened of the dog?'

'Elena, stop. Please stop. Yes, I am intimidated by her brothers. Yes, I am nervous of her dog. But that is not why I refuse to steal the child back. I refuse, that is all. What do you think I am doing in this country where I know no one, where I cannot express my heart's feelings because all human relations have to be conducted in beginner's Spanish? Did I come here to lug heavy bags, day in, and day out, like a beast of burden? No, I came to bring the child to his mother, and that is done now.'

Elena laughs. 'Your Spanish improves when you lose your temper. Maybe you should lose your temper more often. About Inés let us agree to disagree. As for the rest, the truth is we are not here, you and I, to live happy and fulfilled lives. We are here for the sake of our children. We may not feel at home in Spanish, but David and Fidel will. It will be their mother tongue. They will speak it like natives, from the heart. And don't sneer at the work you do at the docks. You arrived in this country naked, with nothing to offer but the labour of your hands. You could have been turned away, but you were not: you were made welcome. You could have been abandoned under the stars, but you were not: you were given a roof over your head. You have a great deal to be thankful for.'

He is silent. At last he speaks. 'Is that the end of the sermon?'

'Yes.'

Chapter 14

Four o'clock, and the last sacks from the freighter at Wharf Two are being stacked on the dray. El Rey and her companion stand in harness, placidly chomping at their feed-bags.

Álvaro stretches his arms and gives him a smile. 'Another job done,' he says. 'Makes you feel good, doesn't it?'

'I suppose so. But I can't help asking myself why the city needs so much grain, week after week.'

'It's food. We can't do without food. And it's not just for Novilla. It's for the hinterland too. That's what it means to be a port: you have a hinterland to serve.'

'Still, what is it all for, in the end? The ships bring the grain from across the seas and we haul it off the ships and someone else mills it and bakes it, and eventually it gets eaten and turned into – what shall I call it? – waste, and the waste flows back into the sea. What is there to feel good about in that? How does it fit into a larger picture? I don't see any larger picture, any loftier design. It's just consumption.'

'You are in a bad mood today! Surely one doesn't need a

lofty design to justify being part of life. Life is good in itself; helping food to flow so that your fellows can live is doubly good. How can you dispute that? Anyway, what do you have against bread? Remember what the poet said: bread is the way that the sun enters our bodies.'

'I don't want to argue, Álvaro, but objectively speaking all that I do, all that we dockers do, is move stuff from point A to point B, one bag after another, day after day. If all our sweat were for the sake of some higher cause, it would be a different matter. But eating in order to live and living in order to eat – that is the way of the bacterium, not the . . .'

'Not the what?'

'Not the human being. Not the pinnacle of creation.'

Usually it is the lunchtime breaks that are given over to philosophical disputation – Do we die or are we endlessly reincarnated? Do the farther planets rotate around the sun or around one another reciprocally? Is this the best of all possible worlds? – but today, instead of making their way home, several of the stevedores drift over to listen to the debate. To them Álvaro now turns. 'What do you say, comrades? Do we need a grand plan, as our friend demands, or is it good enough for us to be doing our job and doing it well?'

There is silence. From the first the men have treated him, Simón, with respect. To some of them he is old enough to be their father. But they respect their foreman too, even revere him. Clearly they do not want to take sides.

'If you don't like the work we do, if you don't think it is good,' says one of them – in fact Eugenio – 'what work would you like to do instead? Would you like to work in an office? Do you think office work is a better kind of work for a man to do? Or factory work perhaps?'

'No,' he replies. 'Emphatically not. Please don't misunderstand me. In itself this is good work we do here, honest work. But that is not what Álvaro and I were discussing. We were discussing the goal of our labours, the ultimate goal. I would not dream of disparaging the work we do. On the contrary, it means a great deal to me. In fact' – he is losing the thread but that does not matter – 'there is nowhere I would rather be than here, working side by side with you. In the time I have spent here I have experienced nothing but comradely support and comradely love. It has brightened my days. It has made it possible –'

Impatiently Eugenio interrupts him: 'Then surely you have answered your own question. Imagine having no work. Imagine having to spend your days sitting on a public bench with nothing to do, waiting for the hours to pass, with no comrades around you to share a joke with, no comradely goodwill to support you. Without labour, and the sharing of labour, comradeship is not possible, it is no longer substantial.' He turns and glances around. 'Is that not so, comrades?'

There is a murmur of agreement.

'But what of football?' he responds, trying another tack, though with no confidence. 'Surely we would love each other and support each other just as well if we all belonged to a football team, playing together, winning together, losing together. If comradely love is the ultimate good, why do we need to move these heavy bags of grain, why not just kick a football?'

'Because by football alone you cannot live,' says Álvaro. 'In order to play football you must be alive; and to be alive you must eat. Through our labour here we enable people to live.' He shakes his head. 'The more I think about it, the more I am convinced that labour cannot be compared to football, that the two belong to different philosophical realms. I cannot see, I truly cannot see, why you should want to disparage our labour in this way.'

All eyes are turned on him. There is a grave silence.

'Believe me, I do not mean to disparage our labour. To prove my sincerity, I will come to work an hour early tomorrow morning, and cut short my lunch break too. I will move as many bags per day as any man here. But I will continue to ask: Why are we doing this? What is it for?'

Álvaro steps forward, throws a brawny arm around him. 'Heroic feats of labour won't be necessary, my friend,' he says. 'We know where your heart is, you do not need to prove yourself.' And other men come up too to clap him on the back or give him a hug. He smiles at all and sundry; tears come to his eyes; he cannot stop smiling.

'You have not seen our main storehouse yet, have you?' says Álvaro, still gripping his hand.

'No.'

'It is an impressive facility, if I say so myself. Why not pay it a visit? You can go right now, if you like.' He turns to the driver, hunched on his seat waiting for the stevedores' debate

131

to be over. 'Our comrade can ride with you to the storehouse, can't he? Yes, of course he can. Come!' – he helps him clamber up beside the driver – 'Maybe you will appreciate our work better once you have had a sight of the storehouse.'

The storehouse is further from the wharves than he had expected, on the south bank at the bend where the river begins to narrow. At an ambling pace – the driver has a whip but does not use it, merely clucking to the horses now and then to encourage them – it takes them the best part of an hour to get there, time during which not a word is said.

The storehouse stands alone in a field. It is vast, as big as a football pitch and as high as a two-storey house, with great sliding doors through which the loaded dray passes with ease.

The working day seems to be over, for there is no crew to do the unloading. While the driver manoeuvres the dray beside the loading platform and sets about unharnessing the horses, he wanders deeper into the great building. Light filtering through gaps between wall and roof reveals sacks stacked metres high, mountain upon mountain of grain stretching back into the dark recesses. Idly he tries to do the computation, but loses track. A million sacks at least, perhaps several million. Can there be enough millers in Novilla to mill all this grain, enough bakers to bake it, enough mouths to consume it?

There is a dry crunch underfoot: spilled grain. Something soft bumps against his ankle, and involuntarily he kicks out. A squeal; all of a sudden he is aware of a subdued whispering all around him, like the noise of flowing water. He utters a cry.

The floor around him is heaving with life. Rats! There are rats everywhere!

'There are rats all over the place!' he calls out, hurrying back, confronting the drayman and the gatekeeper. 'There is grain all over the floor, and you have a plague of rats! It's appalling!'

The two exchange a glance. 'Yes, we certainly have our share of rats,' says the gatekeeper. 'Mice too. More than you can count.'

'And you do nothing about it? It's insanitary! They are nesting in the food, contaminating it!'

The gatekeeper shrugs. 'What do you want us to do? Where you have grain you have rodents. That is how the world is. We tried bringing in cats, but the rats have grown fearless, and there are too many of them anyway.'

'That's not an argument. You could set traps. You could lay down poison. You could fumigate the building.'

'You can't pump poisonous gases into a food store – have some sense! And now, if you don't mind, I need to lock up.'

First thing next morning he raises the matter with Álvaro. 'You boast about the storehouse, but have you ever been there yourself? It is crawling with rats. What is there to be proud of in working to feed a host of vermin? It is not just absurd, it is insane.'

Álvaro bestows on him a benign and infuriating smile. 'Wherever you have ships you have rats. Wherever you have warehouses you have rats. Where our species flourishes rats flourish too. Rats are intelligent creatures. You might say they are our shadow. Yes, they consume some of the grain we offload. Yes, there is spoilage in the warehouse. But there is spoilage all along the way: in the fields, in the trains, in the ships, in the warehouses, in the bakers' storerooms. There is no point in getting upset about spoilage. Spoilage is part of life.'

'Just because spoilage is part of life does not mean we cannot fight against it! Why store grain by the ton, by the thousands of tons, in rat-infested sheds? Why not import just enough for our needs, from one month to the next? And why can't the whole trans-shipment process be more efficiently organized? Why do we have to use horses and carts when we could use trucks? Why does the grain have to come in bags and be lugged on the backs of men? Why can't it just be poured into the hold at the other end, and pumped out at this end through a pipe?'

Álvaro reflects at length before he replies. 'What do you think would become of us all, Simón, if the grain were pumped en masse as you propose? What would become of the horses? What would become of El Rey?'

'There would no longer be work for us here at the docks,' he replies. 'That I concede. But instead we would find jobs assembling pumps or driving trucks. We would all have work, just as before, only it would be a different kind of work, requiring intelligence, not just brute strength.'

'So you would like to liberate us from a life of bestial labour. You want us to quit the wharves and find some other kind of work, where we would no longer be able to hoist a load onto our shoulders, feeling the ears of grain in the bag shift as they take the shape of our body, hearing their rustle, where we would lose touch with the thing itself — with the food that feeds us and gives us life.

'Why are we so sure we need to be saved, Simón? Do you think we live the lives of stevedores because we have been found too stupid to do anything else — too stupid to assemble a pump or drive a truck? Of course not. You know us by now. You are our friend, our comrade. We are not stupid. If we had needed to be saved, we would have saved ourselves by now. No, it is not we who are stupid, it is the clever reasoning you rely on that is stupid, that gives you the wrong answers. This is our dock, our wharf — right?' He glances left and right; the men murmur their approval. 'There is no place for cleverness here, only for the thing itself.'

He cannot believe his ears. He cannot believe that the person spouting this obscurantist nonsense is his friend Álvaro. And the rest of the crew seems to be marshalled solidly behind him — intelligent young men with whom he every day discusses truth and appearance, right and wrong. If he were not fond of them he would simply walk away — walk away and leave them to their futile labours. But they are his comrades whom he wishes well, whom he owes the duty of trying to convince that they are following the wrong path.

'Listen to yourself, Álvaro,' he says. '*The thing itself.* Do you think the thing remains forever itself, unchanging? No. Everything flows. Did you forget that when you crossed the ocean to come here? The waters of the ocean flow and in flowing they change. You cannot step twice into the same waters. As the fish live in the sea, so we live in time and must change with time. No matter how firmly we may pledge ourselves to follow the venerable traditions of stevedoring, we will in the end be overtaken by change. Change is like the rising tide. You can build barriers, but it will always seep in through the chinks.'

The men have by now closed in to form a half-circle around Álvaro and him. In their bearing he can detect no hostility. On the contrary, he feels he is being quietly urged on, urged to make his best case.

'I am not trying to save you,' he says. 'There is nothing special about me, I claim to be no one's saviour. Like you I crossed the ocean. Like you I bring no history with me. What history I had I left behind. I am simply a new man in a new land, and that is a good thing. But I have not let go of the idea of history, the idea of change without beginning or end. Ideas cannot be washed out of us, not even by time. Ideas are everywhere. The universe is instinct with them. Without them there would be no universe, for there would be no being.

'The idea of justice, for instance. We all desire to live under a just dispensation, a dispensation in which honest toil brings due reward; and that is a good desire, good and admirable. But what we are doing here at the docks will not help to bring about that dispensation. What we do here amounts to no more than a pageant of heroic labour. And that pageant depends on an army of rats to keep it going – rats who will work night and day gobbling down these tons of grain we unload so as to make space in the shed for more grain. Without the rats the pointlessness of our labour would be laid bare.'

He pauses. The men are silent. 'Don't you see that?' he says. 'Are you blind?'

Álvaro looks around. 'The spirit of the agora,' he says. 'Who is going to respond to our eloquent friend?'

One of the young stevedores raises a hand. Álvaro nods to him.

'Our friend invokes the concept of the real in a confusing way,' says the young man, speaking fluently and confidently, like a star student. 'To demonstrate his confusion, let us compare history with climate. The climate we live in, we can agree, is greater than we. None of us can ordain what the climate shall be. But it is not the quality of being greater than us that makes climate real. Climate is real because it has real manifestations. Those manifestations include wind and rain. Thus when it rains we get wet; when the wind rises our caps get blown off. Rain and wind are transitory, second-order realities, such as are accessible to our senses. Above them in the hierarchy of the real sits climate.

'Consider now history. If history, like climate, were a higher reality, then history would have manifestations which we would be able to feel through our senses. But where are these manifestations?' He looks around. 'Which of us has ever had his cap blown off by history?' There is silence. 'No one. Because history has no manifestations. Because history is not real. Because history is just a made-up story.'

'To be more accurate' – the speaker is Eugenio, who yesterday wanted to know whether he would prefer to work in an office – 'because history has no manifestations in the present.

History is merely a pattern we see in what has passed. It has no power to reach into the present.

'Our friend Simón says that we should get machines to do our work for us, because history so ordains. But it is not history that tells us to give up honest labour, it is idleness and the lure of idleness. Idleness is real in a way that history is not. We can feel it with our senses. We feel its manifestations each time we lie down on the grass and close our eyes and vow we will never get up again, even when the whistle blows, so sweet is our pleasure. Which of us, loafing on the grass on a sunny day, will say, *I can feel history in my bones telling me not to get up*? No: it is idleness that we feel in our bones. That is why we have the idiom: *He does not have an idle bone in his body.*'

As Eugenio has spoken he has grown more and more excited. Perhaps out of fear that he will never stop, his comrades interrupt him with a round of applause. He pauses, and Álvaro grasps the opportunity. 'I don't know whether our friend Simón wants to respond,' he says. 'Our friend dismissed our labours here as a useless pageant, a remark which some of us may have found hurtful. If the remark were merely unconsidered, if on further reflection he would like to withdraw or amend it, I am sure the gesture would be appreciated.'

His turn. The tide is against him, unmistakably. Does he have the will to resist?

'Of course I withdraw my thoughtless remark,' he says, 'and apologize moreover for any hurt it may have caused. As for history, all I can say is that while today we may refuse to heed it, we cannot refuse for ever. Therefore I have a proposal to make. Let us gather again on this wharf in ten years' time, or even in five years' time, and let us see then whether grain is still being unloaded by hand and being stored in sacks in an open shed for the sustenance of our enemies the rats. My guess is that it will not.'

'And what if you are proved wrong?' says Álvaro. 'If in ten years' time we are still unloading grain exactly as we do today, will you concede that history is not real?'

'I will indeed,' he replies. 'I will bow my head to the force of the real. I will call it submitting to the verdict of history.'

Chapter 15

For a while, after his speech against the rats, he finds the atmosphere at work constrained. Though his comrades are as kindly as ever, a hush seems to fall when he is around.

And indeed, as he looks back on his outburst, he flushes with shame. How could he have belittled the work of which his friends are so proud, work in which he is grateful to be allowed to join?

But then gradually things become easier again. During a morning break Eugenio comes up to him proffering a paper bag. 'Biscuits,' he says. 'Take one. Take two. A gift from a neighbour.' And when he expresses his appreciation (the biscuits are delicious, he can taste ginger in them and perhaps cinnamon too), Eugenio adds, 'You know, I've been thinking about what you said the other day, and maybe you have a point. Why should we feed rats when they do nothing to feed us? There are some people who eat rat, but I certainly don't. Do you?'

'No,' he says. 'I don't eat rat either. I much prefer your biscuits.'

At the end of the work day Eugenio returns to the subject. 'I have been worried that we might have hurt your feelings,' he says. 'Believe me, there was no animus. We all feel the utmost goodwill towards you.'

'I am not hurt at all,' he replies. 'We had a philosophical disagreement, that is all.'

'A philosophical disagreement,' agrees Eugenio. 'You live in the East Blocks, don't you? I'll walk with you as far as the bus stop.' So to keep up the fiction that he lives at the Blocks he has to accompany Eugenio to the bus stop.

'There is a question that has been preoccupying me,' he remarks to Eugenio as they wait for the Number 6 bus. 'It is entirely non-philosophical. How do you and the other men spend your free time? I know many of you are interested in football, but what about the evenings? You don't seem to have wives and children. Do you have girlfriends? Do you go to clubs? Álvaro tells me there are clubs one can join.'

Eugenio colours. 'I don't know anything about clubs. I go to the Institute, mainly.'

'Tell me about that. I have heard mention of an Institute, but I have no idea of what goes on there.'

'The Institute offers classes. It offers lectures, films, discussion groups. You should join up. You would enjoy it. It's not just for young people, there are lots of older people too, and it's free. Do you know how to get there?'

'No.'

'It's on New Street, near the big intersection. A tall white building with glass doors. You have probably passed by many times without knowing. Come tomorrow night. You can join our group.'

'All right.'

As it turns out, the course in which Eugenio is enrolled, along with three other of the stevedores, is on philosophy. He takes a seat in the back row, apart from his comrades, so that he can slip out if he gets bored.

The teacher arrives and silence falls. She is a woman of middle age, rather dowdily dressed, to his eye, with tightly cropped iron-grey hair and no make-up. 'Good evening,' she says. 'Let us resume where we left off last week, and continue our exploration of the table – the table and its close relative the chair. As you will remember, we were discussing the diverse kinds of table that exist in the world, and the diverse kinds of chair. We were asking ourselves what unity lies behind all the diversity, what it is that makes all tables tables, all chairs chairs.'

Quietly he rises and slips out of the room.

The corridor is empty save for a figure in a long white robe hurrying in his direction. As the figure comes nearer he sees it is none other than Ana from the Centre. 'Ana!' he calls out. 'Hello,' replies Ana – 'sorry, I can't stop, I'm late.' But then she does stop. 'I know you, don't I? I have forgotten your name.'

'Simón. We met at the Centre. I had a young boy with me. You kindly gave us shelter on our first night in Novilla.'

'Of course! How is your son doing?'

The white robe is in fact a white towelling bathrobe; her feet are bare. Strange attire. Is there a swimming pool in the Institute?

She notes his puzzled look and laughs. 'I'm modelling,' she says. 'I do modelling two evenings a week. For a life class.'

'A life class?'

'A drawing class. Drawing from life. I am the class model.' She stretches out her arms as if yawning. The fold of the robe at her throat opens; he catches a glimpse of the breasts he had so admired. 'You should come along. If you want to learn about the body, there is no better way.' And then, before he can overcome his confusion: 'Goodbye – I'm late. Say hello to your son.'

He wanders down the empty corridor. The Institute is larger than he had guessed from outside. From behind a closed door comes music, a woman singing mournfully to the accompaniment of a harp. He pauses before a noticeboard. A long list of courses on offer. Architectural Drawing. Bookkeeping. Calculus. Course after course on Spanish: Beginner's Spanish (twelve sections), Intermediate Spanish (five sections), Advanced Spanish, Spanish Composition, Spanish Conversation. He should have come here instead of struggling with the language all alone. No Spanish literature that he can see. But perhaps literature falls under Advanced Spanish.

No other language courses. No Portuguese. No Catalan. No Galician. No Basque.

No Esperanto. No Volapük.

He looks for Life Drawing. There it is: Life Drawing, Mondays to Fridays 7 to 9 p.m., Saturdays 2 to 4 p.m.; enrolment per section 12; Section 1 CLOSED, Section 2 CLOSED, Section 3 CLOSED. Clearly a popular course.

Calligraphy. Weaving. Basketwork. Flower Arranging. Pottery. Puppetry.

Philosophy. Elements of Philosophy. Philosophy: Selected Topics. Philosophy of Labour. Philosophy and Everyday Life.

A bell rings to mark the hour. Students emerge into the corridor, first a trickle, then a torrent, not just young folk but people of his age too and older, just as Eugenio said. No wonder the city is like a morgue after dark! Everyone is here at the Institute, improving himself. Everyone is busy becoming a better citizen, a better person. Everyone save he.

A voice hails him. It is Eugenio, waving from out of the human tide. 'Come! We are going to get something to eat! Come and join us!'

He follows Eugenio down a flight of stairs into a brilliantly lit cafeteria. Already there are long lines of people waiting to be served. He helps himself to a tray, to cutlery. 'It's Wednesday, which means it's noodles,' says Eugenio. 'Do you like noodles?'

'Yes, I do.'

Their turn comes. He holds out a plate and a counter hand slaps a big helping of spaghetti onto it. A second hand adds a dollop of tomato sauce. 'Take a bread roll as well,' says Eugenio. 'In case you need to fill up.'

'Where do we pay?'

'We don't pay. It's free.'

They find a table and are joined by the other young steve-dores.

'How was your class?' he asks them. 'Did you work out what a chair is?'

It is meant as a joke, but the young men stare at him blankly.

'Don't you know what a chair is?' says one of them finally. 'Look down. You are sitting on one.' He glances around at his companions. They all burst out laughing.

He tries to join in, to show he is a good sport. 'I meant,' he says, 'did you find out what constitutes . . . I don't know how to say it . . .'

'*Sillicidad*,' offers Eugenio. 'Your chair' – he gestures towards the chair – 'embodies *sillicidad*, or partakes of it, or realizes it, as our teacher likes to say. That is how you know it is a chair and not a table.'

'Or a stool,' adds his companion.

'Has your teacher ever told you,' says he, Simón, 'about the man who, when asked how he knew a chair was a chair, gave the chair in question a kick and said, *That, sir, is how I know*?'

'No,' says Eugenio. 'But that isn't how you learn a chair is a chair. That is how you learn it is an object. The object of a kick.'

He is silent. The truth is, he is out of place in this Institute. Philosophizing just makes him impatient. He does not care about chairs and their chairness.

The spaghetti lacks seasoning. The tomato sauce is simply pureed tomatoes, warmed up. He looks around for a salt cellar, but there is none. Nor is there pepper. But at least spaghetti is a change. Better than everlasting bread.

'So – which courses do you think you will enrol in?' asks Eugenio.

'I haven't decided yet. I had a look at the list. Quite a range of offerings. I thought of Life Drawing, but I see it is full.'

'So you won't be joining our class. That's a pity. The discussion grew more interesting after you left. We talked about infinity and the perils of infinity. What if, beyond the ideal chair, there is a yet more ideal chair, and so forth for ever and ever? But Life Drawing is interesting too. You could take Drawing this semester – ordinary Drawing. Then you would get preference for Life Drawing next semester.'

'Life Drawing is always very popular,' explains another of the boys. 'People want to learn about the body.'

He searches for the irony, but there is none, as there is no salt.

'If you want to learn about the human body, wouldn't a course in anatomy be better?' he asks.

The boy disagrees. 'Anatomy tells you only about the parts of the body. If you want to learn about the whole you need to take something like Life Drawing or Modelling.'

'By the whole you mean . . . ?'

'I mean first the body as body, then later the body in its ideal form.'

'Won't ordinary experience teach you that? I mean, won't spending a few nights with a woman teach you all you need to know about the body as body?'

The boy blushes and looks around for help. He curses himself. These stupid jokes of his!

'As for the body in its ideal form,' he presses on, 'we will probably have to wait for the next life before we get to see that.' He pushes the spaghetti aside half-eaten. It is too much for him, too much stodge. 'I must go,' he says. 'Goodnight. I'll see you at the docks tomorrow.'

'Goodnight.' They make no effort to detain him. And rightly so. How must he seem to them, to these fine young men, hard-working, idealistic, innocent? What can they possibly learn from the bitter miasma he gives off?

'How is your boy doing?' asks Álvaro. 'We miss him. Have you found a school for him?'

'He isn't old enough for school yet. He is with his mother. She doesn't want him to spend too much time with me. His affections will remain divided, she says, as long as there are two adults laying claim to him.'

'But there are always two adults laying claim to us: our father and our mother. We are not bees or ants.'

'That may be so. But in any case I am not David's father. His mother is the mother but I am not the father. That is the difference. Álvaro, I find this a painful subject. Can we drop it?'

Álvaro grips him by the arm. 'David is no ordinary boy. Believe me, I have watched him, I know what I am speaking about. Are you sure you are acting in his best interests?'

'I have handed him over to his mother. He is in her care. Why do you say he is no ordinary boy?'

'You say you have handed him over, but does he really want to be handed over? Why did his mother abandon him in the first place?'

'She did not abandon him. He and she were parted. For a while they lived in different spheres. I helped him to find her.

He found her, and they were united. Now they have a natural relationship, that of mother and son. Whereas he and I don't have a natural relationship. That's all.'

'If his relationship with you is not natural, what is it?'

'Abstract. He has an abstract relationship with me. A relationship with someone who cares for him in the abstract but has no natural duty of care to him. What did you mean by saying he was not an ordinary boy?'

Álvaro shakes his head. 'Natural, abstract . . . It makes no sense to me. How do you think a mother and a father come together in the first place – the mother and father of the future child? Because they owe each other a natural duty? Of course not. Their paths cross haphazardly, and they fall in love. What could be less natural, more arbitrary, than that? Out of their random conjuncture a new being comes into the world, a new soul. Who, in this story, owes what to whom? I can't say, and I'm sure you can't either.

'I used to watch you and your boy together, Simón, and I could see: he trusts you utterly. He loves you. And you love him. So why give him away? Why cut yourself off from him?'

'I haven't cut myself off from him. His mother has cut him off from me, as is her right. If I could choose, I would be with him still. But I can't choose. I don't have the right to choose. I have no rights in this matter.'

Álvaro is silent, seems to withdraw into himself. 'Tell me where I can find this woman,' he says at last. 'I would like to have a word with her.'

'Be careful. She has a brother who is a nasty piece of work.

You shouldn't tangle with him. In fact she has two brothers, one as unpleasant as the other.'

'I can take care of myself,' says Álvaro. 'Where will I find her?'

'Her name is Inés and she has taken over my old apartment in the East Blocks: block B, number 202 on the second floor. Don't say I sent you because that would not be true. I don't send you. This is not my idea at all, it is your idea.'

'Don't worry, I will make it clear to her it is my idea, you have nothing to do with it.'

The next day, during the midday break, Álvaro beckons him over. 'I spoke to your Inés,' he says without preamble. 'She accepts that you can see the boy, only not yet. At the end of the month.'

'That is wonderful news! How did you persuade her?'

Álvaro waves a dismissive hand. 'It doesn't matter how. She says you can take him for walks. She will inform you when. She asked for your telephone number. I didn't know it, so I gave her mine. I said I would pass on messages.'

'I can't tell you how grateful I am. Please assure her that I won't upset the boy – I mean, I won't upset his relationship with her.'

Chapter 16

The summons from Inés comes sooner than expected. The very next morning Álvaro calls him over. 'There's an emergency at your apartment,' he says. 'Inés phoned as I was leaving home. She wanted me to come over, but I told her I couldn't spare the time. Don't be alarmed, it has nothing to do with your boy, it's just the plumbing. You will need tools. Take the toolbox from the shed. Hurry. She is in quite a state.'

Inés meets him at the door, wearing (why? – it is not a cold day) a heavy overcoat. She is indeed in quite a state, quite a fury. The toilet is blocked, she says. The building supervisor came to inspect, but refused to do anything about it because (he said) she was not the legal tenant, he did not know her (he said) from a bar of soap. She telephoned her brothers at La Residencia, but they fobbed her off with excuses, being too fastidious (she says bitterly) to get their hands dirty. So this morning, as a last resort, she contacted his colleague Álvaro, who being a working man ought to know about plumbing. And now she has not Álvaro but him.

She talks on and on, pacing angrily about the living room. She has lost weight since he last saw her. There are pinched lines at the corners of her mouth. In silence he listens; but his eyes are on the boy, who, sitting up in his cot — has he only just woken up? — stares at him incredulously, as if he has come back from the land of the dead.

He flashes the boy a smile. *Hello!* he mouths silently.

The boy takes his thumb out of his mouth but does not speak. His hair, naturally curly, has been allowed to grow long. He is wearing a pale blue pyjama suit with a design in red of gambolling elephants and hippopotami.

Inés has not ceased talking. 'That toilet has been giving trouble ever since we moved in,' she is saying. 'I wouldn't be surprised if the people in the flat below are to blame. I asked the supervisor to investigate downstairs, but he wouldn't even listen to me. I have never met such a rude man. He doesn't care that you can already smell the stink from the corridor.'

Inés speaks of sewage without embarrassment. It strikes him as odd: if not intimate, the matter is at least delicate. Does she regard him simply as a workman come to do a job for her, someone whom she need never lay eyes on again; or is she gabbling to hide discomfiture?

He crosses the room, opens the window, leans out. The outflow pipe from the toilet leads directly into a sewage line down the outside wall. Three metres below it is the outflow pipe from the flat downstairs.

'Have you spoken to the people in number 102?' he asks. 'If the whole line is blocked, they will be having same problem as you. But let me take a look at the toilet first, just in case the fault is something obvious.' He turns to the boy. 'Are you going to give me a hand? Isn't it time you got up, you lazy-bones! Look how high the sun is in the sky!'

The boy squirms and gives him a delighted smile. His heart lifts. How he loves this child! 'Come here!' he says. 'Surely you're not too old to give me a kiss?'

The boy leaps out of his cot and dashes over to hug him. He breathes in the deep, unwashed, milky smells. 'I like your new pyjamas,' he says. 'Shall we go and inspect?'

The toilet bowl is full nearly to the brim with water and waste. In the toolbox he has brought is a roll of steel wire. He bends the end of the wire into a hook, probes blindly down the throat of the bowl, and comes up with a wad of toilet paper. 'Have you got a pottie?' he asks the boy. 'A pot for wee-wee?' asks the boy. He nods. The boy scampers off and returns bearing a chamber pot draped with a cloth. A moment later Inés rushes in, snatches up the pot, and exits without a word.

'Find me a plastic bag,' he tells the boy. 'Make sure there are no holes in it.'

He fishes up a considerable mass of paper from the blocked pipe, but the water level does not fall. 'Get dressed and we will go downstairs,' he tells the boy. And to Inés: 'If there is no one at home in 102 I will try opening the hatch at ground level. If the blockage is beyond that point, I won't be able to do anything about it. It will be the responsibility of the local authority. But let us see.' He pauses. 'By the way, something like this can happen to anyone. It is no one's fault. It is just bad luck.'

He is trying to make things easier for Inés, and hopes she will recognize that. But she will not meet his eyes. She is embarrassed, she is angry; more than that he cannot guess.

Accompanied by the boy he knocks at the door of flat 102. After a long wait a bolt is withdrawn and the door opens a crack. In the half-light he can make out a dark figure, whether man or woman he cannot tell.

'Good morning,' he says. 'I am sorry to intrude. I am from the flat above, where we have a blocked toilet. I wonder whether you are having a similar problem.'

The door opens wider. It is a woman, old and bent, whose eyes are of a glassy greyness that suggests she cannot see.

'Good morning,' he repeats. 'Your toilet. Are you having any problems with your toilet? Any blockages, *atascos*?'

No reply. She stands stock-still, her face directed interrogatively towards him. Is she deaf as well as blind?

The boy steps forward. '*Abuela*,' he says. The old woman stretches out a hand, strokes his hair, explores his face. For a moment he presses confidingly against her; then he slips past into the apartment. A moment later he is back. 'It's clean,' he says. 'Their toilet is clean.'

'Thank you, señora,' he says, and bows. 'Thank you for your assistance. I am sorry to have disturbed you.' And to the boy: 'Their toilet is clean, therefore – therefore what?'

The boy frowns.

'Here, downstairs, the water flows freely. There, upstairs' – he points up the flight of stairs – 'the water will not flow. Therefore what? Therefore the pipes are blocked where?'

'Upstairs,' says the boy confidently.

'Good! So where should we go to fix it: upstairs or down-stairs?'

'Upstairs.'

'And we go upstairs because water flows which way, up or down?'

'Down.'

'Always?'

'Always. It always flows down. And sometimes up.'

'No. Never up. Always down. Such is the nature of water. The question is, how does the water get upstairs to our apartment without contradicting its nature? How does it happen that when we turn the tap or flush the toilet, water flows for us?'

'Because for us it flows up.'

'No. That is not a good answer. Let me put the question in a different form. How can water get to our apartment *without* flowing upward?'

'From the sky. It falls from the sky into the taps.'

True. Water does fall from the sky. 'But,' he says, and he raises a cautionary finger, 'but how does the water get into the sky?'

Natural philosophy. Let us see, he thinks, how much natural philosophy there is in this child.

'Because the sky breathes in,' says the child. 'The sky breathes in' – he draws a deep breath and holds it, a smile on his face, a smile of pure intellectual delight, then dramatically he breathes out – 'and the sky breathes out.'

The door closes. He hears the snick of the bolt being shot.

'Did Inés tell you about that – about the breathing of the heavens?'

'No.'

'Did you think it up all by yourself?'

'Yes.'

'And who is it in the heavens who breathes in and breathes out and makes the rain?'

The boy is silent. He wears a frown of concentration. At last he shakes his head.

'You don't know?'

'I can't remember.'

'Never mind. Let's go and tell your mother our news.'

The tools he has brought are useless. Only the primitive length of wire holds any promise.

'Why don't the two of you go for a walk,' he suggests to Inés. 'What I am going to do isn't particularly appetizing. I don't see why our young friend should be exposed to it.'

'I would prefer to call in a proper plumber,' says Inés.

'If I can't do the job then I will go and find you a proper plumber, I promise. One way or another your toilet will be fixed.'

'I don't want to go for a walk,' says the boy. 'I want to help.'

'Thank you, my boy, I appreciate that. But this is not the kind of work where one needs help.'

'I can give you ideas.'

He exchanges a glance with Inés. Something unspoken passes between them. *My clever son!* says her look.

'That's true,' he says. 'You are good at ideas. But alas, toilets are not receptive to ideas. Toilets are not part of the realm of ideas, they are just brute things, and working with them is nothing but brute work. So go for a walk with your mother while I get on with the job.'

'Why can't I stay?' says the boy. 'It's just poo.'

There is a new note in the boy's voice, a note of challenge that he does not like. It is going to his head, all this praise.

'Toilets are just toilets, but poo is not just poo,' he says. 'There are certain things that are not just themselves, not all the time. Poo is one of them.'

Inés tugs at the boy's hand. She is blushing furiously. 'Come!' she says.

The boy shakes his head. 'It's my poo,' he says. 'I want to stay!'

'It was your poo. But you evacuated it. You got rid of it. It's not yours any more. You no longer have a right to it.'

Inés gives a snort and retires to the kitchen.

'Once it gets into the sewer pipes it is no one's poo,' he goes on. 'In the sewers it joins all the other people's poo and becomes general poo.'

'Then why is Inés cross?'

Inés. Is that what he calls her: not *Mommy*, not *Mother*?

'She is embarrassed. People don't like to talk about poo. Poo is smelly. Poo is full of bacteria. Poo isn't good for you.'

'Why?'

'Why what?'

'It's her poo too. Why is she cross?'

'She is not cross, she is just sensitive. Some people are sensitive, that is their nature, you can't ask why. But there is no need to be sensitive, because, as I told you, from a certain point it is no one's poo in particular, it is just poo. Talk to any plumber and he will tell you the same. The plumber doesn't look at poo and say to himself, *How interesting, who would have thought that señor X or señora Y would have poo like that!* It's like an undertaker. An undertaker doesn't say to himself, *How interesting! . . .*' He stops. *I am getting carried away*, he thinks, *I am talking too much*.

'What's an undertaker?' asks the boy.

'An undertaker undertakes the care of dead bodies. He is like a plumber. He sees that dead bodies are sent to the right place.'

And now you are going to ask, What is a dead body?

'What are dead bodies?' asks the boy.

'Dead bodies are bodies that have been afflicted with death, that we no longer have a use for. But we don't have to be troubled about death. After death there is always another life. You have seen that. We human beings are fortunate in that respect. We are not like poo, that has to stay behind and be mixed again with the earth.'

'What are we like?'

'What are we like if we are not like poo? We are like ideas. Ideas never die. You will learn that at school.'

'But we make poo.'

'That is true. We partake of the ideal but we also make poo. That is because we have a double nature. I don't know how to put it more simply.'

The boy is silent. *Let him chew on that*, he thinks. He kneels down beside the toilet bowl, rolls his sleeve up as high as it will go. 'Go for a walk with your mother,' he says. 'Go on.'

'And the undertaker?' says the boy.

'The undertaker? Undertaking is just a job like any other. The undertaker is no different from us. He too has a double nature.'

'Can I see him?'

'Not right now. We have other things to do right now. Next time we go to the city I will see if we can find an undertaker's shop. Then you can have a look.'

'Can we look at dead bodies?'

'No, certainly not. Death is a private matter. Undertaking is a discreet profession. Undertakers don't show off dead bodies to the public. Now that is enough of that.' He probes with the wire into the back of the bowl. Somehow he must make the wire follow the S of the trap. If the blockage is not in the trap, then it must be at the junction outside. If that is the case, he has no idea how to fix it. He will have to give up and find a plumber. Or the idea of a plumber.

The water, in which clots of Inés's poo still float, closes over his hand, his wrist, his forearm. He forces the wire along the S-bend. *Antibacterial soap*, he thinks: *I will need to wash with anti-bacterial soap afterwards, brushing scrupulously under the nails. Because poo is just poo, because bacteria are just bacteria.*

He does not feel like a being with a double nature. He feels like a man fishing for an obstruction in a sewage pipe, using primitive tools.

He withdraws his arm, withdraws the wire. The hook at the end has flattened out. He forms the hook again.

'You can use a fork,' says the boy.

'A fork is too short.'

'You can use the long fork in the kitchen. You can bend it.'

'Show me what you mean.'

The boy trots away, comes back with the long fork that was in the apartment when they arrived, that he has never had a use for. 'You can bend it if you are strong,' says the boy.

He bends the fork into a hook and forces it along the S-bend until it will go no further. When he tries to withdraw the fork, he feels a tug of resistance. First slowly, then more quickly, the obstruction comes up: a wad of cloth with a plastic lining. The water in the bowl recedes. He pulls the chain. Clean water roars through. He waits, pulls the chain again. The pipe is clear. All is well.

'I found this,' he says to Inés. He holds out the object, still dripping. 'Do you recognize it?'

She blushes, standing before him like a guilty thing, not knowing where to look.

'Is that what you usually do – flush them down the toilet? Has no one told you never to do that?'

She shakes her head. Her cheeks are flushed. The boy tugs at her skirt anxiously. 'Inés!' he says. She pats his hand distractedly. 'It's nothing, my darling,' she whispers.

He shuts the bathroom door, strips off his befouled shirt, and washes it in the basin. There is no antibacterial soap, just the soap from the Commissariat that everyone uses. He wrings the shirt out, rinses it, wrings it out again. He is going to have to wear a wet shirt. He washes his arms, washes under his armpits, dries himself. He may not be as clean as he might wish, but at least he does not smell of shit.

Inés is sitting on the bed with the boy clasped to her breast like a baby, rocking back and forth. The boy is drowsing, a string of drool coming from his mouth. 'I'll go now,' he whispers. 'Call me again if you need me.'

What strikes him about the visit to Inés, when he reflects afterwards, is how strange it was as an episode in his life, how unpredictable. Who would have thought, at the moment when he first beheld this young woman on the tennis court, so cool, so serene, that a day would come when he would be having to wash her shit off his body! What would they make of it at the Institute? Would the lady with the iron-grey hair have a word for it: the pooness of poo?

Chapter 17

'If relief is what you are after,' says Elena, 'if getting relief will make life easier for you, there are places where a man can go. Haven't your friends told you about them, your male friends?'

'Not a word. What precisely do you mean by relief?'

'Sexual relief. If sexual relief is what you are after, I need not be your sole port of call.'

'I am sorry,' he says stiffly. 'I didn't realize you looked on it that way.'

'Don't take offence. It's a fact of life: men need relief, we all know that. I am merely telling you what you can do about it. There are places you can go. Ask your friends at the docks, or if you are too embarrassed ask at the Relocation Centre.'

'Are you talking about bordellos?'

'Call them bordellos if you like, but from what I hear there is nothing sleazy about them, they are quite clean and pleasant.'

'Do the girls in attendance wear uniforms?'

She regards him quizzically.

'I mean, do they wear a standard outfit, like nurses? With standard underwear?'

'That you will have to find out for yourself.'

'And is it an accepted profession, working in a bordello?' He knows he is irritating her with his questions, but the mood is on him again, the reckless, bitter mood that has plagued him since he gave up the child. 'Is it something a girl can do and yet hold her head up in public?'

'I have no idea,' she says. 'Go and find out. And now you must excuse me, I am expecting a student.'

He was in fact lying when he told Elena he knew nothing about places where men could go. Álvaro has recently mentioned a club for men not far from the docks called Salón Confort.

From Elena's apartment he goes straight to Salón Confort. *Leisure and Recreational Centre*, reads the engraved plate at the entrance. *Hours of opening 2 p.m.–2 a.m. Closed on Mondays. Right of admission reserved. Membership on application.* And in smaller letters: *Personal counselling. Stress relief. Physical therapy.*

He pushes the door open. He is in a bare anteroom. Along one wall is a padded bench. The desk, marked RECEPTION, is bare save for a telephone. He takes a seat and waits.

After a long while someone emerges from a back room, a woman of middle age. 'Sorry to keep you waiting,' she says. 'How can I help you?'

'I'd like to become a member.'

'Certainly. I'll just get you to fill out these two forms, and then I will need proof of identity.' She passes him a clipboard and a pen.

He glances at the first form. Name, address, age, employment. 'You must get sailors coming in off ships,' he remarks. 'Do they have to fill out forms too?'

'Are you a sailor?' asks the woman.

'No, I work at the docks but I am not a sailor. I mention sailors because they are on shore for only a night or two. Do they have to become members if they visit you?'

'You have to be approved as a member to use the facility.'

'And how long does it take, being approved?'

'To be approved, not long. But after that you have to establish a slot with a therapist.'

'*I* have to establish a slot?'

'You have to be accepted on the list of one of our therapists. That may take time. Often their lists are full.'

'So if I were one of the sailors I was talking about, a sailor with only a night or two on shore, there would be no point in coming here. My ship would be back on the high seas by the time I could get an appointment.'

'Salón Confort isn't here for the benefit of sailors, señor. Sailors will have their own facilities back where they come from.'

'They may have their own facilities back home, but they cannot make use of them. Because they are here, not there.'

'Yes indeed: we have our facilities, they have theirs.'

'I understand. If you don't mind my saying so, you speak like a graduate of the Institute – the Institute for Further Studies, I think it is called – in the city.'

'Really.'

'Yes. Of one of their philosophy courses. Logic maybe. Or rhetoric.'

'No, I am not a graduate of the Institute. Now: have you made up your mind? Are you going to apply? If so, please go ahead and fill out the forms.'

The second form gives him more trouble than the first. *Application for Personal Therapist*, it is headed. *Use the space below to describe yourself and your needs*.

'I am an ordinary man with ordinary needs,' he writes. 'That is to say, my needs are not extravagant. Until recently I was full-time guardian to a child. Since giving up the child (terminating the guardianship) I have been somewhat lonely. Have not known what to do with myself.' He is repeating himself. That is because he is using a pen. If he had a pencil with an eraser he could present himself more economically. 'I find myself in need of a friendly ear, to unburden myself. I have a close female friend, but her mind has been elsewhere of late. My relations with her lack true intimacy. It is only in conditions of intimacy that one can unburden oneself, I find.'

What else?

'I am starved of beauty,' he writes. 'Feminine beauty. Somewhat starved. I crave beauty, which in my experience awakens awe and also gratitude – gratitude at one's great good fortune to be holding in one's arms a beautiful woman.'

He considers crossing out the whole paragraph about beauty, but then does not. If he is going to be judged, let it be on the movements of his heart rather than the clarity of his thought. Or his logic.

'Which is not to say that I am not a man, with a man's needs,' he concludes robustly.

Qué tontería! What a farrago! What moral confusion!

He hands over the two forms. The receptionist peruses them – does not pretend not to be perusing them – from beginning to end. She and he are alone in the waiting room. Not a busy time of day. Beauty awakens awe: does he detect the faintest of smiles when she comes to that pronouncement? Is she a receptionist pure and simple, or does she have a background of her own in gratitude and awe?

'You haven't ticked a box,' she says. '*Length of sessions: 30 minutes, 45 minutes, 60 minutes, 90 minutes*. Which length would you prefer?'

'Let us say the maximum of relief: ninety minutes.'

'You may have to wait some time to get a ninety-minute session. For reasons of scheduling. Nonetheless, I'll put you down for a long first session. You can change that later, should you so decide. Thank you, that is all. We will be in touch. We will write, informing you of when your first appointment will be.'

'Quite a procedure. I can see why sailors are not welcome.'

'Yes, the Salón is not set up for transients. But being a transient is itself a transient state. Someone who is a transient here will be at home where he comes from, just as someone whose home is here would be a transient elsewhere.'

'*Per definitionem*,' he says. 'Your logic is impeccable. I will await your letter.'

On the form he has given Elena's apartment as his address. The days pass. He checks with Elena: there is no letter for him.

He returns to the Salón. The same receptionist is on duty. 'Do you remember me?' he says. 'I was here the week before last. You said I would hear from you. I have heard nothing.'

'Let me take a look,' she says. 'Your name is . . . ?' She opens a filing cabinet and brings out a file. 'No problem with the application itself that I can see. The delay seems to be in marrying you to the right therapist.'

'*Marrying* me? Perhaps I haven't made myself clear. Ignore what I wrote on the form about beauty and so forth. I am not looking for some ideal match, I am simply looking for company, female company.'

'I understand. I will inquire. Give me a few days.'

Days pass. No letter. He should not have used the word *awe*. What young woman trying to earn a few reals on the side wants such a responsibility thrust upon her? The truth may be good, but less than the truth is sometimes better. Thus: *Why are you applying for membership of Salón Confort?* Answer: *Because I am new in town and lack contacts.* Question: *What sort of therapist are you looking for?* Answer: *Someone young and pretty.* Question: *How long do you want sessions to be?* Answer: *Thirty minutes will do.*

Eugenio seems intent on showing that their disagreement about rats, history, and the organization of dockside labour has left no hard feelings. More often than not, when he leaves work, he finds Eugenio dogging his steps, and has then to repeat the charade of catching the Number 6 bus to the Blocks.

'Have you made up your mind yet about the Institute?' asks

Eugenio during one of their treks to the bus stop. 'Do you think you will sign up?'

'I'm afraid I haven't given the Institute much thought of late. I have been trying to enrol at a recreation centre.'

'A recreation centre? You mean, like Salón Confort? Why would you want to join a recreation centre?'

'Don't you and your friends use them? What do you do about – what shall I call them? – physical urges?'

'Physical urges? Urges of the body? We were discussing those in class. Would you like to hear what conclusion we came to?'

'Please.'

'We started by noting that the urges in question have no specific object. That is to say, it is not some particular woman towards whom they impel us but towards woman in the abstract, the womanly ideal. Thus when, in order to still the urge, we resort to a so-called recreation centre, we in fact traduce the urge. Why so? Because the manifestations of the ideal on offer at such places are inferior copies; and union with an inferior copy can only leave the searcher disappointed and saddened.'

He tries to imagine Eugenio, this earnest young man with his owlish glasses, in the arms of an inferior copy. 'You blame your disappointment on the women you meet at the Salón,' he replies, 'but perhaps you should reflect on the urge itself. If it is of the nature of desire to reach for what lies beyond its grasp, should we be surprised if it is not satisfied? Did your teacher at the Institute not tell you that embracing inferior copies may be a necessary step in the ascent towards the good and the true and the beautiful?'

Eugenio is silent.

'Think about it. Ask yourself where we would be if there were no such things as ladders. Here is my bus. Until tomorrow, my friend.'

'Is there something wrong with me that I am not aware of?' he asks Elena. 'I am referring to the club I tried to join. Why did they turn me down, do you think? You can be frank.'

In the last violet light of evening he and she are sitting by the window watching the swallows swoop and dive. Companionable: that is what they have become, over time. *Compañeros* by mutual agreement. Companionate marriage: if he offered, would Elena consent? Living with Elena and Fidel in their flat would certainly be more comfortable than making do in his lonely shed at the docks.

'You can't be sure they have turned you down,' says Elena. 'They probably have a long waiting list. Though I am surprised you persist with them. Why not try another club? Or why not simply withdraw?'

'Withdraw?'

'Withdraw from sex. You are old enough to do so. Old enough to seek your satisfactions elsewhere.'

He shakes his head. 'Not yet, Elena. One more adventure, one more failure, then perhaps I will think of retiring. You did not answer my question. Is there something about me that alienates people? The way I speak, for example: does it put people off? Is my Spanish all wrong?'

'Your Spanish is not perfect, but it improves every day. I

hear plenty of new arrivals whose Spanish is not as good as yours.'

'It's sweet of you to say so, but the fact is I don't have a good ear. Often I can't make out what people are saying, and have to resort to guessing. The woman at the club, for instance: I thought she was saying she wanted to marry me to one of the girls working there; but maybe I misheard her. I told her I wasn't hunting for a bride, and she looked at me as if I were crazy.'

Elena is silent.

'It is the same with Eugenio,' he presses on. 'I am beginning to think there is something in my speech that marks me as a man stuck in the old ways, a man who has not forgotten.'

'Forgetting takes time,' says Elena. 'Once you have properly forgotten, your sense of insecurity will recede and everything will become much easier.'

'I look forward to that blessed day. The day when I will be made welcome in Salón Confort and Salón Relax and all the other salons of Novilla.'

Elena regards him sharply. 'Or else you can cling to your memories, if that is what you prefer. But then don't come complaining to me.'

'Please, Elena, don't mistake me. I place no value on my tired old memories. I agree with you: they are just a burden. No, it is something else that I am reluctant to yield up: not memories themselves but the feel of residence in a body with a past, a body soaked in its past. Do you understand that?'

'A new life is a new life,' says Elena, 'not an old life all over again in new surroundings. Look at Fidel —'

'But what is the good of a new life,' he interrupts her, 'if we are not transformed by it, transfigured, as I certainly am not?'

She gives him time to say more, but he is done.

'Look at Fidel,' she says. 'Look at David. They are not creatures of memory. Children live in the present, not the past. Why not take your lead from them? Instead of waiting to be transfigured, why not try to be like a child again?'

Chapter 18

He and the boy are taking a walk in the parklands, on the first of the excursions sanctioned by Inés. The gloom has lifted from his heart, there is a spring in his step. When he is with the child the years seem to fall away.

'And how is Bolívar getting on?' he asks.

'Bolívar ran away.'

'Ran away! That's a surprise! I thought Bolívar was devoted to you and Inés.'

'Bolívar doesn't like me. He only likes Inés.'

'But surely you can like more than one person.'

'Bolívar only likes Inés. He is her dog.'

'You are Inés's son, but you don't love only Inés. You love me too. You love Diego and Stefano. You love Álvaro.'

'No, I don't.'

'I'm sorry to hear that. So Bolívar has departed. Where do you think he has gone?'

'He came back. Inés put his food outside and he came back. Now she won't let him out at all.'

'I'm sure he is just unused to his new home.'

'Inés says it is because he smells lady dogs. He wants to mate with a lady dog.'

'Yes, that is one of the trials of keeping a gentleman dog – he wants to be with the lady dogs. It's the way of nature. If gentleman dogs and lady dogs no longer wanted to mate, there would be no baby dogs born, and then after a while there would be no dogs at all. So it may be best to allow Bolívar a little freedom. How about your sleeping? Are you sleeping better? Have the bad dreams gone away?'

'I dreamed about the boat.'

'Which boat?'

'The big boat. Where we saw the man with the hat. The pirate.'

'The pilot, not the pirate. What did you dream?'

'It sank.'

'It sank? And what happened next?'

'I don't know. I can't remember. The fishes came.'

'Well, I'll tell you what happened. We were saved, you and I. We must have been saved, otherwise how would we be here now? So it was just a bad dream. Fishes don't eat people anyway. Fishes are harmless. Fishes are good.'

It is time to turn back. The sun is setting, the first stars are coming out.

'Do you see those two stars there, where I am pointing – the two bright ones? They are the Twins, so called because they are always together. And that star there, just above the horizon, with the reddish tinge – that is the evening star, the first star to appear when the sun goes down.'

'Are the twins brothers?'

'Yes. I forget their names, but once upon a time they were famous, so famous that they were turned into stars. Maybe Inés will remember the story. Does Inés ever tell you stories?'

'She tells me bedtime stories.'

'That's good. Once you have learned to read by yourself, you won't have to rely on Inés or me or anyone else. You will be able to read all the stories in the world.'

'I can read, only I don't want to. I like Inés to tell me stories.'

'Isn't that a bit short-sighted? Reading will open new windows to you. What kind of stories does Inés tell you?'

'Third Brother stories.'

'Third Brother stories? I don't know any of those. What are they about?'

The boy stops, clasps his hands before him, stares into the distance, and begins to speak.

'Once upon a time there were three brothers and it was winter and it was snowing and the mother said, Brothers Three, Brothers Three, I feel a great pain in my insides and I fear I am going to die unless one of you will seek out the Wise Woman who guards the precious herb of cure.

'Then the First Brother said, Mother, Mother, I will find the Wise Woman. And he put on his cloak and went out in the snow and he met a fox and the fox said to him, Where are you going, Brother? and the Brother said, I am seeking the Wise Woman who guards the precious herb of cure, so I have no time to talk to you, Fox. And the fox said, Give me food and I will show you the way, and the Brother said, Out of my way,

Fox, and he gave the fox a kick and went into the forest and was never heard of again.

'Then the Mother said, Brothers Two, Brothers Two, I feel a great pain in my insides and I fear I am going to die unless one of you will seek out the Wise Woman who guards the precious herb of cure.

'So the Second Brother said, Mother, Mother, I will go, and he put on his cloak and went out in the snow and he met a wolf and the wolf said, Give me food and I will show you the way to the Wise Woman, and the Brother said, Out of my way, Wolf, and gave him a kick and went into the forest and was never heard of again.

'Then the Mother said, Third Brother, Third Brother, I feel a great pain in my insides and I fear I am going to die unless you bring me the precious herb of cure.

'Then the Third Brother said, Never fear, Mother, I will find the Wise Woman and bring back the precious herb of cure. And he went out in the snow and he met a bear and the bear said, Give me food and I will show you the way to the Wise Woman. And the Third Brother said, Gladly, Bear, will I give whatever you ask. Then the bear said, Give me your heart to devour. And the Third Brother said, Gladly will I give you my heart. So he gave the bear his heart and the bear devoured it.

'Then the bear showed him a secret path, and he came to the Wise Woman's house and he knocked on the door and the Wise Woman said, Why are you bleeding, Third Brother? And the Third Brother said, I gave my heart to the bear to devour so that he would show me the way, for I must bring back the precious herb of cure that will heal my mother.

'Then the Wise Woman said, Behold, here is the precious herb of cure whose name is Escamel, and because you had faith and gave up your heart to be devoured, your mother shall be healed. Follow the drops of blood back through the forest and you will find your way home.

'Then the Third Brother found his way home and he said to his mother, Behold, Mother, here is the herb Escamel, and now goodbye, I must leave you because the bear has devoured my heart. And his mother tasted the herb Escamel and at once she was healed, and she said, My Son, My Son, I see you are shining with a great light, and it was true, he was shining with a great light and then he was borne up into the sky.'

'And?'

'That's all. That's the end of the story.'

'So the last brother was turned into a star and the mother was left alone.'

The boy is silent.

'I don't like that story. The ending is too sad. Anyway, you can't be the third brother and be borne up into the sky like a star because you are the one and only brother and therefore the first brother.'

'Inés says I can have more brothers.'

'Does she! And where are these brothers to come from? Does she expect me to bring them to her as I brought you?'

'She says she is going to have them out of her tummy.'

'Well, no woman can make children all by herself, she will

need a father to help her, she ought to know that. It's a law of nature, the same law for us as for dogs and wolves and bears. But even if she does have more sons, you will still be the first son, not the second or the third.'

'No!' The boy's voice is angry. 'I want to be the third son! I told Inés and she said yes. She said I can go back in her tummy and come out again.'

'Inés said that?'

'Yes.'

'Well, if you can bring that off it would be a miracle. I have never heard of a big boy like you going back into his mother's tummy, let alone coming out again. Inés must have meant something else. Maybe she was trying to say that you will always be the best beloved.'

'I don't want to be the best beloved, I want to be the third son! She promised me!'

'One comes before two, David, and two before three. Inés can make promises until she is blue in the face but she can't change that. One-two-three. It's a law even stronger than a law of nature. It is called the law of numbers. Anyway, you only want to be the third son because the third son is the hero of these stories she tells you. There are lots of other stories where the eldest son is the hero, not the third son. There don't even have to be three sons. There can be just one son, and he doesn't have to have his heart devoured. Or the mother can have a daughter and no sons. There are many, many kinds of story and many kinds of hero. If you learned to read you would find that out for yourself.'

'I can read, I just don't want to. I don't like reading.'

'That's not very smart. Besides, you are going to be six years old one of these days, and when you turn six you will have to go to school.'

'Inés says I don't have to go to school. She says I am her treasure. She says I can learn all by myself at home.'

'I agree you are her treasure. She is very lucky to have found you. But are you sure you want to stay at home with Inés all the time? If you went to school you would meet other children of your age. You could learn to read properly.'

'Inés says I won't get individual attention at school.'

'Individual attention! What does that mean?'

'Inés says I must have individual attention because I am clever. She says that at school clever children don't get individual attention and then they get bored.'

'And what makes you think you are so clever?'

'I know all the numbers. Do you want to hear them? I know 134 and I know 7 and I know' – he draws a deep breath – '4623551 and I know 888 and I know 92 and I know –'

'Stop! That's not knowing the numbers, David. Knowing the numbers means being able to count. It means knowing the order of the numbers – which numbers come before and which come after. Later on it will also mean being able to add and subtract numbers – getting from one number to another in a single jump, without counting all the steps between. Naming numbers isn't the same as being clever with numbers. You could stand here and name numbers all day and you wouldn't come to the end of them, because the numbers have no end. Didn't you know that? Didn't Inés tell you?'

'It's not true!'

'What is not true? That there is no end to the numbers? That no one can name them all?'

'I can name them all.'

'Very well. You say you know 888. What is the next number after 888?'

'92.'

'Wrong. The next number is 889. Which of the two is bigger, 888 or 889?'

'888.'

'Wrong. 889 is bigger because 889 comes after 888.'

'How do you know? You have never *been* there.'

'What do you mean, *been* there? Of course I haven't been to 888. I don't need to have been there to know 888 is smaller than 889. Why? Because I have learned how numbers are constructed. I have learned the rules of arithmetic. When you go to school you will learn the rules too, and then numbers won't any longer be such a' – he hunts for the word – 'such a complication in your life.'

The boy does not respond, but regards him levelly. Not for a moment does he think his words pass him by. No, they are being absorbed, all of them: absorbed and rejected. Why is it that this child, so clever, so ready to make his way in the world, refuses to understand?

'You have visited all the numbers, you tell me,' he says. 'So tell me the last number, the very last number of all. Only don't say it is Omega. Omega doesn't count.'

'What is Omega?'

'Never mind. Just don't say Omega. Tell me the last number, the very last one.'

The boy closes his eyes and draws a deep breath. He frowns with concentration. His lips move, but he utters no word.

A pair of birds settle on the bough above them, murmuring together, ready to roost.

For the first time it occurs to him that this may be not just a clever child – there are many clever children in the world – but something else, something for which at this moment he lacks the word. He reaches out and gives the boy a light shake. 'That's enough,' he says. 'That's enough counting.'

The boy gives a start. His eyes open, his face loses its rapt, distant look and contorts. 'Don't touch me!' he screams in a strange, high-pitched voice. 'You are making me forget! Why do you make me forget? I hate you!'

'If you don't want him to go to school,' he says to Inés, 'at least let me teach him to read. He is ready for it, he will pick it up in no time.'

There is a tiny library in the East Blocks community centre, with a couple of shelves of books: *Teach Yourself Carpentry*, *The Art of Crocheting*, *One Hundred and One Summer Recipes*, and so forth. But flat on its face under other books, its spine torn off, lies *An Illustrated Children's Don Quixote*.

Triumphantly he displays his find to Inés.

'Who is Don Quixote?' she asks.

'A knight in armour, from the old days.' He opens the book to the first illustration: a tall, scrawny man with the wisp of a beard, clad in a suit of armour, mounted on a tired-looking nag; beside him a tubby fellow on a donkey. Before them the road winds into the distance. 'It's a comedy,' he says. 'He will enjoy it. No one is drowned, no one is killed, not even the horse.'

He settles down at the window with the boy on his knee. 'You and I are going to read this book together, a page each day, sometimes two pages. First I will read the story aloud, then we will go through it word by word, looking at how the words are put together. Is that agreed?'

The boy nods.

'There was a man living in La Mancha – La Mancha is in Spain, where the Spanish language originally came from – a man no longer young but not yet old, who one day got the idea into his head that he would become a knight. So he took down the rusty suit of armour that hung on the wall, and strapped it on, and whistled for his horse, who was named Rocinante, and called his friend Sancho, and said to him, *Sancho, I am of a mind to ride in search of knightly adventures – will you join me?* See, there is *Sancho* and there is *Sancho* again, the same word, beginning with the big *S*. Try to remember the way it looks.'

'What are knightly adventures?' asks the boy.

'The adventures of a *caballero*, a knight. Rescuing beauteous ladies in distress. Battling with ogres and giants. You will see. The book is full of knightly adventures.

'Now, Don Quixote and his friend Sancho – you see, *Don Quixote* with the curly *Q* and *Sancho* again – had not ridden far when they beheld, standing by the roadside, a towering giant with no fewer than four arms ending in four huge fists, which he waved menacingly at the travellers.

'*Behold, Sancho, our first adventure*, said Don Quixote. *Until I have vanquished this giant no wayfarer will be safe.*

'Sancho gave his friend a puzzled look. *I see no giant*, he said. *All I see is a windmill with four sails spinning in the wind.*'

'What is a windmill?' asks the boy.

'Look at the picture. Those big arms are the four sails of the windmill. As the sails spin in the wind, they turn the wheel, and the wheel turns a big stone inside the mill, called a millstone, and the millstone grinds wheat into flour so that the baker can bake bread for us to eat.'

'But it isn't really a windmill, is it?' says the boy. 'Go on.'

'*A windmill may be what you see, Sancho*, said Don Quixote, *but that is only because you have been enchanted by the sorceress Maladuta. If your eyes were unclouded, you would see a giant with four arms bestriding the road.* Do you want to know what a sorceress is?'

'I know about sorceresses. Go on.'

'With these words Don Quixote couched his lance and clapped his spurs to the flanks of Rocinante and charged at the giant. With one of his four fists the giant easily parried Don Quixote's lance. *Ha ha ha, poor ragged knight*, he laughed, *do you really believe you can best me?*

'Then Don Quixote unsheathed his sword and charged again. But just as easily, with his second fist, the giant smote the sword aside, together with the knight and his steed.

'Rocinante struggled to her feet, but as for Don Quixote, he had suffered such a blow to the head that he was quite dizzy. *Alas, Sancho*, said Don Quixote, *unless some healing balm shall be applied to my wounds by the hand of my mistress the fair Dulcinea, I fear I will not live to see another dawn. — Nonsense, your honour,* replied Sancho, *it is only a bump on the head, you will be right as rain as soon as I get you away from this windmill. — Not a windmill but a giant, Sancho*, said Don Quixote. *— As soon as I get you away from this giant*, said Sancho.'

'Why doesn't Sancho also fight the giant?' asks the boy.

'Because Sancho is not a knight. He is not a knight, therefore he has no sword or lance, just a pocketknife for peeling potatoes. All he can do — as we will see tomorrow — is to load Don Quixote onto his donkey and convey him to the nearest inn to rest and recover.'

'But why doesn't Sancho hit the giant?'

'Because Sancho knows the giant is really a windmill, and you can't fight against a windmill. A windmill is not a living thing.'

'He's not a windmill, he's a giant! He's only a windmill in the picture.'

He puts down the book. 'David,' he says, '*Don Quixote* is an unusual book. To the lady in the library who lent it to us it looks like a simple book for children, but in truth it isn't simple at all. It presents the world to us through two pairs of eyes, Don Quixote's eyes and Sancho's eyes. To Don Quixote, it is a giant he is fighting. To Sancho, it is a windmill. Most of us — not you, perhaps, but most of us nevertheless — will agree with Sancho that it is a windmill. That includes the artist who drew a picture of a windmill. But it also includes the man who wrote the book.'

'Who wrote the book?'

'A man named Benengeli.'

'Does he live in the library?'

'I don't think so. It is not impossible, but I would say it is unlikely. I certainly haven't noticed him there. He would be easy to recognize. He wears a long robe and has a turban on his head. '

'Why are we reading Bengeli's book?'

'Benengeli. Because I came across it in the library. Because I thought you might enjoy it. Because it will be good for your Spanish. What else do you want to know?'

The boy is silent.

'Let us stop there and go on tomorrow with the next adventure of Don Quixote and Sancho. By tomorrow I will expect you to be able to point out *Sancho* with the big *S* and *Don Quixote* with the curly Q.'

'It's not the adventures of Don Quixote and Sancho. It's the adventures of Don Quixote.'

Chapter 19

One of the larger freighters has arrived at the docks, what Álvaro calls a double-belly freighter, with holds fore and aft. The dockers split into two crews. He, Simón, joins the fore crew.

At mid-morning on the first day of the unloading, down in the hold, he hears commotion on the deck and the shrilling of a whistle. 'That's the fire signal,' says one of his companions. 'Let's get out quick!'

He smells smoke even as they scramble up the ladder. It comes billowing up from the aft hold. 'All out!' bellows Álvaro from his position on the bridge beside the ship's master. 'All ashore!'

No sooner have the stevedores hauled up their ladders than the ship's crew drag the huge hatch covers to.

'Aren't they going to put out the fire?' he asks.

'They are starving it,' replies his companion. 'In an hour or two it will be dead. But the cargo will be ruined, no doubt about that. We may as well dump it to the fishes.'

The stevedores gather on the quayside. Álvaro begins to call the roll. 'Adriano ... Agustín ... Alexandre ...' 'Here ... Here ... Here ...' come the responses. Until he reaches Marciano. 'Marciano ...' Silence. 'Has anyone seen Marciano?' Silence. From the sealed hatch a wisp of smoke drifts into the windless air.

The sailors drag the hatch covers off again. At once they are enveloped in dense grey smoke. 'Close up!' commands the ship's master; and to Álvaro, 'If your man is there, it's all up with him.'

'We are not abandoning him,' says Álvaro. 'I will go down.'

'Not while I am in command you won't.'

At noon the aft hatch covers are briefly reopened. The smoke is as thick as ever. The captain orders the hold to be flooded. The dockers are dismissed.

He recounts the day's events to Inés. 'As for Marciano, we won't know for sure until they pump the hold dry in the morning,' he says.

'What won't you know about Marciano? What happened to him?' asks the boy, coming in on the conversation.

'My guess is that he fell asleep. He was careless and breathed in too much smoke. If you take in too much smoke you grow weak and dizzy and fall asleep.'

'And then?'

'Then I am afraid to say you don't wake up in this life.'

'Do you die?'

'Yes, you die.'

'If he died he will go on to the next life,' says Inés. 'So there is no need to be worried about him. It is time for your bath. Come on.'

'Can Simón give me my bath?'

He has not seen the boy naked in a long time. He notes with pleasure how his body is filling out.

'Stand up,' he says, and rinses the last of the soap off him and wraps him in a towel. 'Let us dry you quickly, then you can put on your pyjamas.'

'No,' says the boy. 'I want Inés to dry me.'

'He wants you to dry him,' he reports to Inés. 'I am not good enough.'

Stretched out on his cot, the boy allows Inés to attend to him, drying between his toes, in the crack between his legs. His thumb is in his mouth; his eyes, drugged with omnipotent pleasure, follow her lazily.

She dusts him with talcum powder as if he were a baby; she helps him into his pyjamas.

It is time for bed, but he will not let go of the story of Marciano. 'Maybe he isn't dead,' he says. 'Can we go and look, Inés and you and I? I won't breathe in any smoke, I promise. Can we?'

'There is no point in that, David. It is too late to save Marciano. And the ship's hold is full of water anyway.'

'It's not too late! I can swim down into the water and save him, like a seal. I can swim anywhere. I told you, I am an escape artist.'

'No, my boy, swimming down into a flooded hold is too dangerous, even for an escape artist. You could get trapped and never come back. Besides, escape artists don't save other people, they save themselves. And you aren't a seal. You haven't learned how to swim. It is time you understood one doesn't get to swim or be an escape artist just by wishing so. It takes years of training. Anyhow, Marciano doesn't want to be saved, to be brought back to this life. Marciano has found peace. He is probably crossing the seas at this very moment, looking forward to the next life. It will be a great adventure for him, to start anew, washed clean. He won't have to be a stevedore any more, and carry heavy bags on his shoulders. He can be a bird. He can be anything he likes.'

'Or a seal.'

'A bird or a seal. Or even a great big whale. There are no limits to what you can be in the next life.'

'Will you and I go to the next life?'

'Only if we die. And we are not going to die. We are going to live a long time.'

'Like heroes. Heroes don't die, do they?'

'No, heroes don't die.'

'Will we have to speak Spanish in the next life?'

'Definitely not. On the other hand, we may have to learn Chinese.'

'And Inés? Will Inés come too?'

'That is for her to decide. But I am sure that if you go to the next life, Inés will want to follow. She loves you very much.'

'Will we see Marciano?'

'Undoubtedly. However, we may not recognize him. We may think we are just seeing a bird or a seal or a whale. And

Marciano – Marciano will think he is seeing a hippopotamus while it will really be you.'

'No, I mean the real Marciano, at the docks. Will we see the real Marciano?'

'As soon as the hold is pumped dry, the captain will send men down to fetch Marciano's body. But the real Marciano will no longer be among us.'

'Can I see him?'

'Not the real Marciano. The real Marciano is invisible to us. As for the body, the body that Marciano has escaped from, by the time we get to the docks it will have been taken away. The men will do that at first light, while you are still asleep.'

'Taken where?'

'Taken to be buried.'

'But what if he isn't dead? What if they bury him and he isn't dead?'

'That won't happen. The people who bury the dead, the gravediggers, are careful not to bury someone if he is still alive. They listen for a heartbeat. They listen for breathing. If they hear even the tiniest heartbeat, they won't bury him. So there is no need to worry. Marciano is at peace –'

'No, you don't understand! What if his tummy is full of smoke but he isn't really dead?'

'His lungs. We breathe with our lungs, not our tummies. If Marciano took smoke into his lungs he will certainly have died.'

'It's not true! You are just saying that! Can we go to the docks before the gravediggers get there? Can we go now?'

'Now, in the dark? No, we certainly can't. Why are you so eager to see Marciano, my boy? A dead body isn't important. It is the soul that is important. The soul of Marciano is the real Marciano; and the soul is on its way to the next life.'

'I want to see Marciano! I want to suck the smoke out of him! I don't want him to be buried!'

'David, if we could bring Marciano back by sucking the smoke out of his lungs, then the sailors would have done so long ago, I promise you. Sailors are just like us, full of good-will. But you can't return people to life by sucking their lungs, not after they are dead. It's one of the laws of nature. Once you are dead you are dead. The body doesn't come back to life. Only the soul lives on: Marciano's soul, my soul, your soul.'

'That's not true! I don't have a soul! I want to save Marciano!'

'I won't allow it. We will all go to Marciano's funeral, and at the funeral you will have a chance, like everyone else, to kiss him goodbye. That is how it will be, and that is the end of it. I am not going to discuss Marciano's death any further.'

'You can't tell me what to do! You are not my father! I am going to ask Inés!'

'I can assure you Inés won't tramp down to the docks with you in the dark. Be sensible. I know you like to save people, and that is admirable, but sometimes people don't want to be saved. Let Marciano be. Marciano is gone. Let us remember the good things about him, and let go of his shell. Come now: Inés is waiting to tell you your bedtime story.'

★ ★ ★

By the time he presents himself for duty the next morning, the pumping of the aft hold is almost completed. Within an hour a team of seamen is able to descend; and soon afterwards, while the dockers watch in silence from the quayside, the body of their deceased comrade, strapped to a stretcher, is borne up on deck.

Álvaro addresses them. 'In a day or two we will have a chance to say a proper goodbye to our friend, lads,' he says. 'But for now it is work as usual. There is an unholy mess in the hold, and it is our job to clean it up.'

For the rest of the day the stevedores are down in the hold, ankle deep in water, enveloped in the acrid smell of wet ash. Every single sack of grain has burst; it is their task to shovel the sticky mess into buckets and pass these by relay up to the deck, from where they are dumped overboard. It is a joyless labour, carried out in silence in a place of death. When he calls at Inés's apartment that evening, he is exhausted and in a dark mood.

'You don't happen to have anything to drink, do you?' he asks her.

'Sorry, I'm out of everything. I'll make you some tea.'

Sprawled in his cot, the boy is absorbed in his book. Marciano is forgotten.

'Hello,' he greets him. 'How is the Don today? What is he up to?'

The boy ignores the question. 'What does that word say?' he asks, pointing.

'It says *Aventuras*, with a big letter *A*. The Adventures of Don Quixote.'

'And that word?'

'*Fantástico,* with an *f.* And that word – remember the big letter *Q*? – is *Quixote.* You can always recognize Quixote by the big *Q.* I thought you told me you knew the letters.'

'I don't want to read letters. I want to read the story.'

'That is not possible. A story is made up of words, and words are made up of letters. Without letters there would be no story, no Don Quixote. You have to know the letters.'

'Show me which is *fantástico.*'

He places the boy's forefinger on the word. 'There.' The fingernails are clean and neatly pared; whereas his own hand, which used to be as soft and clean, is cracked and dirty, with grime worked deep into the cracks.

The boy squeezes his eyes shut, holds his breath, opens his eyes wide. '*Fantástico.*'

'Excellent. You have learned to recognize the word *fantástico.* There are two ways of learning to read, David. One way is to learn the words one by one, as you are doing. The other way, which is quicker, is to learn the letters that make up the words. There are only twenty-seven of them. Once you have learned them, you can spell out strange words for yourself, without having me tell you each time.'

The boy shakes his head. 'I want to read the first way. Where is the giant?'

'The giant who was really a windmill?' He turns the pages. 'There is the giant.' He places the boy's forefinger on the word *gigante.*

The boy closes his eyes. 'I'm reading through my fingers,' he announces.

'It doesn't matter how you read, through your eyes or through your fingers like a blind person, as long as you read. Show me *Quixote*, with a *Q*.'

The boy stabs at the page with his finger. 'There.'

'No.' He moves the boy's finger to the right place. 'There is *Quixote*, with the big *Q*.'

The boy snatches his hand away petulantly. 'That's not his real name – don't you know?'

'It may not be his worldly name, the name his neighbours know him by, but it is the name he chooses for himself and the name we know him by.'

'It's not his *real* name.'

'What is his *real* name?'

Abruptly the boy withdraws into himself. 'You can go,' he mutters. 'I am going to read by myself.'

'Very well, I will go. When you come to your senses again, when you decide you want to learn to read properly, call me. Call me and tell me the Don's real name.'

'I won't. It's secret.'

Inés is absorbed in culinary tasks. She does not even look up as he leaves.

A day passes before his next visit. He finds the boy poring over the book as before. He tries to speak, but the boy gestures impatiently – 'Ssh!' – and turns the page with a quick, whipping motion as though a snake lay behind it that might strike him.

The picture shows Don Quixote, trussed in a cradle of rope, being lowered into a hole in the earth.

'Do you want me to help? Shall I tell you what is happening?' he asks.

The boy nods.

He takes up the book. 'This is an episode called "The Cave of Montesinos"'. Having heard much about the Cave of Montesinos, Don Quixote resolved to see for himself its famed wonders. So he instructed his friend Sancho and the learned scholar – the man with the hat must be the learned scholar – to lower him into the dark cave, and then to wait patiently for his signal to haul him up again.

'For a full hour Sancho and the scholar sat waiting at the mouth of the cave.'

'What is a scholar?'

'A scholar is a man who has read lots of books and learned lots of things. For a full hour Sancho and the scholar sat waiting until at last they felt a tug on the rope and began to haul, and thus Don Quixote came riding up into the light.'

'So Don Quixote wasn't dead?'

'No, he wasn't dead.'

The boy heaves a happy sigh. 'That's good, isn't it?' he says.

'Yes, of course it's good. But why did you think he was dead? He is Don Quixote. He is the hero.'

'He is the hero *and* he is a magician. You tie him up with ropes and put him in a box and when you open the box he isn't there, he has escaped.'

'Oh, did you think Sancho and the scholar tied Don Quixote up? No, if you were to read the book instead of just looking at the pictures and guessing at the story, you would know that they use the rope to haul him out of the cave, not to tie him up. Shall I go on?'

The boy nods.

'Graciously Don Quixote thanked his friends. Then he regaled them with an account of all that had passed in the Cave of Montesinos. In the three days and three nights he had spent under the earth, he said, he had seen many wondrous sights, not least of them waterfalls whose cascades were not drops of water but sparkling diamonds, and processions of princesses in satin robes, and even, the greatest marvel of all, the Lady Dulcinea mounted on a white steed with a jewel-encrusted bridle, who stopped and kindly spoke to him.

'*But your honour*, said Sancho, *surely you are mistaken, for you were under the earth not three days and three nights but a mere hour at most.*

'*No, Sancho*, said Don Quixote gravely, *three days and three nights I was absent; if it seemed to you a mere hour, that was because you fell into a slumber while you waited, and were oblivious of the passing of time.*

'Sancho was about to argue, but then thought better of himself, remembering how obstinate Don Quixote could be. *Yes, your honour*, he said, glancing at the learned scholar and winking, *you must be right: for three whole days and three whole nights we two were in a slumber, until your return. But pray tell us more of the Lady Dulcinea and what passed between her and yourself.*

'Gravely Don Quixote regarded Sancho. *Sancho*, he said, *O friend of little faith, when will you learn, when will you learn?* And he fell silent.

'Sancho scratched his head. *Your honour,* he said, *I will not deny it is hard to believe you spent three days and three nights in the Cave of Montesinos when to us it seemed a mere hour; and so I will not deny it is hard to believe that there are at this very minute troops of princesses beneath our feet, and ladies prancing on snow-white steeds, and suchlike. Now if the Lady Dulcinea had bestowed on your honour some token of her troth, such as a ruby or a sapphire from the bridle of her mount, which you could show to miserable doubters like ourselves, it would be a different matter.*

'*A ruby or a sapphire,* mused Don Quixote. *I should show you a ruby or a sapphire as proof I am not lying.*

'*So to speak,* said Sancho. *So to speak.*

'*And if I were to show you such a ruby or sapphire, Sancho, what then?*

'*Then I would fall to my knees, your honour, and kiss your hand, and beg your pardon for ever doubting you. And I would be your faithful follower to the end of time.*'

He closes the book.

'And?' says the boy.

'And nothing. That is the end of the chapter. Until tomorrow there is no more.'

The boy takes the book from his hands, reopens it to the picture of Don Quixote in his rope truss, stares hard at the surrounding body of print. 'Show me,' he says in a small voice.

'Show you what?'

'Show me the end of the chapter.'

He points to the end of the chapter. 'See, here begins a new chapter, called *Don Pedro y las marionetas*, Don Pedro and the Puppets. The Cave of Montesinos is behind us.'

'But did Don Quixote show Sancho the ruby?'

'I don't know. Señor Benengeli does not say. Perhaps he did, perhaps he didn't.'

'But *really* did he have a ruby? *Really* was he under the ground three days and three nights?'

'I don't know. Maybe for Don Quixote time is not as it is for us. Maybe what is for us the blink of an eyelid is for Don Quixote a whole aeon. But if you are convinced that Don Quixote ascended from the cave with rubies in his pockets, maybe you should write your own book saying so. Then we can return señor Benengeli's book to the library and read yours instead. Unfortunately, however, before you can write your book you will have to learn to read.'

'I can read.'

'No, you can't. You can look at the page and move your lips and make up stories in your head, but that is not reading. For real reading you have to submit to what is written on the page. You have to give up your own fantasies. You have to stop being silly. You have to stop being a baby.'

Never before has he spoken so directly to the child, so harshly.

'I don't want to read your way,' says the child. 'I want to read my way. There was a man of double deed and nandynan-dynandy need, and when he rode he was a horse and when he walked he was a porse.'

'That is nothing but nonsense. There is no such thing as a

porse. Don Quixote is not nonsense. You can't just make up nonsense and pretend you are reading about him.'

'I can! It's not nonsense and I can read! It's not your book, it's my book!' And with a frown he returns to whipping furiously through the pages.

'On the contrary, it's señor Benengeli's book that he gave to the world, therefore it belongs to all of us – to all of us in one sense, and to the library in another sense, but not to you alone in any sense. And stop tearing at the pages. Why are you handling the book so roughly?'

'Because. Because if I don't hurry a hole will open.'

'Open up where?'

'Between the pages.'

'That's nonsense. There is no such thing as a hole between the pages.'

'There is a hole. It's inside the page. You don't see it because you don't see anything.'

'Stop that now!' says Inés.

For an instant he thinks she is addressing the child. For an instant he thinks she has at last aroused herself to rebuke him for his wilfulness. But no, it is he at whom she is glaring.

'I thought you wanted him to learn to read,' he says.

'Not at the cost of all this bickering. Find another book. Find a simpler book. This *Don Quixote* is too difficult for a child. Take it back to the library.'

'No!' The boy clutches the book tightly. 'You are not going to take it! It's my book!'

Chapter 20

Since Inés took over, the apartment has lost its once austere air. It has, in fact, become cluttered, and not only with her many possessions. Worst is the corner by the boy's bed, where a cardboard box overflows with objects he has collected and brought home: pebbles, pine cones, withered flowers, bones, shells, bits of crockery and old metal.

'Isn't it time to throw out that mess?' he suggests.

'It's not a mess,' says the boy. 'It's things I am saving.'

He gives the box a push with his foot. 'It's rubbish. You can't save every last thing you come across.'

'It's my museum,' says the boy.

'A load of old rubbish is not a museum. Things need to have some value before they find a place in a museum.'

'What is value?'

'If things have value it means that people in general prize them, agree they are valuable. An old broken cup has no value. No one prizes it.'

'I prize it. It's my museum, not yours.'

He turns to Inés. 'Does this have your blessing?'

'Let him be. He says he feels sorry for old things.'

'You can't feel sorry for an old cup without a handle.'

The boy stares at him uncomprehendingly.

'A cup has no feelings. If you threw it away it wouldn't care. It wouldn't be hurt. If you are going to feel sorry for an old cup, you may as well feel sorry for' – he casts about in exasperation – 'for the sky, the air, the earth beneath your feet. You might as well feel sorry for everything.'

The boy continues to stare.

'Things are not meant to last for ever,' he says. 'Each thing has its natural term. That old cup had a good life; now it is time for it to retire and make way for a new cup.'

The stubborn look with which he is by now so familiar settles on the boy's face. 'No!' he says. 'I am going to keep it! I am not going to let you take it! It's mine!'

As Inés gives way to him on every front, the boy grows more and more headstrong. Not a day passes without an argument, without raised voices and stamped feet.

He urges her to send him to school. 'The apartment is becoming too small to hold him,' he says. 'He needs to face up to the real world. He needs wider horizons.' But she continues to resist.

'Where does money come from?' asks the boy.

'It depends on what kind of money you have in mind. Coins come from a place called the Mint.'

'Is the Mint where you get your money?'

'No, I get my money from the paymaster at the docks. You saw that.'

'Why don't you go to the Mint?'

'Because the Mint won't just give us money. We have to work for it. We have to earn it.'

'Why?'

'Because that is the way the world is. If we didn't have to work for our money, if the Mint just handed money out to everyone, it would cease to have any value.'

He takes the boy to a football match, and pays at the turnstile.

'Why do we have to pay?' asks the boy. 'We didn't have to pay before.'

'This is the championship game, the last game of the season. At the end of the game the winners get cake and wine. Someone has to collect money to buy the cake and the wine. Unless the baker gets money for his cake, he won't be able to buy the flour and sugar and butter for the next cake. That's the rule: if you want to eat cake then you have to pay for it. And the same goes for wine.'

'Why?'

'Why? The answer to all your *Why?* questions, past, present and future, is: *Because that is the way the world is*. The world was not made for our convenience, my young friend. It is up to us to fit in.'

The boy opens his mouth to reply. Swiftly he presses a finger to his lips. 'No,' he says. 'No more questions. Be quiet and watch the football.'

After the game they return to the apartment. Inés is busy at the stove; a smell of scorched meat is in the air.

'Supper time!' she calls out. 'Go and wash your hands!'

'I'll be off now,' he says. 'Goodbye, I'll see you tomorrow.'

'Do you have to go?' says Inés. 'Wouldn't you like to stay and watch him have his supper?'

The table is set for one, for the little prince. From the frying pan Inés transfers two slim sausages to his plate. In an arc around them she sets the halves of a boiled potato, slices of carrot, and florets of cauliflower, over which she drips grease from the pan. Bolívar, who has been sleeping by the open window, rouses himself and pads over.

'Mm, sausages!' says the boy. 'Sausages are the best food.'

'I haven't seen sausages in a long while,' he remarks to Inés. 'Where did you buy them?'

'Diego got them. He is friendly with someone in the kitchen at La Residencia.'

The boy cuts his sausages into bits, cuts his potatoes, chews vigorously. He seems quite untroubled by the two adults standing over him, or by the dog resting his head on his knee, watching his every move.

'Don't forget your carrots,' says Inés. 'They make you see in the dark.'

'Like a cat,' says the boy.

'Like a cat,' says Inés.

The boy eats his carrots. 'What is cauliflower good for?' he asks.

'Cauliflower is good for your health.'

'Cauliflower is good for your health, and meat makes you strong, right?'

'That's right, meat makes you strong.'

'I must go,' he says to Inés. 'Meat does make you strong, but maybe you should think twice before feeding him sausages.'

'Why?' says the boy. 'Why should Inés think twice?'

'Because of what they put in sausages. What goes into sausages is not always good for you.'

'What do they put in sausages?'

'Well, what do you think?'

'Meat.'

'Yes, but what kind of meat?'

'Kangaroo meat.'

'Now you are being silly.'

'Elephant meat.'

'They put pig meat in sausages, not always but sometimes, and pigs aren't clean animals. They don't eat grass, like sheep and cows. They eat anything they come across.' He glances at Inés. She glares back, tight-lipped. 'For instance, they eat poo.'

'Out of the toilet?'

'No, not out of the toilet. But if they happen to come across poo in a field, they will eat it. Without thinking twice. They are omnivorous, which means they eat anything. They even eat each other.'

'That's not true,' says Inés.

'Is there poo in sausages?' says the boy. He has laid his fork down.

'He is talking nonsense, don't listen to him, there is no poo in your sausage.'

'I am not saying there is actual poo in your sausage,' he says. 'But there is poo meat in it. Pigs are unclean animals. Pig meat is poo meat. But that is just my opinion. Not everyone will agree. You must decide for yourself.'

'I don't want any more,' says the boy, pushing his plate aside. 'Bolívar can have it.'

'Finish your plate and I'll give you a chocolate,' says Inés.

'No.'

'I hope you feel proud of yourself,' says Inés, turning on him.

'It's a matter of hygiene. Ethical hygiene. If you eat pig you become like a pig. In part. Not wholly, but in part. You partake of the pig.'

'You are crazy,' says Inés. She addresses the boy. 'Don't listen to him, he has gone crazy.'

'I'm not crazy. It is called consubstantiation. Why else do you think there are cannibals? A cannibal is a person who takes consubstantiation seriously. If we eat another person we embody that person. That is what cannibals believe.'

'What is a cannibal?' asks the boy.

'Cannibals are savages,' says Inés. 'You don't have to worry, there are no cannibals here. Cannibals are just a fable.'

'What is a fable?'

'A story from the old days that isn't true any more.'

'Tell me a fable. I want to hear a fable. Tell me a fable about the three brothers. Or about the brothers in the sky.'

'I don't know anything about brothers in the sky. Now finish your supper.'

'If you won't tell him about brothers, tell him about Little Red Riding Hood,' he says. 'Tell him about how the wolf gobbles up the little girl's grandmother and turns into a grandmother, a wolf grandmother. By consubstantiation.'

The boy gets up, scrapes the food from his plate into the dog's bowl, and puts the plate in the kitchen sink. The dog gobbles down the sausages.

'I'm going to be a lifesaver,' the boy announces. 'Diego is going to teach me in the swimming pool.'

'That's nice,' he says. 'What else are you planning to be, besides a lifesaver and an escape artist and a magician?'

'Nothing. That's all.'

'Pulling people out of swimming pools and escaping from boxes and doing magic tricks are hobbies, not a career, not a life's work. How are you going to earn an actual living?'

The boy casts a glance at his mother, as if searching for guidance. Then, emboldened, he says: 'I don't have to earn a living.'

'We all have to earn a living. It's part of the human condition.'

'Why?'

'*Why? Why? Why?* That is not how we carry on a proper conversation. How are you going to eat if you spend all your time saving people and escaping from chains and refusing to work? Where will you get the food to make you strong?'

'From the shop.'

'You will go to the shop and they will give you food. For nothing.'

'Yes.'

'And what will happen when the people in the shop have given all their food away for nothing? What will happen when the shop is empty?'

Serenely, with a strange little smile on his lips, the child answers: 'Why?'

'Why what?'

'Why is the shop empty?'

'Because if you have X loaves of bread and you give them all away for nothing then you have no loaves left and no money with which to buy new loaves. Because X minus X equals zero. Equals nothing. Equals emptiness. Equals an empty stomach.'

'What is X?'

'X is any number, ten or a hundred or a thousand. If you have something and you give it away, you don't have it any more.'

The boy screws his eyes shut and pulls a funny face. Then he begins to giggle. He grips his mother's skirt and presses his face against her thigh and giggles and giggles until he is red in the face.

'What is it, my darling?' says Inés. But the boy will not stop laughing.

'You had better go,' says Inés. 'You are upsetting him.'

'I am educating him. If you would send him to school, there would be no need for these home lessons.'

★ ★ ★

The boy has made friends with an old man in Block E who keeps a pigeon-cote on the roof. According to the letter box in the lobby his name is Palamaki, but the boy calls him señor Paloma, Mr Dove. Señor Paloma lets the boy feed the birds by hand. He has even given him a pigeon of his own, a pure white bird whom the boy names Blanco.

Blanco is a placid, even torpid bird who allows himself to be taken for walks sitting on the boy's outstretched wrist or sometimes on his shoulder. He shows no inclination to fly away, or indeed to fly at all.

'I think Blanco's wings may have been clipped,' he says to the boy. 'That would explain why he doesn't fly.'

'No,' says the boy. 'Look!' He tosses the bird in the air. It flaps its wings languidly, circles once or twice, then settles on his shoulder again and preens itself.

'Señor Paloma says Blanco can carry messages,' says the boy. 'He says if I get lost I can tie a message to Blanco's leg and Blanco will fly home and then señor Paloma will come and find me.'

'That's very kind of señor Paloma. You will have to make sure you carry a pencil and paper around with you, and a piece of string so that you can tie the paper to Blanco's leg. What will you write? Show me what you will write when you want to be rescued.'

They are crossing the empty playground. In the sandpit the boy squats down, smoothes the surface, and with a finger begins to write. He reads over his shoulder: *O* then *E* then a character he cannot make out then *O* again then *X* and again *X*.

The boy rises. 'Read it,' he says.

'I am having difficulty. Is it Spanish?'

The boy nods.

'No, I give up. What does it say?'

'It says, *Follow Blanco, Blanco is my best friend.*'

'Indeed. It used to be that Fidel was your best friend, and before that El Rey. What has happened that Fidel is no longer your friend and his place has been taken by a bird?'

'Fidel is too old for me. Fidel is rough.'

'I have never seen Fidel being rough. Did Inés tell you he was rough?'

The boy nods.

'Fidel is a perfectly gentle boy. I am fond of him and you used to be fond of him too. Let me tell you something. Fidel is hurt because you no longer play with him. In my opinion you are treating Fidel badly. In fact, you are treating him roughly. In my opinion you should spend less time with señor Paloma on the roof and more time with Fidel.'

The boy strokes the bird on his arm. The rebuke is accepted without demur. Or perhaps he simply lets the words wash over him.

'Furthermore, I think you should inform Inés it is time for you to go to school. You should insist on it. I know you are very clever and have taught yourself to read and write, but in real life you have to be able to write like other people. It is no use sending Blanco off with a message tied to his leg if no one can read it, not even señor Paloma.'

'I can read it.'

'You can read it because you are the one who wrote it. But the whole point about messages is that other people need to be able to read them. If you get lost and send a message to señor Paloma to come and save you, he must be able to read your message. Otherwise you will have to tie yourself to Blanco's leg and tell him to fly you home.'

The boy gives him a puzzled look. 'But –' he says. Then he sees it is a joke and they both laugh and laugh.

They are in the playground of the East Blocks. He has been pushing the boy on the swings, so high that he has been crying out with fear and pleasure. Now they sit side by side, catching their breath, drinking in the last of the twilight.

'Can Inés have twins out of her tummy?' asks the boy.

'Of course she can. It may be uncommon but it is possible.'

'If Inés had twins then I could be the third brother. Do twins always have to be together?'

'They don't have to, but usually they prefer it. Twins are naturally fond of each other, like the star twins. If they were not, then they might go wandering off separately and be lost in the sky. But their love for each other holds them together. It will go on holding them together until the end of time.'

'But they are not together, the star twins, not really together.'

'No, that is true, they are not tight up against each other in the sky, there is a tiny gap between them. That is the way of nature. Think of lovers. If lovers were tight up against each other all the time they would no longer need to love each other. They would be one. There would be nothing for them to want. That is why nature has gaps. If everything were packed tightly together, everything in the universe, then there would be no you or me or Inés. You and I would not be talking to each other right now, there would just be silence – oneness and silence. So, on the whole, it is good that there should be gaps between things, that you and I should be two instead of one.'

'But we can fall. We can fall down the gap. Down the crack.'

'A gap is not the same thing as a crack, my boy. Gaps are part of nature, part of the way things are. You can't fall down a gap and disappear. It just doesn't happen. A crack is quite different. A crack is a break in the order of nature. It is like cutting yourself with a knife, or tearing a page in two. You keep saying we must watch out for cracks, but where are these cracks? Where do you see a crack between you and me? Show me.'

The boy is silent.

'The twins in the sky are like twins on earth. They are also like numbers.' Is this all too difficult for a child? Perhaps. But the boy will absorb his words, he must hope for that – absorb them and mull over them and perhaps begin to see the sense in them. 'Like One and Two. One and Two are not the same, there is a difference between them which is a gap but not a crack. That is what makes it possible for us to count, to get from One to Two without worrying about falling.'

'Can we go and see them one day, the twins in the sky? Can we go in a ship?'

'I suppose so, if we can find the right kind of ship. But it would take a long time to get there. The twins are very far away. No one has been to visit them yet, not to my knowledge. This' – he stamps his foot on the ground – 'is the only star we human beings have ever visited.'

The boy stares at him in puzzlement. 'This isn't a star,' he says.

'It is. It just doesn't look like a star from close up.'

'It doesn't shine.'

'Nothing shines from close up. From a distance, however, everything shines. You shine. I shine. The stars certainly shine.'

The boy seems pleased. 'Are all the stars numbers?' he asks.

'No. I said the twins were *like* numbers, but that was just a way of speaking. No, the stars are not numbers. Stars and numbers are quite different things.'

'I think the stars are numbers. I think that is Number 11' – he stabs a finger up at the sky – 'and that is Number 50 and that is Number 33333.'

'Ah, do you mean, can we give each star a number? That would certainly be one way of identifying them, but a very dull way, very uninspired. I think it is better that they have proper names, like Bear and evening star and Twins.'

'No, silly, I said each star *is* a number.'

He shakes his head. 'Each star is *not* a number. Stars are like numbers in a few respects, but in most respects they are quite unlike them. For instance, the stars are scattered all over the heavens chaotically whereas the numbers are like a fleet of ships sailing in order, each knowing its place.'

'They can die. Numbers can die. What happens to them when they die?'

'Numbers can't die. Stars can't die. Stars are immortal.'

'Numbers *can* die. They can fall out of the sky.'

'That is not true. Stars can't fall out of the sky. The ones that do seem to fall, the shooting stars, aren't real stars. As for numbers, if a number were to fall out of the ranks, then there would be a crack, a break, and that is not how the numbers work. There is never any crack between the numbers. No number is ever missing.'

'There is! You don't understand! You don't remember anything! A number can fall out of the sky like Don Quixote when he fell down the crack.'

'Don Quixote didn't fall down a crack. He descended into a cave, using a ladder made of rope. Anyhow, Don Quixote isn't relevant. He isn't real.'

'He is! He is a hero!'

'I'm sorry. I didn't mean to say what I said. Of course the Don is a hero and of course he is real. What I meant to say is that what happened to him doesn't happen to people any more. People live their lives from beginning to end without falling down cracks.'

'They do fall! They fall down cracks and you can't see them any more because they can't get out. You said so yourself.'

'Now you are confusing cracks with holes. You are thinking of people dying and getting buried in graves, in holes in the ground. A grave is made by gravediggers using spades. It is not something unnatural like a crack.'

There is a rustle of clothing and Inés materializes out of the dark. 'I have been calling and calling,' she says crossly. 'Does no one ever listen?'

Chapter 21

The next time he comes knocking at the apartment, the door is flung open by the boy in a flushed, excited state. 'Simón, guess what!' he shouts. 'We saw señor Daga! He's got a magic pen! He showed me!'

He has almost forgotten about Daga, the man who humiliated Álvaro and the paymaster at the docks. 'A magic pen!' he says. 'That sounds interesting. May I come in?'

Bolívar approaches him magisterially and sniffs his crotch. Inés is sitting hunched over her sewing: he has a momentary, unsettling vision of what she will be like as an old woman. Without greeting him she speaks. 'We went in to the city, to the Asistencia, to get the child allowance, and this man was there, this friend of yours.'

'He is no friend of mine. I have never so much as exchanged a word with him.'

'He's got a magic pen,' says the boy. 'There's a lady inside it, and you think it is a picture, but it isn't, it's a real lady, a tiny

tiny lady, and when you turn the pen upside down her clothes fall off and she is naked.'

'Mm. What else did señor Daga show you, besides the tiny lady?'

'He said it wasn't his fault that Álvaro got his hand cut. He said Álvaro started it. He said it was Álvaro's fault.'

'That's what people always say. It's always someone else who started it. It's always someone else's fault. Did señor Daga by any chance tell you what has become of the bicycle that he took?'

'No.'

'Well, next time you see him, ask him. Ask him whose fault it is that the paymaster has no bicycle and has to do his tour on foot.'

There is silence. It surprises him that Inés has so little to say about men who take little boys aside and show them pens with naked ladies inside them.

'Whose fault is it?' says the boy.

'What do you mean?'

'You said it is always someone else's fault. Is it señor Daga's fault?'

'That the bicycle is gone? Yes, it is his fault. But when I say it is always someone else's fault I am talking more generally. When something goes wrong we at once claim it is not our fault. We have been taking that line since the beginning of the world. It seems to be ingrained in us, part of our nature. We are never prepared to admit it is our fault.'

'Is it my fault?' asks the boy.

'Is what your fault? No, it isn't your fault. You are just a child, how can it be your fault? But I do think you should steer clear of señor Daga. He is not a good model for a young person to follow.' He speaks slowly and seriously: the warning is directed as much to Inés as to the boy.

A few days later, coming up out of the hold of a ship at the docks, he is surprised to see Inés herself on the quayside, deep in conversation with Álvaro. His heart gives a lurch. She has never been to the docks before: it can only be bad news.

The boy is gone, says Inés, stolen away by señor Daga. She has called the police but they will not help. No one will help. Álvaro must come; he, Simón, must come. They must track Daga down – it cannot be hard, he works with them – and restore her child to her.

Women are a rare enough sight on the dockside. The men glance curiously at the distraught woman with her wild hair and her city clothes.

By degrees he and Álvaro get the story out of her. The queue at the Asistencia was long, the boy was restless, señor Daga chanced to be there, he offered to buy the boy an ice cream, and when next she looked they were gone, as if they had vanished from the face of the earth.

'But how could you have let him go off with a man like that?' he protests.

She brushes the question away with a peremptory toss of the head. 'A growing boy needs a man in his life. He can't be with his mother all the time. And I thought he was a nice man.

I thought he was sincere. David is fascinated by his earring. He wants an earring too.'

'Did you say you would buy him one?'

'I told him he can wear an earring when he is older, but not yet.'

'I'll leave you to your discussion,' says Álvaro. 'Call me if you need me.'

'What about your own part in this?' he asks, when they are alone. 'How could you have entrusted your child to that man? Is there something you are not telling me? Is it possible you too find him fascinating, with his gold earrings and his naked ladies in pens?'

She pretends not to hear. 'I waited and waited,' she says. 'Then I caught the bus because I thought they might have come back home. Then when they weren't there I phoned my brother, and he said he would phone the police, but then he phoned back to say the police wouldn't help because I am not . . . because I don't have the right papers for David.'

She pauses, staring fixedly into the distance. 'He told me . . .' she says, 'he told me he would give me a child. He didn't tell me . . . he didn't tell me he would take my child away.' Suddenly she is sobbing helplessly. 'He didn't tell me . . . he didn't tell me . . .'

His anger does not fade, but his heart goes out to the woman nonetheless. Careless of the watching stevedores, he takes her in his arms. She sobs on his shoulder. 'He didn't tell me . . .'

He told me he would give me a child. His head is whirling. 'Come away,' he says. 'Let us go somewhere private.' He leads her behind the shed. 'Listen to me, Inés. David is safe, I am sure of that. Daga would not dare to do anything to him. Go back to the apartment and wait there. I will find out where he lives and pay him a call.' He pauses. 'What did he mean when he said he would give you a child?'

She pulls herself free. The sobs cease. 'What do you suppose he meant?' she says, a hard edge to her voice.

Half an hour later he is at the Relocation Centre. 'I need some information urgently,' he says to Ana. 'Do you know a man named Daga? He is in his thirties, slim, wears an earring. Worked at the docks briefly.'

'Why do you ask?'

'Because I need to speak to him. He has taken David from his mother and disappeared. If you won't help me I will have to go to the police.'

'His name is Emilio Daga. Everyone knows him. He lives in the City Blocks. At least, that is where he is registered.'

'Where exactly in the City Blocks?'

She retires to the bank of card drawers, comes back with an address on a scrap of paper. 'Next time you are here,' she says, 'tell me how you tracked down his mother. I would like to know, if you have the time.'

The City Blocks are the most desirable of the complexes administered by the Centre. The address Ana has given leads him to an apartment on the top floor of the main block. He knocks. The door is opened by an attractive young woman, rather too heavily made up, teetering unsteadily on high heels. In fact not a woman at all – he doubts she is older than sixteen.

'I am looking for someone named Emilio Daga,' he says. 'Does he live here?'

'Sure,' says the girl. 'Come in. Have you come to fetch David?'

The interior smells of stale cigarette smoke. Daga, dressed in a cotton T-shirt and jeans, barefoot, sits facing a large window with a view of the city and the setting sun. He swivels in his chair, raises a hand in greeting.

'I've come for David,' he says.

'He's in the bedroom watching television,' says Daga. 'Are you the uncle? David! Your uncle is here!'

The boy rushes in from the adjoining room in great excitement. 'Simón, come and see! It's Mickey Mouse! He has a dog named Plato, and he is driving a train, and the Red Indians are shooting arrows at him. Come quickly!'

He ignores the boy, addresses Daga. 'His mother has been frantic with worry. How could you do this?'

He has not been so close to Daga before. The bold head of hair, with its mass of golden curls, turns out to be coarse and greasy. The T-shirt has a hole at the armpit. To his surprise, he feels no fear of the man.

Daga does not rise. 'Calm down, *viejo*,' he says. 'We had a good time together. Then the youngster took a nap. He slept like a log, like an angel. Now he is watching the kids' show. Where is the harm in that?'

He does not reply. 'Come, David!' he says. 'We're leaving. Say goodbye to señor Daga.'

'No! I want to look at Mickey Mouse!'

'You can look at Mickey next time,' says Daga. 'I promise. We will keep him here just for you.'

'And Plato?'

'And Plato. We can keep Plato too, can't we, sweetie?'

'Sure,' says the girl. 'We'll keep them locked up in the mouse-box till next time.'

'Come,' he says to the child. 'Your mother has been worrying herself sick.'

'She's not my mother.'

'Of course she is your mother. She loves you very much.'

'Who is she, young fellow, if she isn't your mother?' says Daga.

'She is just a lady. I haven't got a mother.'

'You have got a mother. Inés is your mother,' he, Simón, says. 'Give me your hand.'

'No! I haven't got a mother and I haven't got a father. I just am.'

'That's nonsense. Every one of us has a mother. Every one of us has a father.'

'Have you got a mother?' says the boy, addressing Daga.

'No,' says Daga. 'I haven't got a mother either.'

'See!' says the boy triumphantly. 'I want to stay with you, I don't want to go to Inés.'

'Come here,' says Daga. The boy trots over; he lifts him onto his knee. The boy nestles against his chest, his thumb in his mouth. 'You want to stay with me?' The boy nods. 'You want to live with me and Frannie, just the three of us?' The boy nods again. 'That OK with you, sweetheart – that David comes and lives with us?'

'Sure,' says the girl.

'He is not competent to choose,' says he, Simón. 'He is just a child.'

'You are right. He is just a child. It is up to his parents to decide. But, as you heard, he hasn't got parents. So what do we do?'

'David has a mother who loves him as much as any mother in the world. As for me, I may not be his father but I care about him. Care about him and care for him and take care of him. He is coming with me.'

Daga hears this little speech in silence and then, to his surprise, gives him a smile, a rather attractive smile, showing off his excellent teeth. 'That's good,' he says. 'You take him back to his lady mother. Tell her he had a good time. Tell her he is always safe with me. You do feel safe with me, don't you, young man?'

The boy nods, his thumb still in his mouth.

'Right, then maybe it's time to go off with your gentleman guardian.' He lifts the boy from his lap. 'Come again soon. Promise? Come and watch Mickey.'

Chapter 22

'Why do I have to speak Spanish all the time?'

'We have to speak some language, my boy, unless we want to bark and howl like animals. And if we are going to speak some language, it is best we all speak the same one. Isn't that reasonable?'

'But why Spanish? I hate Spanish.'

'You don't hate Spanish. You speak very good Spanish. Your Spanish is better than mine. You are just being contrary. What language do you want to speak?'

'I want to speak my own language.'

'There is no such thing as one's own language.'

'There is! *La la fa fa yam ying tu tu.*'

'That's just gibberish. It doesn't mean anything.'

'It does mean something. It means something to me.'

'That may be so, but it doesn't mean anything to me. Language has to mean something to me as well as to you, otherwise it doesn't count as language.'

In a gesture that he must have picked up from Inés, the

boy tosses his head dismissively. '*La la fa fa yam ying!* Look at me!'

He looks into the boy's eyes. For the briefest of moments he sees something there. He has no name for it. *It is like* – that is what occurs to him in the moment. Like a fish that wriggles loose as you try to grasp it. But not like a fish – no, like *like a fish*. Or like *like like a fish*. On and on. Then the moment is over, and he is simply standing in silence, staring.

'Did you see?' says the boy.

'I don't know. Stop for a minute, I am feeling dizzy.'

'I can see what you are thinking!' says the boy with a triumphant smile.

'No you can't.'

'You think I can do magic.'

'Not at all. You have no idea what I am thinking. Now pay attention. I am going to say something about language, something serious, something I want you to take to heart.

'Everyone comes to this country as a stranger. I came as a stranger. You came as a stranger. Inés and her brothers were once strangers. We came from various places and various pasts, seeking a new life. But now we are all in the same boat together. So we have to get along with each other. One of the ways in which we get along is by speaking the same language. That is the rule. It is a good rule, and we should obey it. Not only obey it but obey it with a good heart, not like a mule that keeps digging in its heels. With a good heart and goodwill. If you refuse, if you go on being rude about Spanish and insist on speaking your own language, then you are going to find yourself living in a private world. You will have no friends. You will be shunned.'

'What is shunned?'

'You will have nowhere to lay your head.'

'I don't have friends anyway.'

'That will change once you go to school. At school you will make lots of new friends. Anyway, you do have friends. Fidel and Elena are your friends. Álvaro is your friend.'

'And El Rey is my friend.'

'El Rey is your friend too.'

'And señor Daga.'

'Señor Daga is not your friend. Señor Daga is trying to lead you into temptation.'

'What is temptation?'

'He is trying to lure you away from your mother with Mickey Mouse and ice cream. Remember how sick you were from all the ice cream he fed you that day?'

'He gave me firewater too.'

'What do you mean, firewater?'

'It made my throat burn. He says it is medicine for when you are feeling blue.'

'Does señor Daga carry his medicine in a little silver flask in his pocket?'

'Yes.'

'Please never drink anything from señor Daga's flask again, David. It may be medicine for grown-up people, but it's not good for children.'

He does not report the firewater to Inés but he does tell

Elena. 'He is gaining a hold over the child,' he tells her. 'I can't compete with him. He wears an earring, he carries a knife, he drinks firewater. He has a pretty girlfriend. He has Mickey Mouse at home in a box. I have no idea how to bring the boy to his senses. Inés is under the man's spell too.'

'What else do you expect? Look at it from her point of view. She is at an age when a woman who has not had children – children of her own – begins to feel anxious. It is a matter of biology. She is in a receptive state, biologically speaking. I'm surprised you don't sense it.'

'I don't think of Inés in that way – biologically.'

'You think too much. This has nothing to do with thinking.'

'I don't see why Inés should want another child, Elena. She has the boy. He came to her as a gift, out of the blue, a gift pure and simple. A gift like that ought to be enough for any woman.'

'Yes, but he is not her natural child. She will never forget that. If you don't do something about it, young David is going to have señor Daga as his stepfather one of these days, and then a brood of little Daga stepbrothers and stepsisters. Or if not Daga then some other man.'

'What do you mean, if I don't do something about it?'

'If you don't give her a child yourself.'

'I? I wouldn't dream of it. I am not the father type. I was made to be an uncle, not a father. Besides, Inés doesn't like men – at least, that is the impression I get. Doesn't like male loud-ness and rudeness and hairiness. I wouldn't be surprised if she tried to keep David from growing up a man.'

'Being a father isn't a career, Simón. Nor is it some kind of metaphysical destiny. You don't have to like the woman, she doesn't have to like you. You have intercourse with her, and lo and behold, nine months later you are a father. It's simple enough. Any man can do it.'

'Not so. Fatherhood is not only a matter of having intercourse with a woman, just as motherhood is not only a matter of providing a vessel for male seed.'

'Well, what you describe counts as fatherhood and motherhood in the real world. You can't enter the real world unless you are sparked off by some man's seed and gestated in some woman's womb and come down that same woman's birth canal. You have to be born of man and woman. No exceptions. Excuse my plain speech. So ask yourself: *Is it going to be my friend señor Daga who plants his seed in Inés, or is it going to be me?*'

He shakes his head. 'That's enough, Elena. Can we change the subject? David tells me that Fidel threw a stone at him the other day. What is going on?'

'It wasn't a stone, it was a marble. It's what David must expect if his mother won't let him fraternize with other children, if she encourages him to think of himself as some kind of superior being. Other children will gang up on him. I spoke to Fidel, I scolded him, but it won't have any effect.'

'They used to be best friends.'

'They used to be best friends before you brought Inés into the picture, with her peculiar ideas about child-raising. That is another reason why you should reassert yourself in the household.'

He sighs.

★ ★ ★

'Can we speak in private?' he says to Inés. 'I have something to propose to you.'

'Can it wait?'

'What are you whispering about?' the boy calls from the next room.

'No concern of yours.' And to Inés: 'Please, can we step outside, just for a minute?'

'Are you whispering about señor Daga?' calls the boy.

'This has nothing to do with señor Daga. It is something private between your mother and myself.'

Inés dries her hands and takes off her apron. She and he leave the apartment, cross the playground into the parkland. Perched in the window, the boy keeps watch on them.

'What I have to say concerns señor Daga.' He pauses, draws a breath. 'I understand you wish to have another child. Is it true?'

'Who told you that?'

'David says you are going to give him a brother.'

'I was telling him his bedtime story. It was something that came up in passing; it was just an idea.'

'Well, ideas can become reality, just as seed can become flesh and blood. Inés, I don't want to embarrass you, so let me simply say, with the utmost respect, that if you are considering entering into relations with a man for the purpose of child-bearing, you might consider me. I am prepared to play the part. To play the part and then absent myself, while continuing to be your protector, to provide for you and any children of yours. You can call me their godfather. Or, if you prefer, their uncle. I will forget whatever passed between us, between you and me.

It will be washed from memory. It will be as if it had never happened.

'There. I have said it. Please don't answer at once. Reflect.'

In silence, in the gathering dusk, they turn back to the apartment. Inés strides ahead. She is clearly cross, or upset: she will not so much as look at him. He blames Elena for putting him up to it, blames himself too. What a crude way of offering oneself! As if he were offering to fix the plumbing!

He catches up with her, takes her by the arm, turns her to face him. 'That was unforgiveable,' he says. 'I am sorry. Please forgive me.'

She does not speak. Like a thing carved in wood she stands, her arms at her sides, waiting for him to let go. He loosens his grip and she stumbles away.

From the window high above he hears the boy call: 'Inés! Simón! Come! Señor Daga is here! Señor Daga is here!'

He curses under his breath. If she was expecting Daga, why did she not warn him? What does she see in the man anyhow, with his cocky swagger and his smell of pomade and his flat, nasal voice?

Señor Daga has not come alone. With him is his pretty girl-friend, wearing a white dress with flounces in startling red, and heavy earrings in the shape of chariot wheels that sway as she moves. Inés greets her with frosty reserve. As for Daga, he seems quite at home in the apartment, lounging on the bed, doing nothing to put the girl at ease.

'Señor Daga wants us to go dancing,' announces the boy. 'Can we go dancing?'

'We are due at La Residencia tonight. You know that.'

'I don't want to go to La Residencia! It's boring! I want to go dancing!'

'You can't go dancing. You are too young.'

'I can dance! I'm not too young! I'll show you.' And he whirls around the floor, stepping lightly and not without grace in his soft blue shoes. 'There! Do you see?'

'We are not going dancing,' says Inés firmly. 'Diego is coming to fetch us, and we are going with him to La Residencia.'

'Then señor Daga and Frannie must come too!'

'Señor Daga has plans of his own. You can't expect him to abandon his plans and follow us.' She speaks as if Daga were not in the room. 'Besides, as you know only too well, they don't allow visitors at La Residencia.'

'I am a visitor,' objects the boy. 'They allow me.'

'Yes, but you are different. You are my child. You are the light of my life.'

The light of my life. What a surprising thing to say in front of strangers!

Now Diego makes his appearance, and the other brother too, the one who never opens his mouth. Inés greets them with relief. 'We are ready. David, fetch your things.'

'No!' says the boy. 'I don't want to go. I want to have a party. Can we have a party?'

'There is no time for a party, and we don't have anything to offer our guests.'

'That's not true! We've got wine! In the kitchen!' And in a trice he has clambered onto the kitchen dresser and is reaching for the top shelf. 'See!' he shouts, displaying the bottle triumphantly. 'We've got wine!'

Blushing scarlet, Inés tries to take the bottle from him – 'It's not wine, it's sherry,' she says – but he evades her. 'Who wants wine? Who wants wine?' he chants.

'Me!' says Diego; and 'Me!' says the silent brother. They are laughing, both of them, at their sister's discomfiture. Señor Daga joins in. 'And me!'

There are not enough drinking vessels for all six of them, so the boy goes around the circle with the bottle and a tumbler, pouring sherry for each of them and waiting solemnly for the tumbler to be drained.

He comes to Inés. With a frown she motions the glass away. 'You must!' commands the boy. 'I am the king tonight, and I order that you must!'

Inés takes a ladylike sip.

'Now me,' announces the boy, and before anyone can stop him he raises the bottle to his lips and takes a hearty swig. For an instant he gazes triumphantly around the assembly. Then he chokes, coughs, splutters. 'It's horrible!' he gasps. The bottle drops from his hand; deftly señor Daga rescues it.

Diego and his brother fall about laughing. 'What ails thee, gentle King?' cries Diego. 'Canst thou not hold thy liquor?'

The boy recovers his breath. 'More!' he cries. 'More wine!'

If Inés is not going to act, then it is time for him, Simón, to step in. 'Enough of that!' he says. 'It is late, David, time for our guests to leave.'

'No!' says the boy. 'It's not late! I want to play a game. I want to play Who Am I?'

'Who Am I?' says Daga. 'How do you play that?'

'You have to pretend you are someone and then everyone has to guess who you are. Last time I pretended I was Bolívar and Diego guessed it at once, didn't you, Diego?'

'And what is the penalty?' asks Daga. 'What penalty do you pay if we guess right?'

The boy seems nonplussed.

'The way we used to play in the old days,' says Daga, 'is if we guess right you have to tell a secret, your most cherished secret.'

The boy is silent.

'We have to leave, there is no more time for games,' says Inés feebly.

'No!' says the boy. 'I want to play another game. I want to play Truth or Consequences.'

'That sounds better,' says Daga. 'Tell us how you play Truth or Consequences.'

'I ask a question and you have to answer and you can't lie, you have to tell the truth. If you don't tell the truth you have to pay a penalty. All right? I'll start. Diego, is your bum clean?'

Silence falls. The second brother grows red in the face, then explodes in a great snort of laughter. The boy laughs delightedly, and whirls around in a dance. 'Come on!' he shouts. 'Truth or Consequences!'

'Just one round,' concedes Inés. 'And no more rude questions.'

'No rude questions,' agrees the boy. 'It's my turn again. My question goes' – he looks around the room, from one face to another – 'my question goes to . . . Inés! Inés, who do you like most in the world?'

'You. I like you most.'

'No, not me! Which *man* do you like most in the world, to make a baby in your tummy?'

There is silence. Inés is tight-lipped.

'Do you like him or him or him or him?' the boy asks, pointing in turn at the four men in the room.

He, Simón, the fourth man, intervenes. 'No rude questions,' he says. 'That was a rude question. A woman doesn't make a baby with her brother.'

'Why not?'

'She just doesn't. There is no why.'

'There is a why! I can ask any question I like! It's in the game. Do you want Diego to make a baby inside you, Inés? Or do you want Stefano?'

For Inés's sake he intervenes again. 'That's enough!'

Diego stands up. 'Let's go,' he says.

'No!' says the boy. 'Truth or Consequences! Who do you like most, Inés?'

Diego turns to his sister. 'Say something, say anything.'

Inés is silent.

'Inés doesn't want to have anything to do with men,' says Diego. 'There, you have your answer. She doesn't want any of us. She wants to be free. Now let's go.'

'Is that true?' says the boy to Inés. 'It's not true, is it? You promised I could have a brother.'

Once more he intervenes. 'Only one question each, David. That is the rule. You asked your question, and you got your answer. As Diego says, Inés doesn't want any of us.'

'But I want a brother! I don't want to be the only son! It's boring!'

'If you really want a brother, go out and find one yourself. Start with Fidel. Take Fidel as your brother. Brothers don't all have to come out of the same womb. Start a brotherhood of your own.'

'I don't know what a brotherhood is.'

'I'm surprised to hear that. If two boys agree to call each other brother, they have started a brotherhood. It is as simple as that. They can round up more boys and make them brothers too. They can swear loyalty to one another and choose a name – the Brotherhood of the Seven Stars or the Brotherhood of the Cave or some such. Even the Brotherhood of David, if you like.'

'Or it can be a secret brotherhood,' interjects Daga. His eyes glint, he wears a little smile. The boy, who has barely listened to him, Simón, now seems quite transfixed. 'You can swear an oath of secrecy. No one need ever find out who your secret brothers are.'

He breaks the silence. 'That is enough for tonight. David, go and fetch your pyjamas. You have kept Diego waiting long enough. Think up a good name for your brotherhood. Then when you come back from La Residencia, you can invite Fidel to be your first brother.' He turns to Inés. 'Do you agree? Do you approve?'

Chapter 23

'Where is El Rey?'

The cart is standing at the quayside, empty, ready to be loaded, but El Rey's place has been taken by a horse they have not seen before, a black gelding with a white blaze on his forehead. When the boy comes too close, the new horse rolls his eyes nervously and paws the ground.

'Hey!' Álvaro calls to the driver, who sits drowsing on his seat. 'Where is the big mare? The youngster has come especially to see her.'

'Down with horse flu.'

'His name is El Rey,' says the boy. 'He's not a mare. Can we visit him?'

A guarded look passes between Álvaro and the driver. 'El Rey is back at the stables, resting,' says Álvaro. 'The horse doctor is going to give him medicine. We can visit him as soon as he is better.'

'I want to see him now. I can make him better.'

He, Simón, intervenes. 'Not now, my boy. Let us speak to

Inés first. Then maybe all three of us can make a trip to the stables tomorrow.'

'Better wait a few days,' says Álvaro, and flashes him a look which he does not know how to interpret. 'Let El Rey have a chance to recover properly. Horse flu is a nasty thing, worse than human flu. If you are sick with horse flu, you need rest and quiet, not visitors.'

'He does want visitors,' says the boy. 'He wants me. I am his friend.'

Álvaro takes him, Simón, aside. 'Better if you don't bring the kid to the stables,' he says; and, when he still fails to understand: 'The mare is old. She has had her day.'

'Álvaro has just had a message from the horse doctor,' he reports to the boy. 'They have decided to send El Rey to the horse farm so that he can get better more quickly.'

'What is a horse farm?'

'A horse farm is where young horses are born and old horses go to rest.'

'Can we go there?'

'The horse farm is out in the country, I'm not sure exactly where. I'll make inquiries.'

When the men knock off at four o'clock, the boy is nowhere to be seen. 'He went with the last dray,' says one of the men. 'I thought you knew.'

He sets off at once. By the time he gets to the grain store the sun is setting. The store is deserted, the great doors are locked. His heart beating fast, he searches for the boy. He finds him behind the store, on a loading platform, squatting beside the

234

body of El Rey, stroking her head, waving the flies away. The stout leather belt that must have been used to hoist the mare is still around her belly.

He clambers onto the platform. 'Poor, poor El Rey!' he murmurs. Then he notices the blood that has congealed in the horse's ear, and the dark bullet hole above it, and shuts up.

'It's all right,' says the boy. 'He is going to be well again in three days.'

'Is that what the horse doctor told you?'

The boy shakes his head. 'El Rey.'

'Did El Rey tell you that himself – three days?'

The boy nods.

'But it isn't just horse flu, my boy. Surely you can see. He's been shot with a gun, as a mercy. He must have been suffering. He was suffering and they decided to help him, to ease the pain. He is not going to get better. He is dead.'

'No, he's not.' Tears are running down the boy's cheeks. 'He is going to the horse farm to get better. You said so.'

'He is going to the horse farm, yes, but not to this horse farm, not to the horse farm here; he is going to another horse farm, in another world. Where he will not have to wear harness and pull a heavy cart but can stroll around in the fields in the sunshine eating buttercups.'

'It's not true! He is going to the horse farm to get better. They are going to put him on the cart and take him to the horse farm.'

The boy bends and presses his mouth to the horse's vast

nostril. Hastily he grips the boy by the arm and pulls him away. 'Don't do that! It's not hygienic! You will get sick!'

The boy wrests himself free. He is weeping openly. 'I will save him!' he sobs. 'I want him to live! He's my friend!'

He holds the struggling boy still and clasps him tight. 'My dearest, dearest child, sometimes those we love die and there is nothing we can do about it except look forward to the day when we will all be together again.'

'I want to make him breathe!' the boy sobs.

'He's a horse, he's too big for you to breathe life into.'

'Then you can breathe into him!'

'That won't work. I don't have the right kind of breath. I don't have the breath of life. All I can do is be sad. All I can do is mourn and help you to mourn. Now quick, before it gets dark, why don't you and I go down to the river and look for some flowers to put on El Rey? He will like that. He was a gentle horse, wasn't he, in spite of being a giant. He will enjoy arriving at the horse farm with a wreath of flowers around his neck.'

So he coaxes the boy away from the dead body, leads him to the riverbank, helps him pluck flowers and weave them into a garland. They return; the boy drapes the garland over the dead, staring eyes.

'There,' he says. 'Now we must leave El Rey. He has a long journey to make, all the way to the great horse farm. When he arrives, the other horses will look at him with his crown of flowers, and they will say to each other, "He must have been a king where he came from! He must be the great El Rey whom we have heard about, the friend of David!"'

The boy takes his hand. Under a rising full moon they trudge back along the path to the docks.

'Is El Rey getting up now, do you think?' asks the boy.

'He is getting up, he is shaking himself, he is giving that whinny of his that you know, he is setting off, clop-clop-clop, towards his new life. End of weeping. No more weeping.'

'No more weeping,' says the boy, and perks up, and even gives a jaunty little smile.

Chapter 24

He and the boy share a birthday. That is to say, because they arrived on the same boat on the same day they have been assigned as their birth date the date of their joint arrival, their joint entry into a new life. The boy was deemed to be five years old because he looked five years old, just as he was deemed to be forty-five (so his card says) because that was how old he looked on that day. (He had been piqued: he had felt himself to be younger. Now he feels older. He feels sixty; there are days when he feels seventy.)

Since the boy has no friends, not even a horse friend, there is no point in holding a birthday party for him. Nonetheless, he and Inés are agreed that the day should be properly celebrated. So Inés bakes a cake and ices it and plants six candles on it, and they secretly buy him gifts, she a sweater (winter is around the corner), he an abacus (he is worried about the boy's resistance to the science of numbers).

The birthday celebration is overshadowed by a letter that comes in the post, reminding him that as of his sixth birthday

David should be enrolled in the public school system, the responsibility for so enrolling him resting with his parent(s) or guardian(s).

Up to now Inés has encouraged the boy to believe that he is too clever to need schooling, that what little tutoring he may require he can receive at home. But his wilfulness over *Don Quixote*, his claims to be able to read and write and count when he clearly cannot, have sown doubt even in her mind. Perhaps it would be best, she now concedes, for him to have the guidance of a trained teacher. So they buy him a third, joint gift, a red leather pouch with the initial letter *D* stamped in gold in one corner, containing two new pencils, a pencil sharpener, and an eraser. This they present to him, along with the abacus and the sweater, on his birthday. The pouch, they tell him, is his surprise gift, to accompany the happy and surprising news that he will soon, perhaps as early as next week, be going to school.

The boy receives the news coolly. 'I don't want to go with Fidel,' he says. They reassure him: being older than he, Fidel is bound to be in a different class. 'And I want to take *Don Quixote* with me,' he says.

He tries to dissuade the boy from taking the book to school. It belongs to the East Blocks library, he says; if it were to be lost he has no idea how they would replace it. Besides, the school is bound to have its own library with its own copy of the book. But the boy will have none of that.

On Monday he arrives early at the apartment to accompany Inés and the boy to the stop where he will catch the bus that will take him to his first day of school. The boy wears his new sweater, carries the red leather pouch with the initial *D* on it, and grips the tattered East Blocks *Don Quixote* under his arm. Fidel is already at the bus stop, along with half a dozen other children from the Blocks. Ostentatiously David does not greet him.

Because they want going to school to seem part of a normal life, they agree not to press the boy for tales of the classroom; and he, for his part, remains tight-lipped, unusually so. 'Did it go well at school today?' he dares to ask, on the fifth day. – 'Uh-huh,' replies the boy. – 'Have you made new friends yet?' The boy does not deign to reply.

Thus it continues for three weeks, four weeks. Then a letter arrives in the mail, with the school's address in the top left-hand corner. Headed 'Extraordinary Communication', it invites the parent(s) of the pupil in question to contact the school secretary at his/her/their earliest convenience to fix a time for a consultation with the relevant class teacher in order to address certain issues that have arisen relating to his/her/their son/daughter.

Inés telephones the school. 'I am free all day,' she says. 'Name a time and I will be there.' The secretary proposes eleven o'clock the next morning, during señor León's free period. 'It will be best if the boy's father comes too,' she adds. 'My son does not have a father,' Inés replies. 'I will ask his uncle to come along. His uncle takes an interest in him.'

Señor León, the first-year class teacher, turns out to be a tall, thin young man with a dark beard and only one eye. The dead eye, made of glass, does not move in its socket; he, Simón, wonders whether the children do not find this disturbing.

'We have only a little time,' says señor León, 'therefore I will speak directly. I find David to be an intelligent boy, very intelligent. He has a quick mind; he grasps new ideas at once. However, he is finding it difficult to adjust to the realities of the classroom. He expects to get his own way all the time. Perhaps this is because he is a little older than the class average. Or perhaps at home he has been used to getting his own way rather too easily. In any event, it is not a positive development.'

Señor León pauses, places the fingers of one hand against the fingers of the other, tip to tip, and waits for their response.

'A child should be free,' says Inés. 'A child should be able to enjoy his childhood. I had my doubts about sending David to school so young.'

'Six is not young to be going to school,' says señor León. 'On the contrary.'

'Nevertheless he is young, and used to his freedom.'

'A child does not give up his freedom by coming to school,' says señor León. 'He does not give up his freedom by sitting still. He does not give up his freedom by listening to what the teacher has to say. Freedom is not incompatible with discipline and hard work.'

'Does David not sit still? Does he not listen to what you say?'

'He is restless, and he makes the other children restless too. He leaves his seat and roams around. He leaves the room without permission. And no, he does not pay attention to what I say.'

'That is strange. At home he does not roam around. If he roams around at school, there must be a reason for it.'

The solitary eye bores into Inés.

'As for the restlessness,' she says, 'he has always been like that. He doesn't get enough sleep.'

'A bland diet will cure that,' says señor León. 'No spices. No stimulants. I come now to specifics. In reading, David has unhappily made no progress, none at all. Other children who are not as naturally gifted read better than he does. Much better. There is something about the activity of reading that he seems unable to grasp. The same goes for figures.'

He, Simón, intervenes. 'But he has a love for books. You must have seen that. He carries *Don Quixote* with him wherever he goes.'

'He clings to the book because it has pictures,' replies señor León. 'It is generally not good practice to learn to read from books with pictures. The pictures distract the mind from the words. And *Don Quixote*, whatever else may be said about it, is not a book for beginning readers. David's spoken Spanish is not bad, but he cannot read. He cannot even sound the letters of the alphabet. I have never come across such an extreme case. I would like to propose that we call in a specialist, a therapist. I have a feeling – and colleagues of mine whom I have consulted share my feeling – that there may be a deficit.'

'A deficit?'

'A specific deficit linked to symbolic activities. To working with words and numbers. He cannot read. He cannot write. He cannot count.'

'At home he reads and writes. He spends hours at it every day. He is absorbed in his reading and writing. And he can count to a thousand, a million.'

For the first time señor León smiles. 'He can recite all kinds of numbers, yes, but not in the right order. As for the marks he makes with his pencil, you may call them writing, he may call them writing, but they are not writing as generally understood. Whether they have some private meaning I cannot judge. Perhaps they have. Perhaps they hint at artistic talent. Which would be a second and more positive reason for him to see a specialist. David is an interesting child. It would be a pity to lose him. A specialist may be able to tell us whether there is some common factor underlying the deficit on the one hand and the inventiveness on the other.'

The bell rings. Señor León takes a notebook from his pocket, scribbles in it, tears off the page. 'This is the name of the specialist I propose, and her telephone number. She visits the school once a week, so you can see her here. Telephone and make an appointment. In the meantime, David and I will continue with our efforts. Thank you for coming to see me. I am sure there will be a fortunate outcome.'

He seeks out Elena, reports on the interview. 'Do you know señor León at all?' he asks. 'Did Fidel have him as a teacher? I find his complaints hard to credit. That David is disobedient,

for instance. He may sometimes be a bit wilful, but not disobedient, not in my experience.'

Elena does not reply but calls Fidel into the room. 'Fidel,
darling, tell us about señor León. David and he don't seem to
be getting on together, and Simón is worried.'

'Señor León is OK,' says Fidel. 'He's strict.'

'Is he strict about children speaking out of turn?'

'I suppose so.'

'Why do you think he and David don't get along?'

'I don't know. David says crazy things. Maybe señor León
doesn't like that.'

'Crazy things? What sort of crazy things?'

'I don't know . . . He says crazy things in the playground.
Everyone thinks he is crazy, even the big boys.'

'But what sort of crazy things?'

'That he can make people disappear. That he can make
himself disappear. He says there are volcanoes everywhere that
we can't see, only him.'

'Volcanoes?'

'Not big volcanoes, little ones. That no one can see.'

'Does he perhaps frighten the other children with his
stories?'

'I don't know. He says he is going to be a magician.'

'He has been saying that for a long time. He told me you and
he are going to perform in the circus one day. He is going to do
magic tricks and you are going to be a clown.'

Fidel and his mother exchange glances.

'Fidel is going to be a musician, not a magician, not a clown,' says Elena. 'Fidel, did you tell David you were going to be a clown?'

'No,' says Fidel, shifting uneasily.

The interview with the psychologist takes place on the school premises. They are ushered into the well-lit, rather antiseptic room where señora Otxoa holds her consultations. 'Good morning,' she says, smiling and offering her hand. 'You are the parents of David. I have met your son. He and I had a long talk together, several talks. What an interesting young man!'

'Before we get down to business,' he interrupts, 'let me clarify who I am. Though I have known David for a long time, and was once a sort of guardian to him, I am not his father. However –'

Señora Otxoa raises a hand. 'I know. David told me. David says he has never met his real father. He also says' – here she turns to Inés – 'that you are not his real mother. Let us discuss these convictions of his before all else. Because, although organic factors may be at work, dyslexia for instance, my sense is that David's unsettled behaviour in the classroom comes out of a – to a child – mystifying family situation: out of uncertainty about who he is, where he comes from.'

He and Inés exchange glances. 'You use the word *real*,' he says. 'You say we are not his real mother and his real father. What exactly do you mean by real? Surely there is such a thing as overvaluing the biological.'

Señora Otxoa purses her lips, shakes her head. 'Let us not

become too theoretical. Let us rather concentrate on David's experience and David's understanding of the real. The real, I want to suggest, is what David misses in his life. This experience of lacking the real includes the experience of lacking real parents. David has no anchor in his life. Hence his withdrawal and retreat into a fantasy world where he feels more in control.'

'But he has an anchor,' says Inés. 'I am his anchor. I love him. I love him more than the world. And he knows that.'

Señora Otxoa nods. 'He does indeed. He told me how much you love him – how much both of you love him. Your goodwill makes him happy; he feels the greatest goodwill in return, towards both of you. Nevertheless, there is still something missing, something that goodwill or love cannot supply. Because, although a positive emotional environment counts for a great deal, it cannot be enough. It is that difference, that lack of a real parental presence, that I have called us together to discuss today. Why? you ask. Because, as I say, I feel that David's learning difficulties stem from a confusion about a world from which his real parents have vanished, a world into which he does not know how he arrived.'

'David arrived by boat, like everyone else,' he objects. 'From the boat to the camp, from the camp to Novilla. None of us knows more than that about our origins. We are all washed clean of memory, more or less. What is so special about David's case? And what has any of this to do with reading and writing, with David's problems in the classroom? You mentioned dyslexia. Does David suffer from dyslexia?'

'I mentioned dyslexia as a possibility. I have not tested for it.

But if it is indeed present, my guess is that it is only a contributory factor. No, to come to your main question, I would say that what is special about David is that he feels himself to be special, even abnormal. Of course he is not abnormal. As for being special, let us set that question aside for the moment. Instead let us, all three of us, make an effort to see the world through his eyes, without imposing on him our way of seeing the world. David wants to know who he really is, but when he asks he receives evasive answers like "What do you mean by real?" or "We have no history, any of us, it is all washed out." Can you blame him if he feels frustrated and rebellious, and then retreats into a private world where he is free to make up his own answers?'

'Are you telling us that the illegible pages he writes for señor León are stories about where he comes from?'

'Yes and no. They are stories for himself, not for us. That is why he writes them in a private script.'

'How do you know that if you can't read them? Has he interpreted them for you?'

'Señor, for David's relationship with me to flourish it is important that he should rely on me not to reveal what has passed between us. Even a child should have a right to his little secrets. But from the talks David and I have had, yes, I believe that in his own mind he is writing stories about himself and his true parentage. Which out of concern for you, for both of you, he keeps hidden, in case you will be upset.'

'And what is his true parentage? Where, according to him, does he really come from?'

'That is not for me to say. But there is the matter of a certain letter. He speaks of a letter containing the names of his true parents. He says you, señor, know about the letter. Is that true?'

'A letter from whom?'

'He says he had the letter with him when he arrived on the boat.'

'Aha, *that* letter! No, you are mistaken, the letter was lost before we came ashore. It was lost during the voyage. I never saw it. It was because he had lost the letter that I took on the responsibility of helping him find his mother. Otherwise he would have been helpless. He would still be in Belstar, in limbo.'

Señora Otxoa writes a vigorous note to herself on her pad.

'We come now,' she says, laying down her pen, 'to the practical problem of David's comportment in the classroom. His insubordination. His failure to make progress. The consequences of that lack of progress, and that insubordination, for señor León and the other children in the class.'

'Insubordination?' He waits for Inés to add her voice, but no, she is leaving it to him to speak. 'At home, señora, David is always polite and well behaved. I find it hard to credit these reports from señor León. What exactly does he mean by insubordination?'

'He means continual challenges to his authority as teacher. He means refusal to accept direction. Which brings me to the main point. I would like to propose that we withdraw David from the regular class, at least for the time being, and enrol him instead in a programme of tuition adapted to his individual needs. Where he can proceed at his own pace, given his difficult family situation. Until he is ready to rejoin his class. Which I am confident he will be able to do, since he is an intelligent child with a quick mind.'

'And this programme of tuition . . . ?'

'The programme I have in mind is run at the Special Learning Centre at Punta Arenas, not far from Novilla, on the coast, in a very attractive setting.'

'How far?'

'Fifty kilometres, more or less.'

'Fifty kilometres! That's a lot of travelling for a small child to do every day, back and forth. Is there a bus?'

'No. David will reside at the Learning Centre, spending every second weekend at home, if he so chooses. Our experience is that it works best if the child is in residence. It allows a certain distance from a domestic situation that may be contributing to the problem.'

He and Inés exchange looks. 'And what if we decline?' he says. 'What if we prefer him to stay in señor León's class?'

'What if we prefer to take him out of this school where he is learning nothing?' Inés now enters, her voice rising. 'Where he is too young to be anyway. That is the real reason why he is having difficulty. He is too young.'

'Señor León is no longer prepared to have David in his class, and after making my own inquiries I can see why. As for his age, David is of normal school-going age. Señor, señora, I offer my advice with David's interests in mind. He is making no progress at school. He is a disruptive influence. To remove him from school and return him to a home environment which he clearly finds unsettling cannot be the solution. Therefore we must take some alternative, bolder step. Which is why I recommend Punta Arenas.'

'And if we refuse?'

'Señor, I wish you would not put it in those terms. Take my word for it, Punta Arenas is the best option before us. If you and señora Inés would like to visit Punta Arenas beforehand, I can arrange it, so that you can see for yourselves what a first-rate institution it is.'

'But if we visit this institution and still refuse, what then?'

'What then?' Señora Otxoa spreads her hands in a gesture of helplessness. 'You told me, at the beginning of this consultation, that you are not the boy's father. There is nothing in his papers about his parentage, his real parentage. I would say . . . I would say that your qualifications to dictate where he should receive his education are extremely weak.'

'So you are going to take our child away from us.'

'Please don't look at it in that way. We are not taking the child away from you. You will see him regularly, every second week. Your home will continue to be his home. In all practical respects you will continue to be his parents, unless he decides that he wishes to be separated from you. Which he does not indicate in any way. On the contrary, he is extremely fond of you, both of you – fond of you and attached to you.

'I repeat, Punta Arenas is in my opinion the best solution to the problem we face, and a generous solution too. Think about it. Take your time. Visit Punta Arenas, if you wish. Then, along with señor León, we can discuss details.'

'And in the meantime?'

'In the meantime I suggest that David go home with you. It is not doing him any good to be in señor León's class, and it is certainly not doing any good to his classmates.'

Chapter 25

'Why are we going home early?'

They are on the bus, the three of them, heading back to the Blocks.

'Because it was all a mistake,' says Inés. 'They are too old for you, those boys in your class. And that teacher, that señor León, doesn't know how to teach.'

'Señor León has a magic eye. He can take it out and put it in his pocket. One of the boys saw him.'

Inés is silent.

'Am I going back to school tomorrow?'

'No.'

'To be specific,' he intervenes, 'you will not be going back to señor León's school. Your mother and I will be discussing a different kind of school for you. Maybe.'

'We are not discussing any other schools,' says Inés. 'School was a bad idea from the beginning. I don't know why I allowed it. What was that woman saying about dyslexia? What is dyslexia?'

'Not being able to read words in the right order. Not being able to read from left to right. Something like that. I don't know.'

'I haven't got dyslexia,' says the boy. 'I haven't got anything. Are they sending me to Punta Arenas? I don't want to go.'

'What do you know about Punta Arenas?' he says.

'It has got barbed wire and you have to sleep in a dormitory and you're not allowed to go home.'

'You are not being sent to Punta Arenas,' says Inés. 'Not as long as I am alive.'

'Are you going to die?' says the boy.

'No, of course not. It is just a manner of speaking. You are not going to Punta Arenas.'

'I forgot my book. My writing book. It's in my desk. Can we go back and fetch it?'

'No. Not now. I'll fetch it some other day.'

'And my pouch.'

'The pencil pouch we gave you for your birthday?'

'Yes.'

'I'll fetch that too. Don't worry.'

'Do they want to send me to Punta Arenas because of my stories?'

'It's not that they want to send you to Punta Arenas,' he says. 'It's more that they don't know what to do with you. You are an exceptional child, and they don't know what to do with exceptional children.'

'Why am I exceptional?'

'That is not a question for you to ask. You just are exceptional, and you will have to live with the fact. Sometimes it will make your way easier, and sometimes it will make it more difficult. This is one of the cases when it makes it more difficult.'

'I don't want to go to school. I don't like school. I can teach myself.'

'I don't think so, David. I think you have been teaching yourself a little too much of late. That is half the problem. A little more humility, a little more readiness to learn from others, is what is called for.'

'You can teach me.'

'Thank you. Very kind of you. As you may remember, I have offered to teach you several times in the past, and been rejected. If you had let me teach you to read and write and count in a normal fashion, we would have had none of this mess.'

The force of his outburst clearly takes the boy aback: he casts him a look of pained surprise.

'But that is all behind us,' he hastens to add. 'We are going to start a new page, you and I.'

'Why doesn't señor León like me?'

'Because he is too full of his own importance,' says Inés.

'Señor León does like you,' he says. 'It is just that he has a whole class to teach, and doesn't have time to give you individual attention. He expects children to work by themselves some of the time.'

'I don't like working.'

'We all have to work, so you had better get used to it. Work is part of the human lot.'

'I don't like working. I like playing.'

'Yes, but you can't play all the time. The time for play is after you have finished your day's work. When you arrive in his class in the morning, señor León expects work from you. It's quite reasonable.'

'Señor León doesn't like my stories.'

'He can't not like your stories, since he can't read them. What kind of story does he like?'

'Stories about vacations. About what people do during vacations. What are vacations?'

'Vacations are empty days, days when you don't have to work. You have been given a vacation for the rest of today. You don't have to do any more studying.'

'And tomorrow?'

'Tomorrow you are going to learn to read and write and count like a normal person.'

'I am going to write a letter to the school,' he tells Inés, 'to notify them formally that we are withdrawing David. That we will take care of his education ourselves. Do you agree?'

'Yes. And while you are about it, write to that señor León too. Ask him what is he doing, teaching small children. Tell him it's not a job for a man.'

'Esteemed señor León,' he writes.

Thank you for introducing us to señora Otxoa.

Señora Otxoa has proposed that our son David be transferred to the special school at Punta Arenas.

On mature consideration we have decided against such a move. David is, in our judgment, too young to live away from his parents. We also doubt that he will receive the right kind of attention at Punta Arenas. We will therefore proceed with his schooling at home. We have every hope that his learning difficulties will soon be a thing of the past. He is, as you concede, a bright child who learns quickly.

We thank you for your efforts on his behalf. We enclose a copy of the letter we have sent your school principal notifying him of the withdrawal.

They receive no reply. Instead, there arrives in the mail a three-page form to be filled in for admission to Punta Arenas, plus a list of clothing and personal items (toothbrush, toothpaste, comb) that a new pupil should bring, and a bus pass. All of this they ignore.

Next comes a telephone call, from neither the school nor Punta Arenas, but, as far as Inés can make out, from some administrative office or other in the city.

'We have decided not to send David back to school,' she informs the woman on the line. 'He was getting no benefit from the teaching. He will be learning at home.'

'It is permitted to educate a child at home only if the parent is an accredited teacher,' says the woman. 'Are you an accredited teacher?'

'I am David's mother, and I and no one else will decide how he is to be educated,' replies Inés, and puts down the receiver.

A week later there arrives a new letter. Headed 'Notice of Tribunal' it instructs the unnamed 'parent(s) and/or guardian(s)' to appear before a board of investigation on February 21st at 9 a.m., to show cause why the child in question should not be transferred to the Special Learning Centre at Punta Arenas.

'I refuse,' says Inés. 'I refuse to attend their tribunal. I am going to take David away to La Residencia and keep him there. If anyone asks where we are, say we have gone up-country.'

'Please think again, Inés. If you do that, you will be turning yourself into a fugitive. Someone or other at La Residencia — that officious porter, for example — will report you to the authorities. Let us appear before this board, you and David and I. Let them have a chance to see that the boy doesn't have horns, that he is just an ordinary six-year-old, far too young to be separated from his mother.'

'This is no longer a game,' he warns the boy. 'If you don't persuade these people that you are willing to learn, they are going to send you away to Punta Arenas and the barbed wire. Fetch your book. You are going to learn to read.'

'But I can read,' says the boy patiently.

'You can only read in your nonsense way. I am going to teach you to read properly.'

The boy trots out of the room, returns with his *Don Quixote*, and opens it to the first page. 'Somewhere in La Mancha,' he reads, slowly but confidently, giving each word its proper weight, 'in a place whose name I do not recall, lived a gentleman who owned a scrawny nag and a dog.'

'Very good. But how do I know you haven't learned that

passage by heart?' He chooses a page at random. 'Read.'

'God knows whether there is a Dulcinea in this world or not,' reads the boy, 'whether she is fatansical or not fatansical.'

'Fantastical. Go on.'

'These are not things that can be proved or disproved. I neither engendered nor gave birth to her. What is engendered?'

'Don Quixote is saying that he is neither the father nor the mother of Dulcinea. Engendering is what the father does to help make the baby. Go on.'

'I neither engendered nor gave birth to her, but I venerate her as one should venerate a lady who has virtues that make her famous through all the world. What is venerate?'

'Venerate is worship. Why didn't you tell me you could read?'

'I did tell you. You wouldn't listen.'

'You pretended you couldn't. Can you write too?'

'Yes.'

'Get your pencil. Write down what I read to you.'

'I haven't got a pencil. I left my pencils at school. You were going to save them. You promised.'

'I haven't forgotten.'

'For my next birthday can I have a horse?'

'You mean a horse like El Rey?'

'No, a little horse that can sleep in my room with me.'

'Be sensible, child. You can't keep a horse in an apartment.'

'Inés keeps Bolívar.'

'Yes, but a horse is much bigger than a dog.'

'I can get a baby horse.'

'A baby horse will grow into a big horse. I will tell you what. If you are good, and show señor León you belong in his class, we will get you a bicycle.'

'I don't want a bicycle. You can't save people on a bicycle.'

'Well, you are not getting a horse, so that is the end of that. Write down: "God knows whether there is a Dulcinea in this world or not." Show me.'

The boy shows him his exercise book. *Deos sabe si hay Dulcinea o no en el mundo*, he reads: the line of words marches steadily from left to right; the letters are evenly spaced and perfectly formed. 'I am impressed,' he says. 'One small point to note: in Spanish God spells his name *Dios*, not *Deos*. Otherwise, very good. First class. So you could read and write all the time, and you were just playing a trick on your mother and me and señor León.'

'I wasn't playing a trick. Who is God?'

'*God knows* is an expression. It is a way of saying no one knows. You can't –'

'Is God no one?'

'Don't change the subject. God is not no one, but he lives too far away for us to converse with him or have dealings with him. As for whether he notices us, *Dios sabe*. What are we going to tell señora Otxoa? What are we going to tell señor León? How are we going to explain to them that you were playing the fool with them, that you knew how to read and write all the time? Inés, come here! David has something to show you.'

He passes the boy's exercise book to her. She reads. 'Who is Dulcinea?' she asks.

'It doesn't matter. She is a woman Don Quixote is in love with. Not a real woman. An ideal. An idea in his mind. Look how well he has made the letters. He could write all the time.'

'Of course he can write. He can do anything – can't you, David? You can do anything. You are your mother's boy.'

With a big and (it seems to him) rather self-satisfied smile on his face, David clambers onto the bed and extends his arms to his mother, who sweeps him up in her embrace. His eyes close; he withdraws into bliss.

'We are going back to the school,' he announces to the boy, 'you and Inés and I. We are going to take *Don Quixote* along. We are going to show señor León that you can read. Once we have done that, you are going to tell him how sorry you are for having caused all this fuss.'

'I'm not going back to school. I don't need to. I can already read and write.'

'The choice is no longer between going to señor León's school and staying at home. The choice is between señor León's school and the barbed-wire school. Besides, school isn't just about reading and writing. It is also about learning to get on with other boys and girls. It is about becoming a social animal.'

'There aren't any girls in señor León's class.'

'Yes. But you meet girls during the breaks and after school.'

'I don't like girls.'

'That's what all boys say. Then suddenly one day they fall in love and get married.'

'I'm not going to get married.'

'That's what all boys say.'

'You're not married.'

'Yes, but I'm a special case. I'm too old to get married.'

'You can marry Inés.'

'I have a special relationship with your mother, David, which you are too young to understand. I am not going to say any more about it except that it is not a marrying relationship.'

'Why not?'

'Because inside each of us there is a voice, sometimes called the voice of the heart, that tells us what kind of feeling we have for a person. And the kind of feeling I have for Inés is more like goodwill than love, the marrying kind of love.'

'Is señor Daga going to marry her?'

'Is that what is worrying you? No, I doubt that señor Daga wants to marry your mother. Señor Daga isn't the marrying kind. Besides, he has a perfectly satisfactory girlfriend of his own.'

'Señor Daga says he and Frannie make fireworks. He says they make fireworks under the moon. He says I can come and watch. Can I?'

'No, you can't. When señor Daga says fireworks he doesn't mean real fireworks.'

'He does! He has a whole drawer full of fireworks. He says that Inés has perfect breasts. He says they are the most perfect breasts in the world. He says he is going to marry her for her breasts and they are going to make babies.'

'He says that, does he! Well, Inés will have thoughts of her own on the subject.'

'Why don't you want señor Daga to marry Inés?'

'Because if your mother really wanted to get married she could find a better husband.'

'Who?'

'Who? I don't know. I don't know all the men your mother knows. She must know lots of men at La Residencia.'

'She doesn't like the men at La Residencia. She says they are too old. What are breasts for?'

'A woman has breasts so that she can give milk to her baby.'

'Is there milk inside Inés's breasts? Will I have milk in my breasts when I grow up?'

'No. You will grow up to be a man, and men don't have breasts, proper breasts. Only women give milk out of their breasts. Men's breasts are dry.'

'I want to have milk too! Why can't I have milk?'

'I told you: men don't make milk.'

'What do men make?'

'Men make blood. If a man wants to give something out of his body, he gives blood. He goes to the hospital and gives his blood to sick people and people who have had accidents.'

'To make them better?'

'To make them better.'

'I am going to give blood. Can I give blood soon?'

'No. You will have to wait until you are older, until you have more blood in your body. Now there is something else I have been meaning to ask. Does it make things difficult for you at school that you don't have a normal father, like other children, that you have only me?'

'No.'

'Are you sure? Because señora Otxoa, the lady at the school, told us you might be worried about not having a proper father.'

'I'm not worried. I'm not worried about anything.'

'I'm glad to hear that. Because, you know, fathers aren't very important, compared with mothers. A mother brings you out of her body into the world. She gives you milk, as I mentioned. She holds you in her arms and protects you. Whereas a father can sometimes be a bit of a wanderer, like Don Quixote, not always there when you need him. He helps to make you, right at the beginning, but then he moves on. By the time you come into the world he may have vanished over the horizon in search of new adventures. That's why we have godfathers, trusty, staid old godfathers, and uncles. So that while the father is away there is someone to hold his place, someone to fall back on.'

'Are you my godfather or my uncle?'

'Both. You can think of me as whichever you like.'

'Who is my real father? What is his name?'

'I don't know. *Dios sabe*. It was probably in the letter you were carrying, but the letter is lost, eaten by the fishes, and shedding tears won't bring it back. As I said, it often happens that we don't know who the father is. Even the mother doesn't always know for sure. Now: are you ready to see señor León? Ready to show him how clever you are?'

Chapter 26

For an hour they wait patiently outside the school office, until the last bell has rung and the last classroom has emptied. Then señor León passes, satchel in hand, on his way home. He is clearly not pleased to see them.

'Just five minutes of your time, señor León,' he pleads. 'We want to show you how much progress David has made with his reading. Please. David, show señor León how you read.'

Señor León gestures them into his classroom. David opens *Don Quixote*. 'Somewhere in La Mancha, in a place whose name I do not recall, lived a gentleman who owned a scrawny nag –'

Señor León cuts him off peremptorily. 'I am not prepared to listen to a recitation.' He strides across the room, flings open a cupboard, returns with a book, and opens it before the child. 'Read to me.'

'Read where?'

'Read the beginning.'

'Juan and María go to the sea. Today Juan and María are going to the sea. Father tells them their friends Pablo and

Ramona may come along. Juan and María are excited. Mother makes sandwiches for the trip. Juan —'

'Stop!' says señor León. 'How did you learn to read in two weeks?'

'He has spent a lot of time on *Don Quixote*,' he, Simón, intervenes.

'Let the boy speak for himself,' says señor León. 'If you could not read two weeks ago, how is it that you can read today?'

The boy shrugs his shoulders. 'It's easy.'

'Very well, if reading is so easy, tell me what you have been reading. Tell me a story from *Don Quixote*.'

'He falls into a hole in the ground and no one knows where he is.'

'Yes?'

'Then he escapes. With a rope.'

'And what else?'

'They lock him up in a cage and he makes poo in his pants.'

'And why do they do that — lock him up?'

'Because they won't believe he is Don Quixote.'

'No. They do it because there is no such person as Don Quixote. Because Don Quixote is a made-up name. They want to take him home so that he can recover his senses.'

The boy casts him, Simón, a dubious glance.

'David has his own reading of the book,' he says to señor León. 'He has a lively imagination.'

Señor León does not deign to respond. 'Juan and Pablo go fishing,' he says. 'Juan catches five fish. Write that on the blackboard: five. Pablo catches three fish. Write that underneath the five: three. How many fish do they catch together, Juan and Pablo?'

The boy stands before the blackboard, his eyes screwed shut, as if listening for a far-off word to be spoken. The chalk does not move.

'Count. Count one-two-three-four-five. Now count three more. How many does that give you?'

The boy shakes his head. 'I can't see them,' he says in a tiny voice.

'You can't see what? You don't need to see fish, you just need to see the numbers. Look at the numbers. Five and then three more. How many is that?'

'This time . . . this time . . .' says the boy in the same tiny, lifeless voice, 'it is . . . eight.'

'Good. Make a line below the three, and write eight. So you were pretending all the time you said you could not count. Now show us how you write. Write, *Conviene que yo diga la verdad*, I must tell the truth. Write it. *Con-viene.*'

Writing from left to right, forming the letters clearly if slowly, the boy writes: *Yo soy la verdad*, I am the truth.

'You see,' says señor León, turning to Inés. 'This is what I had to deal with day after day while your son was in my class. I say, there can be only one authority in the classroom, there cannot be two. Do you disagree?'

'He is an exceptional child,' says Inés. 'What kind of school are you running if you cannot cope with a single exceptional child?'

'Refusing to listen to his teacher does not mean a child is exceptional, it just means he is disobedient. If you insist the boy must have special treatment, let him go to Punta Arenas. They know how to deal with exceptional children there.'

Inés comes erect, her eyes blazing. 'Over my dead body will he go to Punta Arenas!' she says. 'Come, my darling!'

Carefully the boy replaces the chalk in its box. Glancing neither left nor right, he follows his mother out of the room.

At the door Inés turns and hurls a last shaft at señor León: 'You are not fit to teach children!'

Señor León shrugs indifferently.

As the days pass, Inés's sense of outrage only grows stronger. She spends hours on the telephone to her brothers, making and remaking plans to leave Novilla and start a new life elsewhere, beyond the reach of the education authorities.

As for him, mulling over the episode in the classroom, he finds it harder to feel ill-used. He does not like the autocratic señor León; he agrees with Inés that he should not be in charge of small children. But why does the boy resist instruction? Is it just some inborn spirit of rebelliousness flaring up in him, fanned by his mother; or has the bad feeling between pupil and teacher a more specific cause?

He takes the boy aside. 'I know señor León can sometimes be very strict,' he says, 'and you and he have not always got along well. I am trying to understand why. Has señor León ever said anything nasty to you that you haven't reported to us?'

The boy gives him a puzzled look. 'No.'

'As I said, I am blaming no one, I am only trying to under-stand. Is there some reason why you don't like señor León, besides the fact that he is strict?'

'He has a glass eye.'

'I am aware of that. He probably lost it in an accident. He probably feels sensitive about it. But we don't make enemies of people just because they have glass eyes.'

'Why does he say there is no Don Quixote? There is a Don Quixote. He is in the book. He saves people.'

'True, there is a man in the book who calls himself Don Quixote and saves people. But some of the people he saves don't really want to be saved. They are happy just as they are. They get cross with Don Quixote and shout at him. They say he doesn't know what he is doing, he is upsetting the social order. Señor León likes order, David. He likes calm and order in his classroom. He likes order in the world. There is nothing wrong with that. Chaos can be very disturbing.'

'What is chaos?'

'I told you the other day. Chaos is when there is no order, no laws to hold on to. Chaos is just things whirling around. I can't describe it any better.'

'Is it like when the numbers open up and you fall?'

'No, it isn't, not at all. The numbers never open up. We are safe with the numbers. The numbers are what hold the universe together. You should make friends with the numbers. If you were more friendly to them, they would be more friendly to you. Then you would not have to fear they will give way beneath your feet.'

He speaks as earnestly as he can, and the boy appears to hear that. 'Why was Inés fighting with señor León?' he asks.

'They were not fighting. There was a flare-up between them, which they probably both regret, now that they have had time to reflect. But that isn't the same as fighting. Strong words aren't fighting. There are times when we have to stand up for those we love. Your mother was standing up for you. That is what a good mother, a brave mother, will do for her children: stand up for them, protect them, as long as there is breath left in her body. You should be proud to have a mother like that.'

'Inés isn't my mother.'

'Inés is your mother. She is a true mother to you. She is your true mother.'

'Are they going to take me away?'

'Is who going to take you away?'

'The people from Punta Arenas.'

'Punta Arenas is a school. The teachers at Punta Arenas don't kidnap children. That's not how the education system works.'

'I don't want to go to Punta Arenas. Promise you won't let them take me.'

'I promise. Your mother and I won't allow anyone to send you to Punta Arenas. You have seen what a tiger your mother is when it comes to defending you. No one will get past her.'

The hearing takes place at the headquarters of the Office of Education in Novilla. He and Inés are there at the appointed time. After a short wait they are escorted into a huge, echoing chamber, with row upon row of empty seats. At the head, on a raised bench, sit two men and a woman, judges or examiners. Señor León is already in attendance. No greetings pass.

'You are the parents of the boy David?' says the judge in the centre.

'I am his mother,' says Inés.

'And I am his godfather,' says he. 'He does not have a father.'

'His father is deceased?'

'His father is unknown.'

'With which of you does the boy live?'

'The boy lives with his mother. His mother and I do not live together. We do not have a connubial relationship. Nevertheless the three of us are a family. Of sorts. We are both devoted to David. I see him every day, almost.'

'We understand that David attended school for the first time in January, and was assigned to señor León's class. Then after some weeks had passed you were called in together for a consultation. Is that correct?'

'Correct.'

'And what did señor León report to you?'

'He said that David was making poor academic progress, also that he was insubordinate. He recommended that he be removed from the class.'

'Señor León, is that correct?'

Señor León nods. 'I discussed the case with señora Otxoa, the school psychologist. We agreed that David would benefit from being transferred to the school at Punta Arenas.'

The judge looks around. 'Is señora Otxoa present?'

A court official whispers in his ear. The judge speaks: 'Señora Otxoa cannot be present but has submitted a report which . . .' – he shuffles through his papers – 'which, as you say, señor León, recommends a transfer to Punta Arenas.'

The judge on the left speaks. 'Señor León, can you explain why you feel such a move is necessary? It seems a very stern measure, to send a six-year-old to Punta Arenas.'

'Señora, I have twelve years' experience as a teacher. In all that time I have not had a like case. The boy David is not stupid. He is not handicapped. On the contrary, he is both gifted and intelligent. But he will not accept direction and he will not learn. I devoted many hours to him, at the expense of the other children in the class, trying to coax into him the elements of reading, writing, and arithmetic. He made no progress. He grasped nothing. Or rather, he pretended to grasp nothing. I say *pretended* because in fact he could already read and write by the time he came to school.'

'Is this true?' asks the presiding judge.

'Read and write, yes, intermittently,' he, Simón, responds. 'He has good days and bad days. In the case of arithmetic he is experiencing certain difficulties, philosophical difficulties I like to call them, that hinder his progress. He is an exceptional child. Exceptionally intelligent, and exceptional in other ways too. He taught himself to read out of the book *Don Quixote*, in an abridged version for children. I became aware of this only very recently.'

'The point at issue,' says señor León, 'is not whether the boy can read and write, or who taught him, it is whether he can be accommodated in an ordinary school. I do not have the time to deal with a child who refuses to learn and who by his behaviour disrupts the normal activities of the class.'

'He is barely six years old!' Inés bursts out. 'What kind of teacher are you that you cannot control a six-year-old child?'

Señor León stiffens. 'I did not say I cannot control your son. What I cannot do is fulfil my duties to the other children while he is in the classroom. Your son is in need of special attention of a kind that we cannot provide in a normal school. That is why I recommended Punta Arenas.'

A silence falls.

'Do you have anything more to say, señora?' asks the presiding judge.

Inés tosses her head angrily.

'Señor?'

'No.'

'Then I would ask you to retire – you too, señor León – and wait for our decision.'

They retire to the waiting room, the three of them together. Inés cannot bring herself to look at señor León. After a few minutes they are recalled. 'The decision of this tribunal,' says the presiding judge, 'is that the recommendation of señor León, seconded and supported by the school psychologist and by his principal, be upheld. The boy David will be transferred to the school at Punta Arenas, the transfer to take place as soon as possible. That is all. Thank you for attending.'

'Your honour,' he says, 'may I ask whether we have a right of appeal?'

'You may take the matter to the civil courts, of course, that is your right. But an appeal procedure may not be used as a means of forestalling this tribunal's decision. That is to say, the transfer to Punta Arenas will take effect whether or not you go to the courts.'

'Diego will pick us up tomorrow evening,' says Inés. 'It is all settled. He just has to finish off some business.'

'And where are you planning to go?'

'How must I know? Somewhere out of the reach of these people and their persecutions.'

'Are you really going to let a band of school administrators hound you out of the city, Inés? How are you going to live, you and Diego and the child?'

'I don't know. Like gypsies, I suppose. Why don't you help instead of just raising objections?'

'What are gypsies?' intervenes the boy.

'Living like gypsies is just a way of speaking,' he says. 'You and I were gypsies of a kind while we lived in the camp at Belstar. Being a gypsy means that you don't have a proper home, a place to lay your head. It's not much fun being a gypsy.'

'Will I have to go to school?'

'No. Gypsy children don't go to school.'

'Then I want to be a gypsy with Inés and Diego.'

He turns to Inés. 'I wish you had discussed this with me. Do you really mean to sleep under hedges and eat berries while you hide from the law?'

'This has nothing to do with you,' replies Inés icily. 'You don't care if David goes to a reformatory. I do.'

'Punta Arenas is not a reformatory.'

'It is a dumping ground for delinquents – delinquents and orphans. My child is not going to that place, never, never, never.'

'I agree with you. David does not deserve to be sent to Punta Arenas. Not because it is a dumping ground but because he is too young to be separated from his parents.'

'Then why did you not stand up against those judges? Why did you bow and scrape and say *Sí señor, Sí señor*? Don't you believe in the boy?'

'Of course I believe in him. I believe he is exceptional and merits exceptional treatment. But those people have the law behind them, and we are in no position to challenge the law.'

'Even when the law is bad?'

'It is not a question of good or bad, Inés, it is a question of power. If you run away they will send the police after you and the police will catch you. You will be declared an unfit mother and the child will be taken away from you. He will be sent to Punta Arenas and you will have a battle on your hands ever to regain custody.'

'They will never take my child away from me. I will die first.' Her breast heaves. 'Why don't you help me instead of taking their side all the time?'

He reaches out to placate her but she shakes him off, sinks

down on the bed. 'Leave me alone! Don't touch me! You don't really believe in the child. You don't know what it means to believe.'

The boy leans over her, strokes her hair. On his lips there is a smile. 'Ssh,' he says; 'ssh.' He lies down beside her; his thumb goes into his mouth; his eyes take on a glassy, absent look; within minutes he is asleep.

Chapter 27

Álvaro calls the stevedores together. 'Friends,' he says, 'there is a matter we need to discuss. As you will remember, our comrade Simón proposed that we give up unloading cargoes by hand and resort instead to a mechanical crane.'

The men nod. Some glance in his direction. Eugenio flashes him a smile.

'Well, today I have news for you. A comrade from Roadworks tells me there is a crane at their depot that has been standing idle for months. If we wish to borrow it for a trial, he says, we are welcome to have it.

'What shall we do, friends? Shall we accept his offer? Shall we see whether, as Simón claims, a crane will change our lives? Who wants to speak first? Simón, you?'

He is taken completely by surprise. His mind is occupied with Inés and her plans for flight; not in weeks has he given a thought to cranes or rats or the economics of grain transport; indeed, he has come to depend on the unvarying grind of labour to exhaust him and bring him the boon of deep, dreamless sleep.

'Not me,' he says. 'I have said my say.'

'Who else?' says Álvaro.

Eugenio speaks up. 'I say we should try the crane. Our friend Simón has a wise head on his shoulders. Who knows, he may be right. Maybe we should indeed move with the times. We will never know for sure unless we try.'

There is a murmur of agreement from the men.

'Shall we try the crane then?' says Álvaro. 'Shall I tell our comrade in Roadworks to bring it along?'

'Aye!' says Eugenio, and raises his hand. 'Aye!' say the stevedores in chorus, raising their hands. Even he, Simón, raises a hand. The vote is unanimous.

The crane arrives the next morning on the back of a truck. It was once painted white, but the paint has flaked and the metal is rusted. It looks as if it has stood outdoors in the rain for a very long time. It is also smaller than he had expected. It runs on clattering steel tracks; the driver sits in a cab over the tracks, operating the controls that rotate the arm and turn the winch.

It takes the best part of an hour to ease the machine off the back of the truck. Álvaro's friend from Roadworks is impatient to leave. 'Who is going to drive?' he asks. 'I'll give him a quick tour of the controls, then I must be off.'

'Eugenio!' Álvaro calls out. 'You spoke in favour of the crane. Would you like to drive it?'

Eugenio looks around. 'If no one else wants to, I will.'

'Good! Then you are the man.'

Eugenio proves a quick learner. In no time at all he is racing back and forth along the quay and rotating the arm, on which the hook swings gaily.

'I've taught him what I can,' the operator reports to Álvaro. 'Let him go carefully for the first few days and he'll be all right.'

The arm of the crane is just long enough to reach up to the ship's deck. The stevedores bring the bags up one by one from the hold, as before; but now, instead of carrying them down the gangplank, they drop them into a canvas sling. When the sling is full for the first time they give Eugenio a shout. The hook catches the sling; the steel rope tightens; the sling rises over the deck rails; and with a flourish Eugenio swings the load around and down in a wide arc. The men give a cheer; but their cheers turn to cries of alarm as the sling bumps the dockside and begins to spin and lurch out of control. The men scatter, all save he, Simón, who is either too self-absorbed to see what is going on or too sluggish to move. He has a glimpse of Eugenio staring down at him from the cab, mouthing words he cannot hear. Then the swinging load strikes him in the midriff and knocks him backwards. He staggers against a stanchion, trips over a rope, and tumbles into the space between the quay and the steel plates of the freighter. For a moment he is held there, gripped so tightly that it hurts to breathe. He is intensely aware that the ship has to drift only an inch and he will be crushed like an insect. Then the pressure slackens and he drops feet first into the water.

'Help!' he gasps. 'Help me!'

A lifebuoy slaps into the water beside him, painted in bright red and white bands. From above comes the voice of Álvaro: 'Simón! Listen! Hold on and we will pull you clear.'

He grips the buoy; like a fish he is drawn along the quayside into open water. Again Álvaro's voice: 'Hold tight, we are going to pull you up!' But when the buoy begins to rise the pain is suddenly too much. His grip fails and he falls back into the water. There is oil all over him, in his eyes, in his mouth. *Is this then how it ends?* he says to himself. *Like a rat? How ignominious!*

But now Álvaro is beside him, bobbing in the water, his hair plastered to his scalp with oil. 'Relax, old friend,' says Álvaro. 'I will hold you.' Gratefully he relaxes into Álvaro's arms. 'Haul!' calls Álvaro; and the two of them, in tight embrace, rise out of the water.

He comes to himself in confusion. He is on his back looking up into an empty sky. There are vague figures around him, and a buzz of talk, but he cannot make out a word. His eyes close and he is gone again.

He wakes again to a thudding noise. The noise seems to be coming from inside him, from inside his head. 'Wake up, *viejo*!' says a voice. He opens one eye, sees a fat, sweating face above him. *I am awake*, he would like to say, but his voice has gone dead.

'Look at me!' say the fat lips. 'Can you hear me? Blink your eyes if you can hear me.'

He blinks.

'Good. I am going to give you a shot of painkiller, then we will get you out of here.'

Painkiller? *I have no pain*, he wants to say. *Why should I have pain?* But whatever it is that speaks for him will not speak today.

Because he is a member of the stevedores' union – an affiliation of which he was not aware – he is entitled to a private room in the hospital. He is tended in his room by a team of kindly nurses, to one of whom, a middle-aged woman named Clara with grey eyes and a quiet smile, he grows quite attached in the weeks that follow.

The consensus seems to be that he got off lightly from his accident. He has broken three ribs. A sliver of bone had punctured a lung, and a small surgical operation was needed to remove it (would he like to keep the bone as a memento? – it is in a phial by his bedside). There are cuts and bruises on his face and upper body, and he has lost some skin, but there is no evidence of injury to the brain. A few days under observation, a few weeks more of taking things easy, and he should be himself again. In the meantime, controlling the pain will be the first priority.

His most constant visitor is Eugenio, who is full of remorse for his incompetence with the crane. He tries his best to comfort the younger man – 'How could you be expected to master a new machine in so short a time?' – but Eugenio will not be comforted. When he surfaces from his slumbers it is more often than not Eugenio who swims into his vision, watching over him.

Álvaro visits too, as do other comrades from the docks. Álvaro has spoken to the doctors, and bears the news that, even though he may expect a full recovery, it would be unwise for him, at his age, to go back to a life of stevedoring.

'Perhaps I can become a crane operator,' he suggests. 'I couldn't do worse than Eugenio.'

'If you want to be a crane operator you will have to transfer to Roadworks,' replies Álvaro. 'Cranes are too dangerous. They have no future at the docks. Cranes were always a bad idea.'

He hopes that Inés will come visiting, but she does not. He fears the worst: that she has carried out her plan to take the boy and flee.

He mentions his concern to Clara. 'I have a woman friend,' he says, 'whose young son I am very fond of. For reasons I won't go into, the education authorities have been threatening to take him away from her and send him to a special school. Could I ask you a favour? Could you telephone her and find out if there have been any developments?'

'Of course,' says Clara. 'But wouldn't you like to speak to her yourself? I can bring a telephone to your bed.'

He calls the Blocks. The telephone is answered by a neighbour, who goes off, comes back, and reports that Inés is not at home. He calls later in the day, again without success.

Early the next morning, in the nameless space between sleeping and waking, he has a dream or vision. With uncommon clarity he sees a two-wheeled chariot hovering in the air at the foot of his bed. The chariot is made of ivory or some metal inlaid with ivory, and is drawn by two white horses, neither of whom is El Rey. Grasping the reins in one hand, holding the other hand aloft in a regal gesture, is the boy, naked save for a cotton loincloth.

How the chariot and the two horses fit into the little hospital room is a mystery to him. The chariot seems to hang in the air without any effort on the part of horses or charioteer. Far from being frozen, the horses now and then paw the air or toss their heads and snort. As for the boy, he does not seem to tire of holding his arm up. The look on his face is a familiar one: self-satisfaction, perhaps even triumph.

At one point the boy looks straight at him. *Read my eyes*, he seems to be saying.

The dream, or vision, lasts for two or three minutes. Then it fades, and the room is as it was before.

He tells Clara about it. 'Do you believe in telepathy?' he asks. 'I had a feeling David was trying to tell me something.'

'And what was that?'

'I am not sure. Perhaps that he and his mother need help. Or perhaps not. The message was – how shall I put it? – dark.'

'Well, remember that the painkiller you are taking is an opiate. Opiates give us dreams, opium dreams.'

'It wasn't an opium dream. It was the real thing.'

From then onward he declines the painkillers, and suffers accordingly. The nights are worst: even the slightest movement brings an electric stab of pain in his chest.

He has nothing to distract him, nothing to read. The hospital has no library, offers only old numbers of popular magazines (recipes, hobbies, women's fashions). He complains to Eugenio, who responds by bringing him the textbook from his philosophy course ('I know you are a serious person'). The book is, as he feared, about tables and chairs. He lays it aside. 'I'm sorry, it's not my kind of philosophy.'

'What kind of philosophy would you like instead?' asks Eugenio.

'The kind that shakes one. That changes one's life.'

Eugenio gives him a puzzled look. 'Is there something wrong with your life then?' he asks. 'Aside from your injuries.'

'Something is missing, Eugenio. I know it should not be so, but it is. The life I have is not enough for me. I wish someone, some saviour, would descend from the skies and wave a magic wand and say, *Behold, read this book and all your questions will be answered*. Or, *Behold, here is an entirely new life for you*. You don't understand that kind of talk, do you?'

'No, I can't claim that I do.'

'Never mind. It's just a passing mood. Tomorrow I will be my old self again.'

He should plan for his discharge, his doctor tells him. Does he have somewhere to stay? Is there someone who will cook for him, care for him, help him to get around while he mends? Would he like to speak to a social worker? 'No social worker,' he replies. 'Let me discuss the matter with my friends and see what can be arranged.'

Eugenio offers him a room in the apartment that he shares with two comrades. He, Eugenio, will be happy to sleep on the sofa. He thanks Eugenio but declines.

At his request, Álvaro investigates nursing homes. The West Blocks, he reports, have a facility which, though intended for the care of the aged, also takes in convalescents. He asks Álvaro to put his name down on the facility's waiting list. 'It's a bit shameful to say,' he says, 'but I hope there will be a vacancy before too long.' 'If there is no ill will in your heart,' Álvaro reassures him, 'that qualifies as a permissible hope.' 'Permissible?' he queries. 'Permissible,' Álvaro confirms.

Then suddenly all his woes are whisked away. From the corridor come the sounds of bright young voices. Clara appears at the door. 'You have visitors,' she announces. She stands aside, and Fidel and David come rushing in, followed by Inés and Álvaro. 'Simón!' cries David. 'Did you really fall into the sea?'

His heart gives a leap. Gingerly he holds out his arms. 'Come here! Yes, I had a little accident, I fell into the water, but I barely got wet. My friends pulled me out.'

The boy clambers onto the high bed, bumping him, sending stabs of pain through him. But the pain is nothing. 'My dearest boy! My treasure! Light of my life!'

The boy pulls free of his embrace. 'I escaped,' he announces. 'I told you I would escape. I walked through the barbed wire.'

Escaped? Walked through the wire? He is confused. What is the boy talking about? And why this strange new outfit: a tight turtle-neck sweater, short (very short) pants, shoes with little white socks that barely cover his ankles? 'Thank you for coming, all of you,' he says, 'but David – where did you escape from? Are you talking about Punta Arenas? Did they take you to Punta Arenas? Inés, did you let them take him to Punta Arenas?'

'I didn't let them. They came while he was playing outside. They took him away in a car. How was I to stop them?'

'I never dreamed it would come to that. But you escaped, David? Tell me about it. Tell me how you escaped.'

But Álvaro intervenes. 'Before we get into that, Simón, can we discuss your move? When do you think you will be able to walk?'

'Can't he walk?' asks the boy. 'Can't you walk, Simón?'

'Just for the next short while I am going to need help. Until all the aches and pains have gone away.'

'Are you going to ride in a wheelchair? Can I push you?'

'Yes, you can push me in a wheelchair, as long as you don't go too fast. Fidel can push too.'

'The reason I ask,' says Álvaro, 'is that I have been in touch again with the nursing home. I told them you were expecting a full recovery and wouldn't need special care. In that case, they said, they can admit you at once, as long as you don't mind sharing a room. How would you feel about that? It would solve a lot of problems.'

Sharing a room with another old man. Who snores in the night and spits into his handkerchief. Who complains about the daughter who has abandoned him. Who is full of resentment against the newcomer, the invader of his space. 'Of course I don't mind,' he says. 'It's a relief to have somewhere definite to go. It's a weight off everyone's shoulders. Thank you, Álvaro, for seeing to it.'

'And the union will pay, of course,' says Álvaro. 'For your residence, for meals, for all your needs while you are there.'

'That's good.'

'Well, I must get back to work now. I'll leave you to Inés and the boys. I am sure they have lots to tell you.'

Is he imagining things, or does Inés cast Álvaro a furtive glance as he departs? *Don't leave me alone with him, this man we are in the course of betraying!* Parked in some antiseptic room in the far-off West Blocks, where he knows not a soul. Left to moulder. *Don't leave me with him!*

'Sit down, Inés. David, tell me your story from beginning to end. Leave nothing out. We have lots of time.'

'I escaped,' says the boy. 'I told you I would. I walked through the barbed wire.'

'I had a phone call,' says Inés. 'From a complete stranger. A woman. She said she had found David wandering around the streets with no clothes.'

'No clothes? You ran away from Punta Arenas, David, with no clothes? When was this? Did no one try to stop you?'

'I left my clothes in the barbed wire. Didn't I promise you I would escape? I can escape from anywhere.'

'And where did this lady find you, the lady who telephoned Inés?'

'She found him in the street, in the dark, cold and naked.'

'I wasn't cold. I wasn't naked,' says the boy.

'You weren't wearing any clothes,' says Inés. 'That means you were naked.'

'Never mind about that,' he, Simón, interrupts. 'Why did the lady contact you, Inés? Why not the school? That was surely the obvious thing to do.'

'She hates the school. Everyone hates it,' says the boy.

'Is it really such a terrible place?'

The boy nods vigorously.

For the first time Fidel speaks. 'Did they beat you?'

'You have to be fourteen before they can beat you. When you are fourteen they can beat you if you are insubordinate.'

'Tell Simón about the fish,' says Inés.

'Every Friday they made us eat fish.' The boy shudders theatrically. 'I hate fish. They've got eyes like señor León.'

Fidel giggles. In a moment the two boys are laughing uncontrollably.

'What else was so horrible about Punta Arenas besides the fish?'

'They made us wear sandals. And they wouldn't let Inés visit. They said she wasn't my mother. They said I was a ward. A ward is someone who hasn't got a mother or a father.'

'That's nonsense. Inés is your mother and I am your godfather, which is as good as a father, sometimes better. Your godfather watches over you.'

'You didn't watch over me. You let them take me to Punta Arenas.'

'That's true. I was a bad godfather. I slept while I should have watched. But I have learned my lesson. I'll take better care of you in the future.'

'Will you fight them if they come back?'

'Yes, as best I can. I will borrow a sword. I'll say, *Try to steal my boy again and you will have Don Simón to deal with!*'

The boy glows with pleasure. 'Bolívar too,' he says. 'Bolívar can guard me in the night. Are you coming to live with us?' He turns to his mother. 'Can Simón come and live with us?'

'Simón has to go to a nursing home to recuperate. He can't walk. He can't climb stairs.'

'He can! You can walk, can't you, Simón?'

'Of course I can. Normally I can't, because of my aches and pains. But for you I can do anything: climb stairs, ride horses, anything. You have just to say the word.'

'Which word?'

'The magic word. The word that will heal me.'

'Do I know the word?'

'Of course you do. Say it.'

'The word is . . . Abracadabra!'

He pushes aside the sheet (fortunately he is wearing the hospital's pyjamas) and swings his wasted legs over the side of the bed. 'I'll need help, boys.'

Bracing himself on the shoulders of Fidel and David, he stands precariously erect, takes a tottering first step, a second. 'See, you do know the word! Inés, can you bring the wheel-chair closer?' He subsides into the wheelchair. 'Now let's go for a promenade. I'd like to see what the world looks like, after all this time shut up. Who wants to push?'

'Aren't you going to come home with us?' asks the boy.

'Not for a while yet. Not until I have my strength back.'

'But we are going to be gypsies! If you stay in the hospital you can't be a gypsy!'

He turns to Inés. 'What is this? I thought we had given up on the gypsy business.'

Inés stiffens. 'He can't go back to that school. I won't allow it. My brothers are going to come with us, both of them. We will take the car.'

'Four people in that old rattletrap? What if it breaks down? And where will you stay?'

'It doesn't matter. We will do odd jobs. We will pick fruit. Señor Daga lent us money.'

'Daga! So he is behind this!'

'Well, David is not going back to that terrible school.'

'Where they make you wear sandals and eat fish. It doesn't sound so terrible to me.'

'There are boys there who smoke and drink and carry knives. It's a school for criminals. If David goes back he will be scarred for life.'

The boy speaks. 'What does that mean, *scarred for life*?'

'It's just a way of speaking,' says Inés. 'It means the school will have a bad effect on you.'

'Like a wound?'

'Yes, like a wound.'

'I've got lots of wounds already. I got them from the barbed wire. Do you want to see my wounds, Simón?'

'Your mother meant something else. She means a wound to your soul. The kind of wound that does not heal. Is it true that boys at the school carry knives? Are you sure it isn't just one boy?'

'It's lots of boys. And they've got a mother duck and duck-lings and one of the boys trod on a duckling and its inside came out of its bum and I wanted to push them back but the teacher wouldn't let me, he said I must let the duckling die, and I said I wanted to breathe into it, but he wouldn't let me. And we had to do gardening. Every afternoon after school they made us dig. I hate digging.'

'Digging is good for you. If no one were prepared to dig, we would have no crops, no food. Digging makes you strong. It gives you muscles.'

'You can grow seeds on blotting paper. Our teacher showed us. You don't need to dig.'

'One or two seeds, yes. But if you want a proper crop, if you want to grow enough wheat to make bread and feed people, the seed has to go into the ground.'

'I hate bread. Bread is boring. I like ice cream.'

'I know you like ice cream. But you can't live on ice cream, whereas you can live on bread.'

'You can live on ice cream. Señor Daga does.'

'Señor Daga just pretends to live on ice cream. In private I'm sure he eats bread like everyone else. Anyway, you shouldn't take señor Daga as a model.'

'Señor Daga gives me presents. You and Inés never give me presents.'

'That's untrue, my boy, untrue and unkind. Inés loves you and looks after you, and so do I. Whereas señor Daga, in his heart, has no love for you at all.'

'He does love me! He wants me to come and live with him! He told Inés and Inés told me.'

'I am sure she will never agree to that. You belong with your mother. That is what we have been struggling for all this time. Señor Daga may seem glamorous and exciting to you, but when you are older you will realize that glamorous, exciting people aren't necessarily good people.'

'What is glamorous?'

'Glamorous means wearing earrings and carrying a knife.'

'Señor Daga is in love with Inés. He is going to make babies in her tummy.'

'David!' Inés explodes.

'It's true! Inés said I mustn't tell you, you will be jealous. Is it true, Simón? Are you jealous?'

'No, of course I am not jealous. It is none of my business. What I am trying to tell you is that señor Daga is not a good person. He may invite you to his home and give you ice cream, but he doesn't have your best interests at heart.'

'What are my best interests?'

'Your first interest is to grow up to be a good man. Like the good seed, the seed that goes deep into the earth and puts forth strong roots, and then when its time comes bursts forth into the light and bears manyfold. That is what you should be like. Like Don Quixote. Don Quixote rescued maidens. He protected the poor from the rich and powerful. Take him as your model, not señor Daga. Protect the poor. Save the oppressed. And honour your mother.'

'No! My mother must honour me! Anyway, señor Daga says Don Quixote is old-fashioned. He says no one rides a horse any more.'

'Well, if you wanted to you could easily prove him wrong. Mount your horse and raise your sword on high. That will silence señor Daga. Mount El Rey.'

'El Rey is dead.'

'No, he is not. El Rey lives. You know that.'

'Where?' the boy whispers. His eyes suddenly fill with tears, his lips quiver, he can barely bring out the word.

'I don't know, but somewhere El Rey is waiting for you to come. If you will search you will be sure to find him.'

Chapter 28

It is the day of his discharge from hospital. He says his good-byes to the nurses. To Clara he says: 'I will not easily forget your care. I would like to believe there was more than just goodwill behind it.' Clara does not answer; but from the direct look she gives him he knows he is right.

The hospital has set aside a car and driver to convey him to his new home in the West Blocks; Eugenio has offered to accompany him and see that he is safely settled in. Once they are on the road, however, he asks the driver to make a detour past the East Blocks.

'I can't do that,' replies the driver. 'It's outside my commission.'

'Please,' he says. 'I need to pick up some clothes. I will be only five minutes.'

Grudgingly the driver consents.

'You mentioned difficulties you have been having with your youngster's schooling,' says Eugenio as they take the turn-off to the east. 'What difficulties are those?'

'The school authorities want to take him away from us. By force, if necessary. They want to send him back to Punta Arenas.'

'To Punta Arenas! Why?'

'Because they have built a school in Punta Arenas especially for children who are bored with stories about Juan and María and what they did at the seaside. Who are bored and show their boredom. Children who won't obey the rules for addition and subtraction laid down by their class teacher. The man-made rules. Two plus two equalling four and so forth.'

'That's bad. But why won't your boy do sums the way his teacher tells him?'

'Why should he, when a voice inside him says the teacher's way is not the true way?'

'I don't follow. If the rules are true for you and for me and for everyone else, how can they not be true for him? And why do you call them man-made rules?'

'Because two and two could just as well equal three or five or ninety-nine if we so decided.'

'But two and two do equal four. Unless you give some strange, special meaning to *equal*. You can count it off for yourself: one *two* three *four*. If two and two really equalled three then everything would collapse into chaos. We would be in another universe, with other physical laws. In the existing universe two and two equal four. It is a universal rule, independent of us, not man-made at all. Even if you and I were to cease to be, two and two would go on equalling four.'

'Yes, but *which* two and *which* two make four? Most of the time, Eugenio, I think the child simply doesn't understand numbers, the way a cat or dog doesn't understand them. But now and then I have to ask myself: Is there anyone on earth to whom numbers are more real?

'While I was in hospital with nothing else to do, I tried, as a mental exercise, to see the world through David's eyes. Put an apple before him and what does he see? An apple: not *one* apple, just *an* apple. Put two apples before him. What does he see? An apple and an apple: not two apples, not the same apple twice, just an apple and an apple. Now along comes señor León (señor León is his class teacher) and demands: *How many apples, child?* What is the answer? What are *apples*? What is the singular of which *apples* is the plural? Three men in a car heading for the East Blocks: who is the singular of which *men* is the plural – Eugenio or Simón or our friend the driver whose name I don't know? Are we three, or are we one and one and one?

'You throw up your hands in exasperation, and I can see why. One and one and one make three, you say, and I am bound to agree. Three men in a car: simple. But David won't follow us. He won't take the steps we take when we count: *one* step *two* step *three*. It is as if the numbers were islands floating in a great black sea of nothingness, and he were each time being asked to close his eyes and launch himself across the void. *What if I fall?* – that is what he asks himself. *What if I fall and then keep falling for ever?* Lying in bed in the middle of the night, I could sometimes swear that I too was falling – falling under the same spell that grips the boy. *If getting from one to two is so hard*, I asked myself, *how shall I ever get from zero to one?*

From nowhere to somewhere: it seemed to demand a miracle each time.'

'The boy certainly has a lively imagination,' Eugenio muses. 'Floating islands. But he will grow out of it. It must come out of long-standing feelings of insecurity. One can't help noticing how highly strung he is, how agitated he gets for no reason at all. Is there a history behind it, do you know? Did his parents fight a lot?'

'His parents?'

'His real parents. Does he carry some scar, some trauma from the past? No? Never mind. Once he begins to feel more secure in his surroundings, once it begins to dawn on him that the universe – not just the realm of numbers but everything else too – is ruled by laws, that nothing happens by chance, he will come to his senses and settle down.'

'That is what his school psychologist said. Señora Otxoa. Once he finds his feet in the world, once he accepts who he is, his learning difficulties will disappear.'

'I'm sure she is right. It will just take time.'

'Perhaps. Perhaps. But what if we are wrong and he is right? What if between one and two there is no bridge at all, only empty space? And what if we, who so confidently take the step, are in fact falling through space, only we don't know it because we insist on keeping our blindfold on? What if this boy is the only one among us with eyes to see?'

'That is like saying, *What if the mad are really sane and the sane are really mad?* It is, if you don't mind my saying so, Simón, schoolboy philosophizing. Some things are simply true. An apple is an apple is an apple. An apple and another apple make two apples. One Simón and one Eugenio make two passengers in a car. A child doesn't find statements like that hard to accept – an ordinary child. He doesn't find them hard because they are true, because from birth we are, so to speak, attuned to their truth. As for being afraid of the empty spaces between numbers, have you ever pointed out to David that the number of numbers is infinite?'

'More than once. There is no last number, I have told him. The numbers go on for ever. But what has that to do with it?'

'There are good infinities and bad infinities, Simón. We talked about bad infinities before – remember? A bad infinity is like finding yourself in a dream within a dream within yet another dream, and so forth endlessly. Or finding yourself in a life that is only a prelude to another life which is only a prelude, et cetera. But the numbers aren't like that. The numbers constitute a good infinity. Why? Because, being infinite in number, they fill all the spaces in the universe, packed one against another tight as bricks. So we are safe. There is nowhere to fall. Point that out to the boy. It will reassure him.'

'I will do so. But somehow I do not think he will be comforted.'

'Don't misunderstand me, my friend. I am not on the side of the school system. I agree, it sounds very rigid, very old-fashioned. In my view, there is much to be said for a more practical, more vocational kind of schooling. David could learn to be a plumber or a carpenter, for instance. You don't need higher mathematics for that.'

'Or for stevedoring.'

'Or for stevedoring. Stevedoring is a perfectly honourable occupation, as both of us know. No, I agree with you: your youngster is getting a raw deal. Nevertheless, his teachers do have a point, don't they? It is not just a matter of following the rules of arithmetic but of learning to follow rules in general. Señora Inés is a very nice lady, but she does spoil the child excessively, anyone can see that. If a child is continually indulged and told he is special, if he is allowed to make up the rules for himself as he goes, what kind of man will he grow up to be? Perhaps a little discipline at this stage of his life won't do young David any harm.'

Though he feels the greatest goodwill towards Eugenio, though he has been touched by his readiness to befriend an older comrade as well as by his many kindnesses, though he does not blame him at all for the accident at the docks – hustled behind the controls of a crane, he himself would have done no better – he has never found it in his heart actually to like the man. He finds him prim and blinkered and self-important. His criticism of Inés makes him bristle. Nonetheless, he holds his temper in check.

'There are two schools of thought, Eugenio, on the upbringing of children. One says that we should shape them like clay, forming them into virtuous citizens. The other says that we are children only once, that a happy childhood is the foundation of a happy later life. Inés belongs to the latter school; and, because she is his mother, because the bonds between a child and his mother are sacred, I follow her.

Therefore no, I do not believe that more of the discipline of the schoolroom will be good for David.'

They drive on in silence.

At the East Blocks he asks the driver to wait while Eugenio helps him out of the car. Together they slowly make their way up the stairs. Emerging onto the second-floor corridor, they are greeted by a dismaying sight. Outside Inés's apartment stand two persons, a man and a woman, in identical dark blue uniform. The door is open; from within comes the sound of Inés's voice, high-pitched, angry. 'No!' she is saying. 'No, no, no! You have no right!'

What prevents the strangers from entering – he sees as they approach – is the dog, Bolívar, who crouches at the threshold, ears flattened, teeth bared, growling softly, watching their every move, ready to leap.

'Simón!' Inés calls out to him, 'Tell these people to go away! They want to take David back to that awful reformatory. Tell them they have no right!'

He draws a deep breath. 'You have no rights over the boy,' he says, addressing the uniformed woman, small and neat as a bird, in contrast to her rather heavy-set companion. 'I was the one who brought him here to Novilla. I am his guardian. I am in all respects that matter his father. Señora Inés' – he gestures towards Inés – 'is in all respects his mother. You do not know our son as we do. There is nothing wrong with him that needs to be corrected. He is a sensitive boy who has certain difficulties with the school curriculum – nothing more than that. He sees pitfalls, philosophical pitfalls, where an ordinary child would not. You cannot punish him for a philosophical disagreement. You cannot take him away from his home and his family. We will not allow it.'

His speech is followed by a long silence. From behind her watchdog, Inés glares belligerently at the woman. 'We will not allow it,' she repeats at last.

'And you, señor?' asks the woman, addressing Eugenio.

'Señor Eugenio is a friend,' he, Simón, intervenes. 'He has kindly accompanied me from the hospital. He is not part of this imbroglio.'

'David is an exceptional child,' says Eugenio. 'His father is devoted to him. I have seen that with my own eyes.'

'Barbed wire!' says Inés. 'What kind of delinquents do you have in your school that you need barbed wire to keep them in?'

'The barbed wire is a myth,' says the woman. 'A complete fabrication. I have no idea how it originated. There is no barbed wire at Punta Arenas. On the contrary, we have –'

'He walked through the barbed wire!' Inés interrupts, raising her voice again. 'It tore his clothes to shreds! And you have the cheek to say there is no barbed wire!'

'On the contrary, we have an open-door policy,' the woman presses on gamely. 'Our children are free to come and go. There are not even locks on the doors. David, tell us truthfully, is there barbed wire at Punta Arenas?'

Now that he looks more closely, he can see that the boy has been present throughout this altercation, half obscured behind his mother, listening solemnly, his thumb in his mouth.

'Is there really barbed wire?' the woman repeats.

'There is barbed wire,' the boy says slowly. 'I walked through the barbed wire.'

The woman shakes her head, gives a little smile of disbelief. 'David,' she says softly, 'you know and I know that that is a fib. There is no barbed wire at Punta Arenas. I invite you all to come and see for yourselves. We can get in the car and drive there this minute. No barbed wire, none.'

'I don't need to see,' says Inés. 'I believe my child. If he says there is barbed wire, then it is true.'

'But is it true?' says the woman, addressing the boy. 'Is it real barbed wire, that we can see with our own eyes, or is it the sort of barbed wire that only certain people can see and touch, certain people with a lively imagination?'

'It is real. It is true,' says the boy.

A silence falls.

'So this is the issue,' says the woman at last. 'Barbed wire. If I can prove to you that there is no barbed wire, señora, that the child is just making up stories, will you let him go?'

'You can never prove that,' says Inés. 'If the child says there is barbed wire then I believe him, there is barbed wire.'

'And you?' asks the woman.

'I believe him too,' he, Simón, replies.

'And you, señor?'

Eugenio looks uncomfortable. 'I would have to see for myself,' he says at last. 'You can't expect me to commit myself, sight unseen.'

'Well, we seem to be at an impasse,' says the woman. 'Señora, let me put it to you. You have two choices: either you obey the law and release the child to us, or we are forced to call in the police. Which is it to be?'

'Over my dead body will you take him away,' says Inés. She turns to him. 'Simón! Do something!'

He stares back helplessly. 'What must I do?'

'This will not be a permanent separation,' says the woman. 'David can come home every second weekend.'

Inés is grimly silent.

He makes a last appeal. 'Señora, please reflect. What you are proposing to do will break a mother's heart. And for what? Here we have a child who happens to have ideas of his own about, of all things, arithmetic – not history, not language, but humble arithmetic – ideas that he will very likely grow out of before long. What kind of crime is it for a child to say that two and two make three? How is it going to shake the social order? Yet for that you want to tear him away from his parents and lock him up behind barbed wire! A six-year-old child!'

'There is no barbed wire,' the woman repeats patiently. 'And the child has been referred to Punta Arenas not because he can't do sums but because he is in need of specialized care. Pablo,' she says, addressing her silent companion, 'wait here. I would like to have a private word with this gentleman.' And to him: 'Señor, can I ask you to come with me?'

Eugenio takes his arm but he brushes the young man off. 'I am all right, thank you, as long as I don't have to hurry.' To the woman he explains: 'I have just come out of hospital. A work-place injury. I am still a little sore.'

He and she are alone in the stairwell. 'Señor,' says the woman in a low voice, 'please understand, I am not some kind of truant officer. By training I am a psychologist. I work with the children at Punta Arenas. During the brief time when David was with us, before he ran away, I took it upon myself to observe him closely. Because — I agree with you — he is very young to be away from home, and I was concerned that he should not feel forsaken.

'What I saw was a sweet child, very honest, very direct, not afraid to talk about his feelings. I saw something else too. I saw how quickly he was taken to the hearts of the other boys, the older boys in particular. Even the roughest ones. I do not exaggerate when I say they adored him. They wanted to make him their mascot.'

'Their mascot? The only kind of mascot I know is an animal that you crown with a garland and lead around on a string. What is there to be proud of in being a mascot?'

'He was their pet, their universal pet. They don't understand why he ran away. They are heartbroken. They ask after him every day. Why am I telling you this, señor? So that you can understand that from the beginning David found a place for himself in our community at Punta Arenas. Punta Arenas is not like a normal school, where a child spends a few hours each day absorbing instruction, and then goes home. At Punta Arenas teachers and students and advisors are bonded tightly together. Why then did David run away, you may ask? Not because he was unhappy, I can assure you. It was because he has a soft heart and could not bear the thought of señora Inés pining for him.'

303

'Señora Inés is his mother,' he says.

The woman shrugs. 'If he had waited a few days he could have come home on a visit. Can you not persuade your wife to release him?'

'And how do you think I should persuade her, señora? You have seen her. What magic formula do you think I possess that will change the mind of a woman like that? No, your problem is not how to take David away from his mother. You have that power. Your problem is that you cannot keep him. Once he makes up his mind to come home to his parents, he will come. You have not the means to stop him.'

'He will keep running away as long as he believes his mother is calling him. That is why I ask you to speak to her. Persuade her that it is for the best that he come with us. Because it is for the best.'

'You will never persuade Inés that for her child to be taken from her is for the best.'

'Then at least persuade her to let him go without tears and threats, without upsetting him. Because, one way or another, he will have to come. The law is the law.'

'That may be so, but there are higher considerations than obeying the law, higher imperatives.'

'Are there indeed? I would not know. For me, thank you, the law is enough.'

Chapter 29

The two officers are gone. Eugenio is gone. The driver is gone too, his commission unfulfilled. He is left with Inés and the boy, safe for the present behind the locked door of his old apartment. Bolívar, his duty done, has returned to his post in front of the radiator, from where he gravely watches and waits, his ears pricked for the next intruder.

'Shall we sit down and discuss the situation calmly, the three of us?' he suggests.

Inés shakes her head. 'There is no time for yet more discussions. I am going to phone Diego and tell him to fetch us.'

'Fetch you and bring you to La Residencia?'

'No. We are going to drive until we are beyond the reach of those people.'

No long-term plan, no ingenious scheme of escape, that much is clear. His heart goes out to her, this stolid, humourless woman whose life of tennis parties and cocktails at dusk he turned upside down when he gave her a child; whose future has now shrunk to driving aimlessly around back roads until her brothers get bored or their money runs out and she has no choice but to return and surrender her precious cargo.

'How would you feel, David,' he says, 'about going back to Punta Arenas, just for a while – going back and showing them how clever you are by coming top of the class? Show how you can do sums better than anyone else, how you can obey the rules and be a good boy. Once they have seen that, they will let you come home, I promise you. Then you can lead a normal life again, the life of a normal boy. Who knows, maybe one day they might even put up a plaque to you at Punta Arenas: *The famous David was here*.'

'What will I be famous for?'

'We will have to wait and see. Perhaps you will be a famous magician. Perhaps a famous mathematician.'

'No. I want to go with Inés and Diego in the car. I want to be a gypsy.'

He turns back to Inés. 'I plead with you, Inés, think again. Don't go ahead with this reckless move. There must be a better way.'

Inés pulls herself erect. 'Have you changed your mind yet again? You want me to give up my child to strangers – give up the light of my life? What kind of mother do you think I am?' And to the boy, 'Go and pack your things.'

'I'm finished packing. Can Simón swing me before we go?'

'I'm not sure I can swing anybody,' says he, Simón. 'I don't have my old strength, you know.'

'Just a little. Please.'

They make their way down to the playground. It has been

raining; the seat of the swing is wet. He wipes it dry with his sleeve. 'Just a few pushes,' he says.

He can push with only one hand; the swing barely moves. But the boy seems happy. 'Now it's your turn, Simón,' he says. With relief he settles into the swing and allows the boy to push him.

'Did you have a father or did you have a godfather, Simón?' asks the boy.

'I am pretty sure I had a father, and he pushed me on the swings just as you are pushing me. We all have fathers, it's a law of nature, as I told you; unfortunately, some of them vanish or get lost.'

'Did your father push you high?'

'To the very top.'

'Did you fall?'

'I don't remember ever falling.'

'What happens when you fall?'

'It depends. If you are lucky you just get a bump. If you are unlucky, very unlucky, you can break an arm or a leg.'

'No, what happens when you *fall*?'

'I don't understand. Do you mean, while you are falling through the air?'

'Yes. Is it like flying?'

'No, not at all. Flying and falling aren't the same thing. Only birds can fly; we human beings are too heavy.'

'But just for a little, when you are high up, it is like flying, isn't it?'

'I suppose so, if you forget you are falling. Why do you ask?'

The boy gives him an enigmatic smile. 'Because.'

On the stairs they meet a grim-faced Inés. 'Diego has changed his mind,' she says. 'He is not coming any more. I knew this would happen. He says we must catch a train.'

'Catch a train? To where? To the end of the line? What will you do when you get there, you and the child alone? No. Telephone Diego. Tell him to bring the car. I will take over. I have no idea where we will go, but I will go with you.'

'He won't agree. He won't give up the car.'

'It is not his car. It belongs to all three of you. Tell him he has had it long enough, it is your turn now.'

An hour later Diego turns up, surly, itching for a fight. But Inés cuts short his grumbling. Dressed in boots and overcoat, he has never seen her behave so imperiously before. While Diego stands by, his hands thrust in his pockets, she lifts a heavy suitcase onto the roof of the car and ties it down. When the boy comes dragging his box of found objects, she shakes her head firmly. 'Three things, no more,' she says. 'Small things. Choose.'

The boy selects a broken clock mechanism, a stone with a white seam in it, a dead cricket in a glass jar, and the parched breastbone of a gull. Calmly she picks up the bone between two fingers and tosses it away. 'Now throw the rest in the rubbish bin.' The boy stares, dumbstruck. 'Gypsies don't carry museums with them,' she says.

At last the car is packed. He, Simón, climbs gingerly into the back seat, followed by the boy, followed by Bolívar, who settles at their feet. Driving much too fast, Diego takes the road to La

Residencia, where without a word he gets out, slams the door to, and stalks off.

'Why is Diego so cross?' asks the boy.

'He is used to being the prince,' says Inés. 'He is used to getting his own way.'

'And am I the prince now?'

'Yes, you are the prince.'

'And are you the queen and Simón the king? Are we a family?'

He and Inés exchange glances. 'A sort of family,' he says. 'Spanish doesn't have a word for exactly what we are, so let us call ourselves that: the family of David.'

The boy settles back in his seat, looking pleased with himself.

Driving slowly – he feels a jab of pain each time he changes gear – he leaves La Residencia behind and begins to search for the main road north.

'Where are we going?' asks the boy.

'North. Do you have a better idea?'

'No, but I don't want to live in a tent, like in that other place.'

'Belstar? Actually, that is not a bad idea. We can head for Belstar and catch a boat back to the old life. Then all our worries will be over.'

'No! I don't want an old life, I want a new life!'

'I was just joking, my boy. The harbour master at Belstar won't let anyone take the boat back to the old life. He is very strict about that. No return. So it's either a new life or else the life we have. Any suggestions, Inés, for where to find a new life? No? Then let us keep going and see what comes up.'

They find the highway north and follow it, first through the industrial suburbs of Novilla, then through ragged farmland. The road begins to wind into the mountains.

'I need to poo,' announces the boy.

'Can't it wait?' says Inés.

'No.'

There is, as it turns out, no toilet paper. What else, in her haste to be off, has Inés forgotten to bring?

'Do we have *Don Quixote* in the car?' he asks the boy.

The boy nods.

'Will you give up a page of *Don Quixote*?'

The boy shakes his head.

'Then you will just have to have a dirty bum. Like a gypsy.'

'He can use a handkerchief,' says Inés stiffly.

They stop; they drive on. He is beginning to like Diego's car. It may not be much to look at, it handles clumsily, but the engine feels quite sturdy, quite willing.

From the heights they descend into rolling scrubland with dwellings scattered here and there, very different from the sandy wastes south of the city. For long stretches theirs is the only car on the road.

They strike a town named Laguna Verde (why? – there is no lagoon), where they fill the tank. An hour passes, a full fifty kilometres, before they reach the next town. 'It's getting late,' he says. 'We should look for a place to spend the night.'

They coast down the main street. There is no hotel to be

seen. They stop at a filling station. 'Where will we find the nearest lodgings?' he asks the attendant.

The man scratches his head. 'If you want a hotel, you will have to go on to Novilla.'

'We have just come from Novilla.'

'Then I don't know,' says the attendant. 'People usually just camp out.'

They return to the highway, into the gathering night.

'Are we going to be gypsies tonight?' asks the boy.

'Gypsies have caravans,' he replies. 'We have no caravan, just this cramped little car.'

'Gypsies sleep under hedges,' says the boy.

'Very well. Tell me when next you see a hedge.'

They have no map. He has no idea what lies ahead on the road. In silence they drive on.

He glances over his shoulder. The boy has fallen asleep, his arms around Bolívar's neck. He looks into the dog's eyes. *Guard him*, he says, though he utters no word. The icy amber eyes stare back at him, unblinking.

He knows the dog does not like him. But perhaps the dog likes no one; perhaps liking is outside the range of his heart. What does it matter anyway, liking, loving, compared with being faithful?

'He is asleep,' he tells Inés, speaking softly. And then: 'I am sorry it has to be me coming with you. You would have preferred your brother, wouldn't you?'

Inés shrugs. 'I always knew he would let me down. He must be the most self-centred person in the world.'

It is the first time she has criticized either of her brothers in his hearing, the first time she has sided with him.

'One grows very self-centred, living in La Residencia,' she goes on.

He waits for more – about La Residencia, about her brothers – but she has said enough.

'I have never dared ask,' he says: 'Why did you accept the boy? The day we met, you seemed to take such a dislike to us.'

'It was too sudden, too much of a surprise. You came out of nowhere.'

'All great gifts come out of nowhere. You should know that.'

Is it true? Do great gifts really come out of nowhere? What possessed him to say that?

'Do you really think,' says Inés (and he cannot but hear the feeling behind her words), 'do you really think I had not longed for a child of my own? What do you think it was like, being shut up in La Residencia all the time?'

He can now give the feeling a name: bitterness.

'I have no idea what it was like. I have never understood La Residencia or how you landed up there.'

She does not hear the question, or does not think it worthy of reply.

'Inés,' he says, 'let me ask for the last time: Are you sure this is what you want to do – run away from the life you know – and all because the child doesn't get on with his teacher?'

She is silent.

'This is not a life for you, a life of flight,' he presses on. 'Nor does it suit me. As for the boy, he can be a runaway only so long. Sooner or later, as he grows up, he is going to have to make his peace with society.'

Her lips tighten. She stares furiously ahead into the darkness.

'Think about it,' he concludes. 'Think hard. But whatever you decide, be assured, I will' – he pauses, resisting the words that want to come out – 'I will follow you to the ends of the earth.'

'I don't want him to end up like my brothers,' says Inés, speaking so softly that he has to strain to hear her. 'I don't want him to become a clerk or a schoolteacher like that señor León. I want him to make something of his life.'

'I am sure he will. He is an exceptional child, with an exceptional future. We both know it.'

The headlights pick out a painted sign at the roadside. *Cabañas 5 km*. Soon afterwards there is another sign: *Cabañas 1 km*.

The *cabañas* in question are set off from the road, in total darkness. They find the office; he gets out and raps on the door. It is opened by a woman in a dressing gown holding a lantern. For the past three days the electricity has been cut off, she informs them. No electricity, therefore no *cabañas* for hire.

Inés speaks. 'We have a child in the car. We are exhausted. We can't go on driving all night. Don't you have candles we can use?'

He returns to the car, shakes the child. 'Time to wake up, my precious.'

In a single fluid moment the dog rises and slips out of the car, the heavy shoulders brushing him aside like a straw.

The boy rubs his eyes sleepily. 'Are we there?'

'No, not yet. We are going to stop for the night.'

By the light of her lantern the woman shows them over the nearest of the *cabañas*. It is skimpily furnished but it has two beds. 'We will take it,' says Inés. 'Is there anywhere we can get a meal?'

'The *cabañas* are self-catering,' the woman replies. 'You have a gas cooker over there.' She waves the lantern in the direction of the cooker. 'Have you brought no supplies?'

'We have a loaf of bread, and some fruit juice for the child,' says Inés. 'We didn't have time to shop. Can we buy food from you? Perhaps some chops or sausages. Not fish. The child doesn't eat fish. And some fruit. And whatever scraps you have for the dog.'

'Fruit!' says the woman. 'It's a long time since we last saw fruit. But come, let us see what we can find.'

The two women depart, leaving them in darkness.

'I do eat fish,' says the boy, 'only not if it has eyes.'

Inés returns with a can of beans, a can of what the label calls cocktail sausages in brine, and a lemon, as well as a candle and matches.

'What about Bolívar?' asks the boy.

'Bolívar will have to eat bread.'

'He can eat my sausages,' says the boy. 'I hate sausages.'

They eat a frugal meal by candlelight, sitting side by side on the bed.

'Brush your teeth, then it is bedtime,' says Inés.

'I'm not tired,' says the boy. 'Can we play a game? Can we play Truth or Consequences?'

It is his turn to baulk. 'Thank you, David, but I have had enough consequences for one day. I need to rest.'

'Then can I open señor Daga's present?'

'What present?'

'Señor Daga gave me a present. He said I must open it in time of need. It's time of need now.'

'Señor Daga gave him a present to take along,' says Inés, avoiding his eyes.

'It's time of need, so can I open it?'

'This is not the real time of need, the real time of need is yet to come,' he says, 'but yes, open it.'

The boy runs out to the car and returns bearing a cardboard box, which he tears open. It contains a black satin gown. He lifts this out and unfolds it. Not a gown but a cape.

'There is a note,' says Inés. 'Read it.'

The boy brings the paper closer to the candle and reads: *Behold the magic cloak of invisibility. Whoever wears it shall walk the world unseen.* 'I told you!' he cries, dancing with excitement. 'I told you señor Daga knows magic!' He wraps the cape around himself. It is much too large. 'Can you see me, Simón? Am I invisible?'

'Not quite. Not yet. You didn't read the whole note. Listen. *Instructions to the wearer. To attain invisibility, wearer shall don the cloak before a mirror, then set fire to the magic powder and utter the secret spell. Whereupon the earthly body shall vanish into the mirror leaving only the traceless spirit behind.*'

He turns to Inés. 'What do you think, Inés? Shall we let our young friend don the cloak of invisibility and utter the secret spell? What if he vanishes into the mirror and never returns?'

'You can wear the cloak tomorrow,' says Inés. 'It is too late now.'

'No!' says the boy. 'I am going to wear it now! Where is the magic powder?' He rummages in the box, comes up with a glass jar. 'Is this the magic powder, Simón?'

He opens the jar and smells the silvery powder. It has no smell.

There is a full-length mirror, spotted with fly droppings, on the wall of the *cabaña*. He sets the boy before the mirror, buttons the cape at his throat. It descends in heavy folds around his feet. 'Here: hold the candle in one hand. Hold the magic powder in the other. Are you ready with the magic spell?'

The boy nods.

'Very well. Sprinkle the powder over the candle flame and utter the spell.'

'Abracadabra,' says the boy, and sprinkles the powder. It falls to the floor in a brief rain. 'Am I invisible yet?'

'Not yet. Try more of the powder.'

The boy dips the candle flame into the jar. There is a huge eruption of light, then utter darkness. Inés utters a cry; he himself recoils, blinded. The dog begins barking like a thing possessed.

'Can you see me?' comes the boy's voice, tiny, unsure. 'Am I invisible?'

Neither of them speaks.

'I can't see,' says the boy. 'Save me, Simón.'

He gropes his way to the boy, raises him from the floor, kicks the cloak aside.

'I can't see,' says the boy. 'My hand hurts. Am I dead?'

'No, of course not. You are neither invisible nor dead.' He gropes on the floor, finds the candle, lights it. 'Show me your hand. I don't see anything wrong with your hand.'

'It hurts.' The boy sucks his fingers.

'You must have burned it. I will go and see if the lady is still awake. Perhaps she can give us some butter to take away the burn.' He passes the boy into Inés's arms. She embraces him, kisses him, lays him down on the bed, croons softly over him.

'It's dark,' says the boy. 'I can't see anything. Am I inside the mirror?'

'No, my darling,' says Inés, 'you aren't inside the mirror, you are with your mother, and everything is going to be all right.' She turns to him, Simón. 'Fetch a doctor!' she hisses.

'It must have been magnesium powder,' he says. 'I fail to understand how your friend Daga could have given a child such a dangerous present. But then' – malice overcomes him – 'there is much that I fail to understand about your friendship with that man. And please shut the dog up – I am sick of his insane barking.'

'Stop complaining! Do something! Señor Daga is none of your business. Go!'

He leaves the cabin, follows the moonlit path to the señora's office. *Like an old married couple*, he thinks to himself. *We have never been to bed together, not even kissed, yet we quarrel as if we have been married for years!*

Chapter 30

The child sleeps soundly, but when he wakes it is clear that his sight is still impaired. He describes rays of green light travelling across his field of vision, cascades of stars. Far from being upset, he seems enthralled by these manifestations.

He knocks at señora Robles' door. 'We had an accident last night,' he tells her. 'Our son needs to see a doctor. Where is the nearest hospital?'

'Novilla. We can call for an ambulance, but it would have to come from Novilla. It will be quicker to take him yourself.'

'Novilla is quite a distance. Is there no doctor nearby?'

'There is a surgery in Nueva Esperanza, about sixty kilometres from here. I will look up the address for you. The poor child. What happened?'

'He was playing with inflammable material. It caught fire and the glare blinded him. We thought his sight might come back overnight but it hasn't.'

Señora Robles clucks sympathetically. 'Let me come and take a look,' she says.

They find Inés chafing to go. The boy sits on the bed, wearing the black cloak, his eyes closed, a rapt smile on his face.

'Señora Robles says there is a doctor an hour's drive from here,' he announces.

Señora Robles kneels down stiffly before the boy. 'Sweetheart, your father says you can't see. Is it true? Can't you see me?'

The boy opens his eyes. 'I can see you,' he says. 'You've got stars coming out of your hair. If I close my eyes' – he closes his eyes – 'I can fly. I can see the whole world.'

'That's wonderful, being able to see the whole world,' says señora Robles. 'Can you see my sister? She lives in Margueles, near Novilla. Her name is Rita. She looks like me, only younger and prettier.'

The boy frowns with concentration. 'I can't see her,' he says at last. 'My hand is too sore.'

'He burned his fingers last night,' he, Simón, explains. 'I was going to ask you for some butter to put on the burn, but it was late and I didn't want to wake you.'

'I'll fetch the butter. Have you tried washing his eyes with salt?'

'It is the sort of blindness you get from looking into the sun. Salt won't help. Inés, are we ready to leave? Señora, how much do we owe you?'

'Five reals for the cabin and two for the supplies last night. Would you like some coffee before you leave?'

'Thank you, but we don't have time.'

He takes the boy's hand, but the boy tugs himself free. 'I don't want to go,' he says. 'I want to stay here.'

'We can't stay. You need to see a doctor and señora Robles needs to clean the *cabaña* for her next visitors.'

The boy folds his arms tightly, refusing to budge.

'I'll tell you what,' says señora Robles. 'You go off to the doctor and on the way back you and your parents can come and stay with me again.'

'They are not my parents and we are not coming back. We are going to the new life. Will you come with us to the new life?'

'Me? I don't think so, sweetheart. It's kind of you to invite me, but I have too many things to do here, and anyway I get carsick. Where are you going to find this new life?'

'In Estell . . . In Estrellita del Norte.'

Señora Robles shakes her head dubiously. 'I don't think you will find much of a new life in Estrellita. I have friends who moved there, and they say it is the most boring place in the world.'

Inés intervenes. 'Come,' she commands the boy. 'If you don't come I will have to carry you. I am counting to three. One. Two. Three.'

Without a word the boy rises and, lifting the hem of his cloak, trudges down the path to the car. Pouting, he takes his place on the back seat. The dog leaps in easily after him.

'Here is the butter,' says señora Robles. 'Smear it on your sore fingers and wrap a handkerchief around them. The burn will soon go away. Also, here is a pair of dark glasses that my husband doesn't use any more. Wear them until your eyes get better.'

She puts the glasses on the boy. They are far too large, but he does not remove them.

They wave goodbye and take the road north.

'You shouldn't tell people we are not your parents,' he remarks. 'In the first place, it is not true. In the second place, they may think we are kidnapping you.'

'I don't care. I don't like Inés. I don't like you. I only like brothers. I want to have brothers.'

'You are in a bad mood today,' says Inés.

The boy pays no heed. Through the señora's dark glasses he stares into the sun, fully risen now above the line of blue mountains in the distance.

A road sign comes into view: *Estrellita del Norte 475 km, Nueva Esperanza 50 km*. Beside the sign stands a hitch-hiker, a young man wearing an olive-green poncho with a rucksack at his feet, looking very lonely in the empty landscape. He slows down.

'What are you doing?' says Inés. 'We don't have time to pick up strangers.'

'Pick up who?' says the boy.

In the rear-view mirror he can see the hitch-hiker trotting towards the car. Guiltily he accelerates away from him.

'Pick up who?' says the boy. 'Who are you talking about?'

'Just a man begging for a lift,' says Inés. 'We don't have space in the car. And we don't have time. We have to get you to a doctor.'

'No! If you don't stop I am going to jump out!' And he opens the door nearest him.

He, Simón, brakes sharply and switches off the engine. 'Don't ever do that again! You can fall and kill yourself.'

'I don't care! I want to go to the other life! I don't want to be with you and Inés!'

A stunned silence falls. Inés stares at the road ahead. 'You don't know what you are saying,' she whispers.

A crunch of footsteps, and a bearded face appears at the driver's window. 'Thank you!' the stranger pants. He yanks open the back door. 'Hello, young man!' he says, then freezes as the dog, stretched out on the seat beside the boy, raises his head and gives a low growl.

'What a huge dog!' he says. 'What's his name?'

'Bolívar. He is an Alsatian. Be quiet, Bolívar!' Wrapping his arms around the dog, the boy wrestles him off the seat. Reluctantly the dog settles on the floor at his feet. The stranger takes his place; the car is suddenly full of the sour smell of unwashed clothing. Inés winds down her window.

'Bolívar,' says the young man. 'That's an unusual name. And what is your name?'

'I haven't got a name. I've still got to get my name.'

'Then I'll call you señor Anónimo,' says the young man. 'Greetings, señor Anónimo, I am Juan.' He holds out a hand, which the boy ignores. 'Why are you wearing a cloak?'

'It's magic. It makes me invisible. I'm invisible.'

He interrupts. 'David has had an accident, and we are taking him to a doctor. I am afraid we can give you a ride only as far as Nueva Esperanza.'

'That's OK.'

'I burned my hand,' says the boy. 'We are going to get medicine.'

'Is it sore?'

'Yes.'

'I like your glasses. I wish I had glasses like that.'

'You can have them.'

After a chilly early-morning ride on the back of a truck carrying timber, their passenger is glad of the warmth and comfort of the car. From his chatter it emerges that he is in the printing trade, and is making his way to Estrellita, where he has friends and where, if rumour is to be believed, there is plenty of work to be had.

At the turn-off to Nueva Esperanza he stops to let the newcomer off.

'Are we at the doctor?' asks the boy.

'Not yet. This is where we part company with our friend. He is going to continue his journey northward.'

'No! He must stay with us!'

He addresses Juan. 'We can drop you here or else you can come into the town with us. The choice is yours.'

'I'll come with you.'

They find the surgery without difficulty. Dr García is out on a house call, the nurse informs them, but they are welcome to wait.

'I'll go and look for breakfast,' says Juan.

'No, you mustn't go,' says the boy. 'You will get lost.'

'I won't get lost,' says Juan. His hand is on the doorknob.

'Stay, I command you!' the boy barks out.

'David!' he, Simón, reproves the child. 'What has got into you this morning? You don't speak to a stranger like that!'

'He is not a stranger. And don't call me David.'

'What must I call you then?'

'You must call me by my real name.'

'And what may that be?'

The boy is silent.

He addresses Juan. 'Feel free to go exploring. We will meet you here.'

'No, I think I'll stay,' says Juan.

The doctor makes his appearance, a short, burly man with an energetic air and a mass of silvery hair. He gazes upon them with mock alarm. 'What is this? And a dog too! What can I do for all of you?'

'I burned my hand,' says the boy. 'The lady put butter on it, but it is still sore.'

'Let me look . . . Yes, yes . . . It must be painful. Come into the surgery and we will see what we can do.'

'Doctor, the hand is not why we are here,' says Inés. 'We had an accident last night with a fire, and now my son can't see properly. Will you examine his eyes?'

'No!' cries the boy, rising to confront Inés. The dog rouses himself too, pads across the room, and takes his place at the boy's side. 'I keep telling you, I can see, only you can't see me because of the magic cloak of invisibility. It makes me invisible.'

'Can I have a look?' says Dr García. 'Will your guardian let me?'

The boy lays a restraining hand on the dog's collar.

The doctor lifts the dark glasses off the boy's nose. 'Can you see me now?' he asks.

'You are tiny, tiny, like an ant, and you are waving your arms and saying, *Can you see me now?*'

'Aha, I get the picture. You are invisible and none of us can see you. But you also have a sore hand, which happens not to be invisible. So shall you and I go into my surgery, and will you let me look at the hand – look at the visible part of you?'

'All right.'

'Shall I come too?' says Inés.

'In a little while,' says the doctor. 'First the young man and I must have a private word.'

'Bolívar must come with me,' says the boy.

'Bolívar may come with you as long as he behaves himself,' says the doctor.

'What actually happened to your son?' asks Juan, when they are alone.

'His name is David. He was playing with magnesium, and it caught fire and the flash blinded him.'

'He says his name isn't David.'

'He says many things. He has a fertile imagination. David is the name he was given in Belstar. If he wants to take on some other name, let him do so.'

'You came through Belstar? I came through Belstar too.'

'Then you know how the system works. The names we use are the names we were given there, but we might just as well have been given numbers. Numbers, names – they are equally arbitrary, equally random, equally unimportant.'

325

'Actually, there are no random numbers,' says Juan. 'You say, "Think of a random number," and I say, "96513," because that is the first number that comes into my head, but it isn't really random, it's my Asistencia number or my old telephone number or something like that. There is always a reason behind a number.'

'So you are another of the number mystics! You and David should set up a school together. You can teach the secret causes behind numbers and he can teach people how to get from one number to the next without falling down a volcano. Of course there are no random numbers *under the eye of God*. But we don't live under the eye of God. In the world we live in there are random numbers and random names and random events, like being picked up at random by a car containing a man and a woman and a child named David. And a dog. What was the secret cause behind that event, do you think?'

Before Juan can reply to his rant the door to the surgery is thrown open. 'Please come in,' says Dr García.

He and Inés enter. Juan hesitates, but the clear young voice of the boy rises from inside: 'He is my brother, he must come too.'

The boy is sitting on the edge of the doctor's couch, a smile of serene confidence on his lips, the dark glasses perched on top of his head.

'We had a good, long talk, our young friend and I,' says Dr García. 'He explained to me how it comes about that he is invisible to us, and I explained to him why it is that we look to him like insects waving our feelers in the air while he flies high above. I have told him that we would prefer it if he would see us as we really are, not as insects, and in return he has told me that when he returns to visibility he would like us to see him as he really is. Is that a fair account, young man, of our conversation?'

The boy nods.

'Our young friend says furthermore that you' – he looks meaningfully at him, Simón – 'are not his real father, and you' – he turns to Inés – 'are not his real mother. I do not ask you to defend yourselves. I have a family of my own, I know children can say wild things. Nonetheless, is there anything you would like to tell me?'

'I am his true mother,' says Inés, 'and we are saving him from being sent to a reformatory school where he will be turned into a criminal.'

Having said her say, she shuts her lips and glares defiantly.

'And his eyes, Doctor?' he, Simón, inquires.

'There is nothing wrong with his eyes. I have conducted a physical examination and I have tested his vision. As organs of sight his eyes are perfectly normal. As for his hand, I have put on a dressing. The burn is not serious, it will show improvement in a day or two. Now let me ask: Should I be concerned about the story this young man tells me?'

He glances at Inés. 'You should pay due heed to whatever the boy says. If he says he wants to be taken away from us and returned to Novilla, return him to Novilla. He is your patient, in your care.' He turns to the boy. 'Is that what you want, David?'

The boy does not reply, but gestures to him to come nearer. Cupping his hand, the boy whispers in his ear.

'Doctor, David informs me that he does not want to return to Novilla, but does want to know if you will come with us.'

'Come where?'

'North, to Estrellita.'

'To the new life,' says the boy.

'And what about my patients here in Esperanza who depend on me? Who will look after them if I leave them behind just to look after you?'

'You don't need to look after me.'

Dr García casts him, Simón, a mystified look. He takes a deep breath. 'David is suggesting that you abandon your practice and come north with us to start a new life. It would be for your own sake, not for his.'

Dr García rises. 'Ah, I understand! It is most generous of you, young man, to include me in your plans. But the life I have here in Esperanza is happy and fulfilling enough. There is nothing I need to be saved from, thank you.'

They are in the car again, heading north. The boy is in ebullient spirits, the sore hand forgotten. He jabbers to Juan, wrestles with Bolívar in the back seat. Juan joins in too, though he is wary of the dog, who has yet to warm to him.

'Did you like Dr García?' he, Simón, inquires.

'He's OK,' says the boy. 'He has hairs on his fingers like a werewolf.'

'Why did you want him to come along to Estrellita?'

'Because.'

'You can't just invite every stranger you meet to come with us,' says Inés.

'Why not?'

'Because there is no room in the car.'

'There is room. Bolívar can sit on my lap, can't you, Bolívar?' A pause. 'What are we going to do when we get to Estrellita?'

'It's a long way yet to Estrellita. Be patient.'

'But what are we going to *do* there?'

'We are going to find the Relocation Centre and we are going to present ourselves at the desk, you and Inés and I, and –'

'And Juan. You didn't say Juan. And Bolívar.'

'You and Inés and Juan and Bolívar and I, and we are going to say, *Good morning, we are new arrivals, and we are looking for somewhere to stay*.'

'And?'

'That's all. *Looking for somewhere to stay, to start our new life*.'